THE PRICE OF SANCTUARY

GAYLON GREER

Medallion Press, Inc.
Printed in USA

DEDICATION:

To Dee and MEG, for patience and support.

Published 2009 by Medallion Press, Inc.

The MEDALLION PRESS LOGO
is a registered trademark of Medallion Press, Inc.

Printed in the United States of America
Typeset in Baskerville

Library of Congress Cataloging-in-Publication Data

Greer, Gaylon E.
  The price of sanctuary / Gaylon Greer.
    p. cm.
  ISBN 978-1-60542-058-5
  1. Women spies--Fiction. 2. Assassins--Fiction. I. Title.
  PS3607.R47P75 2009
  813'.6--dc22
                        2009004351

10 9 8 7 6 5 4 3 2 1
First Edition

ACKNOWLEDGMENTS:

Members of my writing support group, the FABs, who meet regularly in Austin to share advice and counsel, played a crucial role in the final crafting of this novel—ultimate responsibility for the content, both good and bad, rests of course with the author. Thanks FABs, you are indeed fabulous: Nancy Gore, Jim Haws, Cicilia Jones, Jackie Kelly, Kim O'Brien, Diane Owens, Lottie Shapiro. Thanks also to members of Novel in Progress, an open-forum group in Austin that has provided inspiration and criticism for several years.

CHAPTER ONE

FROM TWENTY-EIGHT THOUSAND FEET and ten miles out, southern Florida's coastal lights appeared as a line of twinkling jewels that broadened and transmuted into a steady glow as landfall drew nearer. Shelby Cervosier, the twin-jet Cessna Citation's only passenger, had begun to unwind during the flight from Haiti, but the reminder that she was minutes from being back in harm's way knotted her chest and ignited a fire in her stomach.

The pilot, flying without a copilot, had invited Shelby to join him in the cockpit during the flight. "Almost there," he said. "We need to go over the plan?"

"I have it. When you stop the plane, I jump out and head for the largest hangar. A woman named Brenda will be waiting in a Dodge van. She'll take me to a place where I can rent a car."

He gave her a thumbs-up. "Runway lights reflect skyward, so the ground will be dark. Watch your step." He talked on the radio, listened, talked again, and adjusted the autopilot. The engines' shrill whine softened. "Air Traffic Control bought the oil-leak story. We're cleared for an emergency landing."

A cloud bank temporarily blocked their view. Then Shelby, sitting in the copilot's seat, saw miles of lights but nothing that looked like an airport. "Where do we land?"

"It's a rural strip—no control tower. I trigger the lights with my radio." The pilot changed frequencies and thumbed his microphone switch several times. In the distance, runway lights glowed and brightened. "I won't shut down the engines or turn off the landing lights, because we don't want prying eyes to know you're abandoning ship. Brenda will probably be sleeping. You'll have to find her and knock on a window."

"No problem." Shelby's throat tightened so that she could barely get the words out. "Chuck, I'm so afraid you'll get in trouble for this."

"Don't sweat it. When I park, I'll make a brief exit and—never mind. The point is, by the time Customs gets here, my starboard engine will be leaking oil worse than the Exxon *Valdez*." He patted her hand. "E-mail me when you've snatched your little sister and found a hideout. Now, you ought to go back to the cabin and buckle yourself in."

Lights on the ground grew brighter and more distinct. The Citation's wheels kissed the runway with a muted screech. At the end of its landing roll, the plane reversed direction and lurched to a stop. Chuck wriggled out of the pilot's seat and pulled a lever to open the cabin door. "Steps are going down. Good luck, beautiful."

Shelby barely cleared the edge of the runway before the sleek little jet's twin engines wound up to an ear-achy whine and it began moving, leaving behind a smelly residue of burned jet fuel. Chuck's warning about the runway lights struck home; they made the ground a dark void. With every step, roots, ruts, and weeds threatened Shelby's balance. Something—palmetto fronds, she guessed—whipped her legs.

When distance rendered the lights less blinding, she picked up her pace. Cloying heat and humidity plastered her T-shirt and jeans to her skin as she jogged across the rugged turf with her blue canvas overnight bag slung over a shoulder.

Look for a Dodge van, Chuck had said, but what if it wasn't there? Maybe she could hibernate until daylight and flag someone down. One way or another, get to a car rental agency, drive to Homestead, and sneak Carmen away.

As she approached the hangars, she slowed her pace. Wiping at sweat that stung her eyes and breathing hard from exertion, she looked for the woman who was supposed to meet her. With solid cloud cover blocking the moon, she almost bumped into the van before she recognized it.

Chuck had guessed wrong about the driver: she wasn't sleeping. She opened the passenger door. "Welcome to Florida."

Shelby climbed in. "Brenda, right?"

"Not really." The old Dodge Caravan's dome light revealed an overweight, middle-aged woman with freckled, sun-leathered skin and unruly blond hair. "Chuck said not to use my real name, in case the feds nab me." She cranked the engine and pulled away from the hangar. "You lean on back, catch some shut-eye. We'll be on the road at least an hour, and your butt's gotta be draggin'."

Shelby reclined the seat and closed her eyes. She was too keyed up to sleep, but God, she was tired. Tired of running. Tired of hiding. Tired of being scared.

As dawn turned low-hanging clouds a deep purple, the women found a car rental agency open for business near Fort Myers. Shelby rented a midsized Chevrolet. The charge to her credit card would reveal her presence in America, but they would know by then anyway. She said good-bye to Brenda and, five hours later, with heavy eyelids and cramping shoulder muscles, parked the Chevy at a Cracker Barrel restaurant in Homestead's outskirts. After lunch, she drove to the suburban tract house where the Caribbean Basin Task Force—the CBTF—had kept her and her little sister for two weeks before sending Shelby on the mission that was supposed to win them political asylum.

Since Krystal Erinyes, her CBTF controller, had expected that she would not survive, they might have shut the place down and moved Carmen. If her sister was no longer there, Shelby had no idea what to do.

One step at a time, she reminded herself. *Don't panic and ruin your only chance.*

She parked in the shade of a pine tree where she could see anyone entering or leaving the house. Carmen, if she was still there, would stay inside during the mid-day heat, and waiting for the air to cool enough for her to play outside was dangerous; those would-be assassins in Haiti would eventually report to Krystal, and she would send someone to stake out the house—if they were still using it. *But if I go in, I might walk into a trap.*

With the car windows open and the seat tilted back, Shelby watched and waited until worry that they had moved Carmen became intolerable. When the bellow of traffic on a nearby freeway signalled the afternoon rush hour, she slipped out of the car and walked to the house's side yard, where shrubs hid her from its windows. Nothing about the run-down bungalow had changed during the three weeks she'd been away. The same stench wafted from garbage cans left to cook under the broiling sun, the grass and shrubs still needed cutting and trimming, and the storm-damaged siding still needed repair. She could even be slapping at the same mosquitoes as she waited and prayed that her sister would come out.

Still no movement, no sign of occupancy. They must have moved, closed the house, and—wait, someone was at the back door.

It opened. Carmen dashed out and sprinted to the swing and slide set in the rear yard.

With her heart in her throat, Shelby watched her little sister struggle to climb up the slick metal slide. Barefooted, Carmen wore blue shorts and the pink, blue, and green tie-dyed T-shirt Shelby had helped her pick out at a street fair. Way too big, the shirt made the child's undersized seven-year-old body look even smaller.

Shelby stepped from behind the shrubs. "Carmen," she called softly, and held a finger to her lips.

"Shelby," Carmen yelped as she ran to her.

Squatting, Shelby pulled her close. "We have to be quiet. We need to—"

Lois, the woman assigned to watch Carmen, stepped onto the back porch. Shading her eyes from the sun with a hand, she stared at Shelby. "What are you doing here?"

As the woman approached, Shelby squelched an impulse to grab Carmen and dash for the street. But with her sister in tow, she couldn't outrun the CBTF agent. Standing, she flashed what she hoped was a disarming smile.

Carmen tugged at her fingers. "Let's run."

Squeezing her sister's hand with gentle pressure, Shelby kept her eyes focused on Lois and the smile pasted on her face. *Stay calm. Brazen it through.* "I finished my job early. Thought I'd surprise you."

"It's a surprise, all right." Lois snatched Carmen's hand from

Shelby's. "Come inside, child."

Carmen tried to jerk away. Then she dug in her heels. Lois, acting as if she didn't notice, dragged her.

Shelby followed but paused for a moment at the door, worrying about who might be in the house. With thudding heart and tense muscles, she pushed inside.

Lois walked through the kitchen into the front hallway. She picked up a telephone.

"Don't do that," Shelby said. The woman started dialing, and Shelby jammed her fingers on the hook.

Lois studied her, letting seconds tick away. Then she pulled a short-barreled, silver pistol from a drawer. "You're not supposed to be here." She handled the weapon with an ease that bespoke competence. "Sit on the couch while I check this out."

Better to die fighting, Shelby decided, than to let them take her somewhere and execute her. Putting on a perplexed expression, she looked over Lois's shoulder. "Krystal? What are you . . . ?"

Lois's gaze shifted for a blink, and Shelby slammed a shoulder into the shorter, heavier woman. Years of daily swimming and tennis had made Shelby strong and fast, and desperation gave her added strength. Gripping Lois's gun hand, she crowded the woman.

They bounced off a wall. Lois staggered but recovered. She butted Shelby and tried to twist free.

Near panic, Shelby clamped her teeth on the hand that held the gun.

"Goddamn," Lois shouted. She slammed a fist into the side of Shelby's head.

Dust motes seemed to cluster before Shelby's eyes, blocking the light. Her legs turned rubbery. *Hang on,* an inner voice commanded. Biting down on the fleshy wedge between Lois's thumb and forefinger, she leaned against the woman to keep from falling.

Lois wrenched her hand free but lost her grip on the pistol. She kneed Shelby's groin, punched her stomach.

Lightning flashed inside Shelby's head. She fell to her knees and braced a hand against the wall. She retched and could not inhale. A dark curtain of despair descended upon her.

"Little bitch," Lois shouted.

Carmen had wrapped both arms around the woman's leg and clamped her teeth on flesh just below the hemline of the woman's skirt. Lois kicked, but Carmen hung on.

Shelby realized she had fallen on the errant pistol. She grasped it and twisted to sit with her back against the wall. Managing shallow breaths, she pointed the weapon at Lois. "I'll shoot," she croaked. "I'll shoot you."

Lois, concentrating on dislodging Carmen, didn't seem to hear.

Holding the pistol with both hands and praying that it had no safety device to keep it from firing, Shelby pointed it at the ceiling. With her eyes closed, she squeezed the trigger, flinching as the explosion reverberated through the hallway.

Carmen rolled away from Lois and protected her head with her arms.

Lois froze. "Put the gun down," she said.

Shelby pointed it at her. "You back up. Back up!"

Moving slowly, Lois backed to the wall. "Take it easy. We don't need this. Relax, now."

"Like hell, relax! Carmen, are you all right?"

"Let's run," Carmen said again. On her feet now, she stood by the door, jogging in place. Her cinnamon-hued complexion had paled. "Come on!"

"We're leaving, sweetie." How loud had the gunshot sounded

from the street? Most nearby residents would be at work or school, and in this neighborhood people usually minded their own business, but someone still might call the police. "We have to do something about Lois."

"You don't have to do anything with me," Lois said. "They don't pay me enough for this."

Shelby studied the woman. *Can I pull the trigger? Look her in the eyes and shoot her?* "You kicked my sister."

"To keep her from gnawing my leg off. I didn't hurt her." Lois raised her hands, palms forward. "Why don't you take your finger off that trigger? We don't want an accident."

"You be still." Keeping the handgun centered on the woman, Shelby struggled to her feet. Pain lanced through her groin. Her stomach churned. "Carmen, where is your kite?"

"My kite?" Carmen seemed disoriented. "Upstairs."

"Run and get the ball of string from it. Hurry."

Fighting the primal urge to flee, Shelby marched Lois into the half bath off the hallway and made her lie on her back. Keeping distance between them, she twisted three strands of the kite string together to increase its strength. A loop with a drawstring formed a miniature lariat, which she tossed to Lois. "Put that over your wrists."

Fixing Shelby with a poisonous glare, Lois obeyed.

Still keeping her distance, Shelby drew the loop tight. "Get on your knees with your back to me. Raise your arms and put your wrists behind your head." She approached from behind and, with the pistol digging into Lois's back, wrapped the string around the woman's neck so that she could not move her bound wrists. "Stand up facing the toilet. Now, straddle it and sit." Confident that the woman no longer posed a threat, Shelby laid the pistol aside and tied her to the toilet, using the entire ball of string. As an extra precaution, she also used the cords from a hair dryer and a curling iron. Adhesive tape from the medicine cabinet sealed the woman's mouth. "They'll find you when they come looking for me."

Carmen waited in the hallway, poised to run out the front door. Both her arms hugged Snaggly, an orange-haired, snaggletoothed rag-doll clown that had been Shelby's gift to her when they moved into the house.

Shelby pushed the short-barreled pistol under the waistband of her jeans and pulled the tail of her T-shirt over it. "Let's go out the back, sweetheart. Don't run. We mustn't attract attention."

As they left Homestead behind, motoring north along Florida's east coast, Shelby felt the knot in her stomach melting. She twisted and rotated her shoulders and neck to relax taut muscles. They had been traveling for half an hour when Carmen asked where they were going.

"Somewhere far away," Shelby said.

"To hide from Lois?"

"From everybody. We're starting new lives."

Shelby's description of their destination—*somewhere far away*—seemed to hang in the air, mocking her as she drove. Somewhere in this vast country there had to be a sanctuary, but where?

Arizona, she decided: Phoenix. She knew something about that city from when she had done graduate work at Arizona State University, knew she and Carmen would be inconspicuous among the ethnically diverse population there.

Carmen's voice, soft and grave, cut into her thoughts. "I knew you'd come back for me."

"I promised, didn't I?"

"Lois said you wouldn't. She said you were gone for good. Said brats like me belong in an instit . . . In a place where they lock kids up."

Reaching across the seat, Shelby caressed her little sister's cheek. "If that ever happened, if I did fail to come back, it wouldn't be on purpose. I would never leave you on purpose."

"I thought she was going to shoot you."

"She might have if you hadn't grabbed her. You saved my life."

Carmen beamed. "She said people like me . . . that people with dark skin are a bad thing. Said we have too many babies and don't want to work."

Shelby took a deep breath. How did you explain bigotry to a seven-year-old? "Sweetie, do you know what ancestors are?"

"Sure, they're the ones that came before us. Grandma's gran and her mama and papa and their grans. Like that."

"Good, that's exactly right. And your skin color depends on where those ancestors lived. If they came from places where it's warm all the time and the sun shines every day, God gave them dark skin so they wouldn't get too much sun. If they came from cold, cloudy places, he gave them less color so they could get enough sun. That's the only difference."

"You don't have much color."

"Because my mother's ancestors came from one of those cloudy places. But our father gave me some color, and I'm grateful for that."

"That's why we're sisters."

Shelby caressed her again. "And because we're sisters, I'll always take care of you."

Night closed around them, and Carmen drifted into sleep, slumped in the corner between her seat back and the door. She twisted and whined, then slipped off her seat belt and curled on the seat with Snaggly clutched to her chest.

At a rest stop, Shelby lifted her onto the rear seat. As she covered the little form with a spare shirt, she thought about their fight with Lois. Most seven-year-olds would have simply cringed and cried. Perhaps what she and Carmen had been through during their nine weeks of running, hiding, and running again had taught the child to attack rather than retreat.

Back on the freeway, she set the rental car's cruise control on seventy and ticked off the miles. They had to get rid of the vehicle; in a matter of hours the CBTF would know its make, model, and license number and would have every highway patrol officer in the country watching for it. Throughout the night, pausing only for a brief nap at a rest area, she barreled north on I-95, then west to intersect I-75, heading for Atlanta. She could ditch the car there and take public transportation. Every mode departed from that city for places all across America.

With no identity documents other than those the CBTF had supplied, they couldn't board a plane. A bus, she decided. Pay cash for tickets to a place farther west, maybe Los Angeles, but get off the bus in Phoenix. Even if the CBTF traced the tickets and guessed her strategy, they would have no way of knowing where she debarked.

Buying the tickets would leave her broke. Easy solution: call a friend. She had two in America. Barbara Worthington, now Barbara Worthington Rogers, had been her roommate in graduate school and was the only college acquaintance with whom she had kept in contact. Elizabeth Fontaine, a middle-aged librarian, had befriended her during the desolate days when she and Carmen lived in that so-called safe house in Arkansas. She decided to ask Elizabeth, because she knew Barbara and her minister husband had recently moved and would be financially strapped.

Elizabeth couldn't wire money, however: that would create electronic footprints. Shelby would have to stop in Arkansas and pick up the cash in person.

At her next refueling stop, she called from a public telephone. Elizabeth already knew how Shelby and Carmen had come to be in America, and she knew that Shelby had been arrested for causing the deaths of a man who had beaten and raped her, the rapist's sidekick, and a rogue immigration agent. Struggling to keep her voice steady, Shelby explained what had happened since her arrest. "A woman from the CBTF got me released from jail. She promised to get the manslaughter charge dropped and arrange for political asylum if I worked for her."

"CBTF? What's that?"

"Caribbean Basin Task Force. One of your government's dirty-tricks agencies. They sent me on a mission back to Haiti. Now, Krystal—she runs the task force—is trying to have me killed to keep everything quiet."

"Oh, honey," Elizabeth said, "surely the government wouldn't do something like that."

"Krystal is doing this on her own. Paying someone to kill an illegal immigrant won't bother her in the least."

"You have to take this to the authorities."

"Krystal *is* the authorities."

"Go over her head. Tell her supervisor what she's doing."

"I don't know who that would be." How could she convince Elizabeth, a middle-aged librarian in a middle-sized, middle-American town, that the authorities weren't always good guys? "The CBTF doesn't even show up on your government's organization chart. From what little I learned, I know there's no Congressional oversight. Something about deniability."

"Newspapers or TV, then. Expose the whole sordid scheme."

"Would anyone believe me? Even if . . ." Shelby rubbed a knuckle under her eyes. *Damned tears.* "There's still that manslaughter charge. Krystal said it would be reinstated if I didn't do a good job for the CBTF. Even if they dropped it, we would be deported."

"Back to Haiti? Would that be so bad?"

"I wouldn't last a day. Our father has disappeared, so Carmen would be alone."

"How can I help?"

Relief washed over Shelby like warm sunshine on a frigid day. "I need money. Enough to live on until I find a job and a hiding place."

"I'll go to the bank as soon as it opens. Where shall I send it?"

"We'll meet you."

"Where?"

"A crowded, public place. Pretend you don't know me. Stroll around, and I'll watch to see if anyone follows you. If they do, I'll avoid contact and try another time."

"How about River Center Mall? The food court? You've been there, and it's usually jammed."

"That's good." Calmer now, increasingly confident that she could make this work, that she and Carmen could lose themselves in America's vast hinterland and establish new identities, Shelby thanked her friend. "I'll call again when I know what time we're due in Perryville."

With all the pieces in place, she could move faster than the CBTF. Back on the freeway, she kept the Chevy at a steady seventy miles per hour and, three hours before sunrise, parked in the long-term lot at Atlanta's Hartsfield International Airport and caught the shuttle to a downtown hotel. Unless an alert security guard noted the license plate, the car would sit at the airport for days before the parking authority considered it abandoned.

From the hotel, with Carmen jabbering nonstop and Shelby desperate for sleep, they took a cab to the Greyhound station. Shelby paid cash for tickets to Dallas, Texas. They would get off the bus at an intermediate stop in Arkansas and catch a local to Perryville. If the ticket seller in Atlanta remembered a young woman traveling with a biracial child, would the change of buses be enough to throw hired killers off the trail?

CHAPTER TWO

HE SHOULD HAVE TAKEN the job, Vlad decided as the gushing shower sluiced soap from his body. He wouldn't have hesitated if it had been a simple matter of wasting a soft target and walking away. But instead of the usual shoot-and-scoot, the contract called for the body to disappear. They expected him to travel from Chicago to a hick town in Arkansas *and* to haul off the carcass.

What really scuttled the deal, however, was its time frame. Tonight was the payoff for several days he'd spent cultivating a little twitch he'd picked up near Chicago's Belmont Harbor. To handle the Arkansas contract, he would have to break his date and catch an evening flight out. A man needed time to play, and toys like this one didn't come around that often.

On the other hand, the target was a real looker. She'd be a nice switch from his usual contracts on shady businessmen, heavily insured spouses, and small-time hoods. The job paid thirty grand, and his lifestyle—never staying more than a week in one place, always going first class—cost a bundle; his kitty was getting lean. Why not go for it? The broad he'd picked up near the harbor would still be there when he got back.

He stepped out of the shower and, with a towel wrapped around his waist, typed his password into his laptop computer for another look at the target's specs. He had chosen *Vlad* for a password and professional name after the *Chicago Tribune*, reporting on one of his local jobs, compared him to the historical Vlad Dracula, whose favorite method of dispatching victims had earned him the nickname The Impaler. Vlad used half a dozen different names in face-to-face dealings, and he had developed a distinct persona to go with each.

Despite the laptop's state-of-the-art configuration, data took a moment to filter through its encryption/decryption program. The computer was operated by an offshore remailer who stripped away all traces of the message's origin before forwarding it to the recipient. Then the target's photo materialized on the screen: full, sensuous mouth; high cheekbones; and wide-set green eyes whose peculiar shape and unusual shade made Vlad think of a jungle cat. Dark brown hair hung to her shoulders and flipped under at the ends. He scrolled down to read details, phrased to avoid keywords that the offshore broker's National Security Agency contact had warned might trigger a NSA intercept and analysis.

Name: Shelby Cervosier   Sex: female

Age: 27   Height: 5'8"

Weight: 120 pounds   Hair color: dark brown

Eye color: green   Nationality: Haitian

Race: northern European mother, southern European (French) father with one African grandparent

Education: PhD (history)

Other Information:
- Subject has terminated three men.
- Termination must not be public, and the subject's body must not be found.
- Forward the subject's thumb to the broker as evidence of contract completion.

Vlad studied the digitized photo again. Nice package, and breaking a bitch who knew what it was like to snuff out lives would be a new experience. He sent the broker an e-mail saying he'd changed his mind and would take the assignment. Minutes later his computer dinged, signaling a message.

It was the broker. "Another contractor took that job. I can offer you the same deal in Arizona."

The same? Vlad typed: "Does the client have two targets?"

"Only one, but they're not sure where she's headed. You get six thousand for a three-day vigil. The additional twenty-four is yours if you ice the target."

"If they don't know where she will show, it's a crapshoot. How many places are they staking out?"

The computer program changed *staking out* to *watching*. Vlad, assuming *stakeout* and its variants were NSA keywords, hit the OK button to accept the change and waited the seconds it took for his message and the broker's response to wind their way through the encryption/decryption program and the offshore remailer's computer.

"Just two," the broker replied. "Gives you a fifty-fifty chance."

Since they had posted the Arkansas contract first, Vlad figured they expected the target to show there. Arizona was just insurance. He could use the six grand for the stakeout, however, and maybe he'd get lucky. "I'll take it."

Throughout his cab ride to the airport and while waiting to board his Arizona-bound flight, Vlad fumed about losing the Arkansas stakeout. The guy down there would probably bag the quarry.

He hated flying. If time permitted, he would have driven to

Arizona. He knew flying was safer, but he had trouble with situations he couldn't control. Even though flight attendants treated first-class passengers with deference, they never let you forget who was in charge. Once they closed the airplane's door, you were their prisoner. And nothing pushed Vlad's buttons more than being locked up.

Not that his prison time had been that long. But his face, still boyish at twenty-two, had doomed him to the role of catcher: an ersatz female for sexually aggressive inmates. Being a model prisoner earned him parole after twenty-three months, the only way to get away from the skinhead cellmate who had treated him as a girlfriend and pimped him for candy and cigarettes.

Leaning back in his seat as the plane began its takeoff roll, he closed his eyes and resorted to a survival technique he'd learned in prison: let good memories push away the bad. Two months after his release, he had found his purpose in life while ending supervised parole by staging his own death. Working for a dentist gave him the run of a neighborhood dental office and enabled him to switch records with one of the dentist's boy-loving male patients. He flirted with the patient and lured him into a country drive. The outing, in Vlad's beat-up old Honda Accord, terminated in a flaming wreck that melted the bastard's skin, body fat, and extremities. The cops ID'd Vlad's car, and medical ghouls had confirmed his death by matching the corpse's teeth with the switched records.

Reliving that first kill eased his tension better than a triple shot of vodka. Nothing in his experience had matched the long-term high from beating the queer to death. His first hit, and there'd been how many since? He'd lost count. He couldn't imagine a better life than the one he'd lived during the three years since faking his death.

Able to relax now, he adjusted his seat, stretched out his legs, and let his thoughts rush ahead. In Phoenix, take a cab downtown and rent a car at a hotel. That way, if something went wrong, there would be no link between the vehicle and this flight, so the cops wouldn't be able to backtrack him to Chicago. Drive to Flagstaff and pick up his weapons at the local UPS office, where he had shipped them to himself via overnight freight.

The stakeout would be a flaming bore, but maybe Cervosier would show. The prospect of combining a payday with the kick of wasting her drove a tremor of excitement through him. *Take her to an isolated spot; make sure she lasts a long time.* He closed his eyes and imagined her expression, her voice, as she begged, pleaded, then screamed away her final moments. If he believed that religion crap, he would have asked God to make her head for Arizona instead of Arkansas.

Hank Pekins stopped to refuel his ten-year-old Buick Skylark in Marianna, Arkansas, and checked his road map. Perryville was near the southeastern corner of the state, maybe another hundred and twenty-five miles. He'd been in Memphis closing a deal for some weapons and was about to shut down his computer and head for the airport when the broker's e-mail came in. Six grand for a three-day stakeout, the message had promised; an additional twenty-four if he bagged the quarry.

Easy money, and the job meshed with a contract he had pending in Las Vegas. But he would be on a tight schedule if the stakeout lasted the full three days. He'd have to swing out to Nevada the day he finished.

Maybe he'd get lucky and score the hit. He could use the additional twenty-four grand, and the target wouldn't be his first kill, just his first as an independent contractor. Not his first female, either, but that wouldn't make it any easier. Old cultural tapes—"Don't play rough with girls, Hank"—refused to stay buried, even though he knew women could be every bit as vicious and dangerous as men. He'd learned that lesson in Bosnia years earlier, almost too late to keep a female sidekick of Slobodan Milosevic from taking him out.

This one was like that, he guessed: beautiful and deadly. The digital photo of her, those haunting eyes, burned in his memory. But she had three kills to her credit. He had to be careful not to become her fourth.

On the other hand, he hadn't been able to corroborate the broker's claim that she'd whacked three men. His Internet check on her revealed only that she was a professor of history at a university in Haiti and had published several scholarly journal articles.

In contrast, an Internet search on his Las Vegas target uncovered a history of violence and corruption: Mob enforcer in Detroit; five years in a state pen for suborning a juror and conspiracy to assault a prosecuting attorney; after his release, a rapid climb up the underworld career ladder, leaving behind a trail of unproven criminal allegations. The mobster was the kind of target Hank had envisioned when he decided to solve his family's money problems by contracting for the same work he'd once done for the government.

After Vegas, he would take some time off and lend a hand back home: harvest the hay, repair fences, store up extra firewood. Maybe drive over to Eldora for a visit with Jason and Sylvia. He hadn't spent nearly enough time with their kids, and he ought to enjoy them while he still could. Then back to the grind, to pile up enough cash to keep the farm going indefinitely, before he got too sick to work.

CHAPTER THREE

AT THE RIVER CENTER Mall in Perryville, Arkansas, Shelby Cervosier dipped into her meager cash hoard to buy clothing for Carmen: sneakers, underwear, jeans, and a red, white, and blue T-shirt with *Super Sister* emblazoned across the front and outlined with glitter. In one of the mall's public restrooms, they brushed their teeth, washed their faces, and changed out of clothing that had turned grungy during the bus ride from Atlanta.

Carmen raised her hands so Shelby could pull the new T-shirt on over her head. "Are we going to stay with Elizabeth?" she asked as Shelby tugged and straightened the shirt.

"No, sweetheart. We'll just visit awhile." Shelby tucked the shirt's tail into Carmen's new jeans and dug a hairbrush from their bag. "We'll find our own place to live," she said as she tried to tame the little girl's curly black hair.

As the words left her mouth, she wondered anew whether or not such a place existed. With Haiti's security service looking for her, she couldn't go home. But American authorities wanted her for manslaughter, or they would when word got out that she was no longer cooperating with the CBTF. And if Krystal's contract killers found her, the interests of both governments would become irrelevant.

Carmen's voice cut through her thoughts: "We'll take care of each other, won't we?"

"We certainly will." Shelby kissed the serious little face. "We'll always look out for each other."

Holding hands, they walked both levels of the mall end to end, and Shelby noted possible escape routes and places to hide, just in case. She had been here once before. When she and her fellow refugees first slipped into America and moved into that "safe house" in a nearby swamp, the man charged with their welfare brought her to the mall, treated her to a shopping spree and dinner, and let her use a public telephone to call her former classmate in Arizona. Only later did Shelby understand his true motive: to learn who she knew in America and to separate her from the other refugees so he could claim her for himself.

Memories of being beaten and raped after spurning his advances peppered her with chill bumps and forced bile into her throat. She welcomed Carmen's voice pulling her from the waking nightmare: "Can we eat now?"

In the food court, Carmen picked their lunch: greasy cheese-and-pepperoni pizza. They dumped their leftovers in a trash can and, with fifteen minutes before their scheduled rendezvous with Elizabeth, walked the mall again. While Carmen admired window displays, Shelby watched for assassins. But what did a killer-for-hire look like? Wouldn't such a person be skilled at blending in, appearing to be an ordinary laborer or businessman or housewife? She checked her watch: five more minutes. Suppose something had happened and Elizabeth didn't show?

"Excuse me, ma'am," said a feminine voice from behind her.

Shelby wheeled to face three girls, none more than fifteen or sixteen, all wearing too little clothing and too much makeup, inexpertly applied. The girls were a study in contrasts: one tall and skinny, another grossly overweight, the third petite and pretty. The small one said, "Is your name Shelby Ker-something?"

Masking her concern with a veneer of nonchalance, Shelby glanced around, looking for adults who might be working with the teenagers. She unzipped the side pocket of her overnight bag, where she had stowed the pistol she'd taken from the phony nanny. "Should I know you?"

"The old lady said to come get you."

"We was just hangin' out," the tall girl said. "Doin' some weed in the john. This old lady says she don't feel good and can we go find you."

"Did she give you her name?"

"Gave us yours," said the small, pretty girl. "Said you'd be hanging in the food court with a little nigg"—she glanced at Carmen and back at Shelby—"with a brown-skinned kid."

The hefty girl looked nervous. She tugged at her petite friend's shoulder. "Come on, Patty. Let's go."

Patty jerked away. "She don't look good. Said she's your friend and we should find you."

"Where is she?"

"Downstairs, in the john. We'll show you." The small girl began walking. Her friends fell in step.

Shelby started to follow but hesitated. This could be a trick to get her away from the crowd, but what if it wasn't? Besides, the girls were young, barely in their teens. They wouldn't be working with a hired killer. Grasping Carmen's hand, she hurried to catch up.

Downstairs, retail stores gave way to shoe shops, insurance agencies, dry cleaners, and game arcades, and the crowd thinned. Giggling and prancing, the girls entered an office annex that looked deserted except for two Sunday workers visible through the storefront window of one office.

Farther down, a middle-aged security guard paced in front of a restroom area. When they approached, he blew out a deep breath. "You Miz Cervosier?"

He looked ordinary and harmless in his ill-fitting, wrinkled brown uniform with its First Alert Security shoulder patch and a name tag identifying him as Randolph. Even so, Shelby kept her distance. And she kept a hand on the pistol in her overnight bag. "What is this about?"

Pointing to the restroom, he said, "Got a sick woman in there. I was gonna call it in, but she said some kids were looking for you. Asked me to wait." He handed the small teenager some folded bills. "You did good, girls. Buy yourselves a treat."

They hurried away, and the security guard turned back to Shelby. "Kids sometimes loiter in the restrooms down here. I was doing a routine check and found the sick lady."

"Where is she?"

"Said she was gonna throw up." He looked at the restroom door and back at Shelby. "It didn't feel right, leaving her in there alone, but it's a woman's place, and . . ." He turned both hands palms up.

Tugging Carmen's hand, her pulse racing, Shelby headed for the restroom door. Behind her, the guard said, "I'll just wait here."

With her hand on the door, Shelby hesitated. Wouldn't the guard have a schedule to keep? Why would he wait around without checking with his supervisor? And why did he give those girls money? Realizing she had let her concern for Elizabeth cloud her reason, she stepped back.

The two weekend office workers she had seen before were not visible from this spot. Paranoid, maybe, but Shelby backed farther from the door. Her hand in the overnight bag gripped the pistol tighter. "Why don't you bring her out? I'll wait."

The guard edged closer. He held what looked like an oversized TV remote, except for its bright yellow color. He pointed it at her.

Get away, her instincts screamed. She jerked the snub-nosed pistol from her overnight bag. It snagged the zipper, and in her panic she almost dropped it.

Before she recovered, blue fire glowed at the tip of the yellow device in the guard's hand. Her chest stung. Intolerable pain shot through her, and her vision blanked out. She tried to scream but could not.

Regaining her senses but with no control over her musculature, she felt herself being dragged. The man dropped her. Curled like a fetus on the restroom floor, she tried in vain to stem the tremors that convulsed her. She couldn't get up or even respond to Carmen, who knelt at her side, shaking her and crying. Unable to raise her head, she cut her eyes sharply to watch the security guard.

He lugged a sign—*Restroom Closed, Cleaning in Progress*—out the door and returned without it. "You gonna be quiet?" he asked. "I need to zap you again?"

"No more," she tried to say. It came out as gibberish, a guttural, animal sound.

"You'll be okay in a couple minutes." Kneeling at her side, across from Carmen, he flashed a hypodermic, twisted its plunger, and tapped the needle. "This will sting." He stabbed it into her thigh and pushed the plunger. "I want you to stay on the floor," he said as he stowed the hypodermic in a pouch on his belt. Still kneeling, he turned his attention to Carmen. "Sprout, that shot ought to make her feel better, but you need to stay close in case it doesn't. Will you do that?"

Carmen, her crying reduced to sniffles, did not answer. But

she remained on her knees, one hand clinging to Shelby, the other clutching Snaggly.

Able to turn her head now, Shelby watched the guard pocket the bullets from the snub-nosed handgun and drop it back into her overnight bag. She willed her arms, then her legs, to move. They obeyed reluctantly, sluggishly. She wanted to get off the floor and run. Wanted to fight, to plead, to scream. But she didn't want him to use that vicious thing on her again. Her body vibrated, her mind whirred, but she stayed on the floor.

The man dragged something from a toilet stall and expanded it: a folding wheelchair. "What put you on the floor was fifty thousand volts driven at seven watts. It's called a stun gun." He pushed the wheelchair close. "I need to use it again?"

She had read about stun guns, knew how they worked and what they could do, but she hadn't imagined they would be so painful. Using all her strength, she lifted her head and shook it. Exhausted from the effort, she rested it on the floor again.

The man smiled at Carmen. "You guys friends?"

"Don't you hurt her," Carmen said, her voice quivering. "She's my sister."

Something—surprise, maybe anger—flashed in the man's eyes. It was gone in a wink, and Shelby, still recovering, barely saw it.

The man fingered the badge on his shirt. "I'm one of the good guys, trying to help. Where's your mother?"

That set Carmen to crying in big hiccoughy gasps. She turned from him and clung to Shelby.

He displayed his stun gun to Shelby again. "You ought to be able to sit up now. Give it a try, but move real slow."

Some of her strength had returned, but her body still trembled. There seemed to be no damage other than bruises where she had hit the floor. "What happened to Elizabeth?" she asked after struggling to a sitting position.

"The librarian? She's running late. Blown tire." He motioned to the wheelchair. "Climb in."

By pulling on the chair's seat, then its arms, Shelby got her knees under her and elevated her torso enough to ease her bottom onto the chair. "How do you know she had a blowout?"

"Tiny detonator glued to a tire. They explode when the rubber heats up." Standing behind Shelby, he reached over her shoulders to fasten a strap that held her in the chair. "What's the kid doing with you?"

Shelby's body no longer trembled, but the restroom had turned fuzzy at the edges of her vision, and everything seemed to be receding. The hypodermic, she realized. "She told you. We're sisters."

"And you let her tag along while you play cat-and-mouse with people like me?" He walked around the chair and stared at Shelby. "She's not part of this. If she gets hurt, it'll be your fault."

He had been on the verge of disappearing. His voice helped Shelby bring him back into focus. "Let her go, then."

"What? Say that again."

Hadn't she spoken clearly? She tried again but forgot what she wanted to say. Her vision narrowed to a tunnel in which he stood far back. She couldn't see Carmen. "Where's my sister?" she tried to ask, but she couldn't get her tongue around the words.

He turned his head and spoke to someone outside Shelby's vision tunnel, something about her being sick and needing to go somewhere. Did he say *hospital*? Yes, and he must have been talking to Carmen.

Carmen! She had to escape. "Run," Shelby tried to say. She knew she had failed but wasn't sure how she knew.

Everything started moving. The door's facing passed around her, and a long passageway zipped by. An outside portal rushed toward her, then trees and cars. Hot, burning sunlight. Where was Carmen? Why was everything in motion?

Vaguely, as if in a dream, she heard Carmen say, "She's really sick."

"Afraid so, sprout," said a heavier voice. "She'll be okay when we get her to the hospital. Hold the door for me. That's it. Let's get her in the seat."

CHAPTER FOUR

SHELBY'S HEAD HURT—A THROBBING somewhere deep inside. Her mouth felt arid, sand-coated. She was in a moving car driven by a man in uniform. A metal handcuff tethered her left wrist to the adjustment lever under the seat.

Memories rushed in: the mall bathroom, the security guard, the stun gun. Turning her head made it hurt worse, but she saw Carmen in the backseat. "You promised to let my sister go."

"Welcome back," the man said. "You behave, and she'll be okay."

"You'll let her go?"

"If you don't give me trouble."

Shelby studied the man, then his car. From the vehicle's obvious age, its faded vinyl and frayed upholstery fabric, she decided he wasn't a CBTF agent. A trained professional wouldn't risk being picked up for auto theft or having his personal car identified. He would use fake or stolen identification and rent a vehicle. That clinched her conviction that having her killed was Krystal's personal decision, not one sanctioned by the American government.

"Shelby?" Carmen reached forward and touched her shoulder. "Do you feel better?"

"I'm fine, honey." She patted Carmen's hand while her mind, still sluggish, processed their situation. They were on a rural, gravel-surfaced road. No houses, no other cars. The man was looking for a place to dispose of their bodies. Once he found it, wouldn't he kill them both?

Panic flared. "You said you would let Carmen go. You said—"

"I'll put the kid out where she'll need some time to find help."

He was saying that to calm her. Why would he leave a witness? "She's just a little girl." Shelby peered at the killer through tears that pooled in her eyes. "She's never hurt anyone."

"What's wrong?" Carmen asked. She started crying. "Shelby, let's go back."

"Please," Shelby said, rubbing her watery eyes and runny nose with the back of her free hand. "She's only a baby."

"Quit blubbering. I told you she'll be okay." The killer braked to a stop and twisted around in his seat. "All right, sprout. This is where you bail."

Carmen sat still, staring at him. "I'm not afraid of you," she declared in a shaky voice.

"You're a brave little girl. You'll be fine." Reaching back, he unlatched her seat belt. "I want you to walk back the way we came." He pointed to the side of the road. "Stay on that side, so you'll be facing traffic. It'll turn dark before you get to the main road, but there's nothing to be afraid of. Just keep walking. Can you do that?"

Relief flooded Shelby so abruptly that she couldn't think. Then Carmen said, "I'm staying with Shelby," and the panic returned.

"No, you aren't," she screamed. "You get out of this car. Get out. Get out!"

"Shelby—"

"Get out!" *Go, baby, before he changes his mind.* "Do as you're told!"

"Don't be so harsh," the killer said. He got out and opened Carmen's door. "You have to walk back to the main road, sprout. There's something Shelby and I need to do, and we can't have a little girl with us."

Carmen edged across the seat and out of the car at a sloth's pace. Standing on the gravel, she hugged Snaggly and stared at Shelby.

Through a fresh flood of tears, Shelby saw the killer turn her sister toward the way they had come, heard him tell her to keep walking, no matter what. "Don't turn back; don't sit down. Just keep going. You'll be all right."

He stripped off the security-guard shirt and tossed it on the backseat. Under it he wore a dark blue, crewneck T-shirt. He got back behind the wheel and, a few yards farther down the road, turned and sped back the way they had come. They whipped by Carmen, enveloping her in a cloud of dust.

Shelby twisted to look out the back window. Carmen had not moved from where the killer had put her out of the car. She simply stood and watched them ride away without her. Shelby bit her lip to keep from crying. She could not control the shaking of her shoulders.

"Someone will see her walking," the killer said. "They'll turn her over to the cops. She'll be okay."

She wouldn't be okay. She was free of the immediate threat of execution, but the authorities would recognize her accent and ship her home. The Haitian government turned orphans over to the church, which housed them in overcrowded camps with minimal supervision. Carmen was too pretty. Thugs would take her out of the camp and sell her into child prostitution. She would be abused, ultimately destroyed. By convincing the killer to let her go, Shelby had condemned her to a slower, more agonizing death. Perhaps to a fate worse than death.

The assassin had gone to all this trouble, so he must care about children. And a professional killer would have finished the job the moment he got them into the car. Maybe she could play on his emotions and get him to make arrangements for Carmen. Given what awaited the child in Haiti, it was worth the gamble. Forcing words through the tightness in her throat, Shelby said, "Will you tell me your name?"

"Hank," he said after hesitating for a moment. "You can call me Hank."

"We're here illegally, Hank. Do you realize what will happen to Carmen?"

"She'll get a free trip home. No big deal."

"No one will meet her when the trip ends. I'm her only family."

He shifted his gaze between her and the road. "She said you're sisters. What about the skin color?"

"We have the same father but different mothers."

"And you're both in the country illegally?"

"How else do Haitians get in?"

"Why isn't she with her mom?"

"Her mother came with us. They—the men who were supposed to be caring for us—took her away. I don't know where."

Hank studied her face as if memorizing its features. "You don't look Haitian."

"Because my ancestors weren't African? Haiti has minorities, the same as America. It's just that the colors are reversed."

He shrugged. "This isn't my problem."

"You must have seen on television how chaotic things are in Haiti, how street gangs are running amok, killing and looting." Shelby made no effort to conceal the pleading in her voice. "You saw how pretty she is. Can you imagine what will happen to her there? What doped-up thugs will do to her?"

He ran fingers though his hair. "What do you have in mind?"

"Elizabeth Fontaine, the woman I was supposed to meet at the mall. She'll take care of her."

"You expect me to back up? Drop her on the librarian's door-step? Why would I do something that stupid?"

"Because you're human? Because you remember what it's like to be small and helpless, so scared you can't think? Maybe you have a sister or a daughter?"

His face paled. Muscles clenched in his jaw. "You're looking for an angle. Trying to delay this."

"If that's what you believe, kill me now. Shoot me or cut my throat, dump my body on the road. Then go back for Carmen and take her to Elizabeth."

"It isn't that simple. I'm supposed to dispose of your body where it won't be found."

"Then let me talk to Elizabeth. I'll explain that I'm going away with you and I need her to watch Carmen. What risk is there? If I get out of line or speak out of turn, you can kill all of us."

"You expect me to believe you'd collaborate in your own ex-ecution?"

"I'll kill myself, if that's what it takes to save my sister."

Several moments of silence. "This was supposed to be simple. Do you, send in your thumb as proof, collect my fee."

Send in my thumb? She shuddered at the thought of having her corpse mutilated. "It will be simple. Just drop Carmen off with Elizabeth. Do whatever you want with me."

Slowing the car, Hank pursed his lips and frowned at her. "You're gonna behave?"

He was going to do it? The gamble had been such a long shot that Shelby had not dared hope. Now, she did. "I'll do whatever you say. I just want her to be safe."

Mumbling too softly for her to understand, he turned the car around. Minutes later, they coasted to a stop by Carmen. She still stood on the spot where Shelby had ordered her out of the car. "You act up while she's with us," Hank said, "give me any trouble at all, you're both dead." He got out and opened the rear door. "Climb in, sprout. Change of plans."

Carmen slid into the backseat. To Shelby she said, "I knew you wouldn't leave me."

Tears filled Shelby's eyes so that she could barely see. Using her free hand, she wiped caked-on dust from the sweaty little face.

Hank dug out a handkerchief and handed it to her.

"Thank you." She cleaned Carmen's face with the handkerchief and used it to blot the tears flooding her own cheeks.

Hank knew the way to Elizabeth's modest bungalow. Since he had known about the mall, their planned meeting, Shelby guessed he had watched the librarian's house and bugged her telephone.

Elizabeth did not have a garage or even a driveway. She always parked on the street in front of her house, but her car wasn't there. "Might take her awhile to get home," Hank said as he circled the block to park in shade across the street. "She'll have to get that tire changed."

With the car windows open to catch the occasional breeze that rustled nearby cottonwoods, they waited. Carmen fidgeted in the backseat, and Hank suggested she play in Elizabeth's yard, where they could watch her.

"Let Shelby come, too," Carmen said.

"She and I have to talk. Grown-up stuff."

"I won't listen."

Shelby had promised to do whatever he said. She had to make certain Carmen did the same. "Go on, honey. We won't leave you again."

With obvious reluctance, Carmen climbed out. Sitting on the grass with her back resting against a shade tree and Snaggly in her lap, she stared at the car.

"Most kids would be jumping and running," Hank said. "Working off energy."

"Most haven't been through what she has."

Neither spoke for several moments. Shifting in his seat, Hank checked the street in both directions. He glanced at his watch. "Your friend shoulda been here by now. Maybe we ought to leave the kid on her doorstep."

"I need to talk to her, explain that I'll be gone indefinitely. That way, she'll arrange a cover story for Carmen."

"You have an hour to live, and you're worried about child care arrangements?"

"Please, just a few more minutes." The tears started again. She blotted them with his handkerchief, still wadded in her hand.

"You know I'll do all three of you if you try anything. If you say anything to make the librarian suspicious."

"I won't cause any trouble. Just give me this chance to get my sister settled. To die knowing she's all right."

He didn't agree, but neither did he refuse. He checked his watch again and stared through the windshield.

Shelby studied him while he watched the road. Taut skin on his face and his obvious physical fitness belied the gray that peppered his hair, but crinkles at the corners of his eyes confirmed time's relentless march. She guessed him to be in his middle-to-late forties. Like the ratty old car, his indecision about Carmen told a story: a middle-aged man, desperate for money and with nowhere to turn, trying his luck as an assassin. If she had him pegged right, he would make mistakes. But she had to talk to him, keep him from growing impatient. *Mustn't give him a chance to think about it and change his mind.*

"I'm not going anywhere." She shook her handcuffed wrist. "Does it make any difference if you kill me in one hour or two?"

"Time is money." He looked at Carmen, who stared at the car, and turned back to Shelby. "Why'd you leave Haiti?"

"To keep from being arrested. I had to . . ." *How could she explain when she didn't understand it herself?* "It's complicated."

"So, you're running from the thugs that took over down there. How did that get you on a hit list in America?"

It was none of the killer's business, but she had to keep him talking until Elizabeth came home. "Krystal, the woman who's paying you to kill me, is with your government. I did something for her to keep from being deported. She wants me dead because of it."

"A government agency?" He shook his head. "Come on. They'd have their own cleanup crew, a hell of a lot more sophisticated than me. No way they'd outsource something like that."

"Not the government, just Krystal. She blackmailed me into helping with a political assassination." *It surprised Shelby that she could discuss this. Having cheated death so many times already, perhaps she subconsciously believed she would find a way out once more. Or had she simply reconciled herself to dying?* "I'm the only witness."

"She wants you axed for personal reasons? A goddamned career move?"

"So far as I can tell. There's no other—"

"Shelby," Carmen said, interrupting them. She stood with one hand on the car door, the other holding Snaggly. "I have to go to the bathroom."

"Elizabeth will be here any minute, sweetheart."

"I have to go now."

Hank sighed and opened his door. "I'll take her inside. You know what'll happen if you act up while we're gone?"

Shelby nodded and centered her attention on Carmen. "Hank will take you inside to use Elizabeth's bathroom."

He tried the front door, then knelt and talked with Carmen. With his hand on her shoulder, they walked around the house.

The moment they were out of sight, Shelby checked the car's glove compartment but found nothing other than a dog-eared owner's manual. Rummaging under the seat with her free hand, she groped for something to use as a weapon. Nothing there. She jerked on the bar that held the handcuff, trying to pull loose. No good. A car passed, but signaling for help would get Carmen killed or sent back to Haiti.

Hank and Carmen came out the front door, Carmen sucking on a purple Popsicle. She giggled at something he said. "He broke a window," she said when they reached the car.

"Door was locked." He got Carmen settled in the backseat and slid behind the wheel. "I made some phone calls. Your friend's in the hospital. Auto accident."

An accident? Pain slapped inside Shelby's chest. "How bad?"

"They said she'll be released tomorrow."

Shelby's heartbeat stumbled. She had come so close to arranging for Carmen. Was it all for naught? "We'll be good. It's just overnight."

"Overnight?" He looked startled. "You can't be serious."

"You've already gone to great lengths for Carmen. You must care about children." Thoughts and words tumbled over each other in Shelby's effort to keep her little sister alive and in America. "We'll do exactly as we're told. Won't cause a bit of trouble. We'll even try to be good company." She grasped his arm with her free hand.

He jerked away as if her touch burned. With both hands gripping the steering wheel, he stared at the road.

"You have to spend the night somewhere," she pleaded. "Why not here?" There had to be some motivational lever she could pull, some emotional button she could push, to convince him. "I'll do anything you want me to—everything—and you'll still earn your fee. You won't be delayed any more than you already are. And you will have done a charitable deed."

With a sigh, he started the engine. "Not here. The neighbors might get suspicious." In silence, he drove through a seedy part of Perryville and pulled in at a down-at-the-heels motel with a blinking VACANCY sign. He turned off the engine but looked as if he was having second thoughts. "This is stupid. Amateurish."

"It's the right thing to do, helping a defenseless child. It's safe, it's convenient for you, and it's decent. You're being a kind, decent human being."

"Being decent ends careers. I swear, one peep, and it's over. You doubt me?"

She had to soothe him, keep him from changing his mind. "We'll be quiet. We'll both do exactly as you say."

He got out and opened Carmen's door, wiped purple Popsicle stains from her lips and chin, and clicked her seat belt open. "Let's go, sprout."

Unmoving, Carmen looked at Shelby.

"Go with him," Shelby said, her head pounding with fear that he would change his mind. "Behave yourself, and don't talk to anyone."

They came back five minutes later, Carmen clutching a key on a ring. Hank opened her door and waited while she sat and arranged Snaggly in her lap. He snapped her seat belt, smoothed her hair, and slid behind the steering wheel. "You believe that guy? Me with a little girl, and he asks if I want the room for the night or by the hour." He shook his head and started the engine. "What's happened to morality in this country?"

He parked midway down a row of rooms and wrapped the security-guard shirt around his stun gun. As they walked to the door, he held the shirt close to Carmen's head but behind her where she couldn't see it.

From what she had seen so far, Shelby doubted that he would use the thing on Carmen, but she dared not risk it. Obeying his order, she walked ahead of them to the room, took the key from Carmen, and opened the door.

Inside, he handcuffed Shelby to a bedpost. She could sit with her wrist at her side or lie down with it over her head. In the car, the cuff had chafed and bruised her wrist; she had learned the futility of trying to slip her hand free.

Glaring at Hank, Carmen climbed onto the bed beside Shelby. "Why did he hook you to the bed?"

With her free hand, Shelby patted her sister's shoulder. "He's supposed to, honey. I'll explain when we're alone."

Hank pulled the phone line from the telephone and the wall jack and dropped the coiled wire into his pocket. Smiling, he turned to Carmen. "I need help with the bags, kiddo."

At Shelby's urging, Carmen handed Snaggly to her and followed Hank outside. They returned with Shelby's bag, a computer case, and a black leather overnight case.

Carmen snagged the television remote from a table and climbed back onto the bed with Shelby. Hank spent time in the bathroom with the door opened enough to keep an eye on them. He shook a capsule from a vial, washed it down with tap water, and stepped out of Shelby's line of vision. Urine splashed in the toilet bowl. It flushed.

He came back into the room and, with Carmen engrossed in learning how to work the TV remote, walked close to Shelby and said in a low voice, "You need to go?" He nodded toward the bathroom.

"Yes, please." She forced a smile, though tension knotted all her muscles. He felt safe now, sure of himself. This would be her chance. She might not get another.

He slipped the stun gun into his bag and pulled out a pistol and a bulky metal cylinder. "This is a noise suppressor," he said as he screwed the cylinder to the pistol's barrel, whispering in her ear, his voice muffled by the blaring television. "I shoot you, it'll sound like a car door slamming. No one will pay attention, but your brain will splatter across the wall behind you. You little sister will carry that image in her head the rest of her life." He stepped back and tossed the handcuff key onto the bed where Shelby could reach it. "Open the end of the cuff that's fastened to the bedpost. Now, slide your feet onto the floor. Stand up, but move real slow." When she was standing with the open end of the handcuff dangling from her wrist, he said, "Put the cuff on your other wrist."

Rubbing her shackled wrist, she stared at him, pretending not to understand. Did she dare risk it? If she tried and failed, would he kill Carmen? Even if he didn't, if he simply abandoned her, she would almost certainly perish in Haiti's child welfare system. But what were her prospects here, with no identity documents and only a middle-aged, small-town librarian to look after her? Anyway, Shelby didn't think she would fail. She was probably twenty years younger than him, and she was fast, in top physical condition. Yes, she could take him, and Carmen would want her to chance it.

"Slip the cuff around your other wrist," he said again.

She grasped the opened cuff and, as she fumbled with it, pushed the grooved end into the catch on the other side, locking it around thin air. When the lock clicked, she dropped the cuff and let it dangle. "Sorry," she said, fear making her voice tremble. "I think I locked it."

He exhaled a grunt of obvious exasperation. "Hand me the key."

She picked it off the bed and stepped closer to drop it into his outstretched palm. Was she close enough to get past that pistol's ugly snout before he pulled the trigger?

"Put your wrists together and hold them out. Arm's length."

She held her breath and stared at him, steeling herself for what had to be done.

His voice turned hard. "Stick out your wrists."

She brought them up fast, and her fist caught him just under his eye. The pistol barrel wavered, and she lashed out with her cuffed hand. The dangling handcuff slashed his temple. Stepping in quickly, she aimed a knee at his groin.

CHAPTER FIVE

THE TARGET'S FIRST BLOW surprised Hank but did no real damage. Her follow-up blow came from the fist with the dangling handcuff, and the flailing end of the cuff slammed into his temple less than an inch from his eye.

Acting on instinct, he pivoted and took her thrusting knee on the inside of his thigh, barely avoiding having his testicles crushed. He snaked an arm around her. Using his hip as a fulcrum, and still gripping the pistol, he flipped her onto her back on the bed. He fell on top of her and heard her lungs empty with an explosive grunt.

That didn't keep her from slapping at him. Then she doubled her fist and swung.

He blocked the blow with a forearm. A hand in her hair pinned her against the mattress. "Behave, now."

Sucking short gasps of air, her face screwed into a wild-animal snarl, she tried to claw his face. Failing that, she dug at his windpipe.

He released her hair and captured both her wrists in one hand.

She reared her head to bite his chest.

"Christ!" He tossed the pistol aside and banged her forehead with the heel of his newly freed hand. Her head hit the mattress. He fisted her hair again and held her there, boiling anger threatening to erupt into rage.

She wrenched an arm from his grasp. Bucking and twisting, pounding his shoulders and chest, she tried to dislodge him. Still gasping, she said, "Get . . . off . . . me."

With his bulk pressing her into the mattress, he accepted the blows she rained on his chest and shoulders and waited for exhaustion to calm her. Disgust with himself for carelessness mixed with his anger at her for lashing out. She was doing what he would have done under the same circumstances: making a last-ditch stand, putting everything she had into a final shot at survival. He'd given her the opening by growing lax, by letting his doubts about the job get in the way of professionalism.

His anger cooled further as her thrashing slowed. Her blows lost force, and he knew it was over. Stupid to feel a sense of betrayal over the attack, since she couldn't know he'd been thinking about setting her free. He would have had less respect for her if she had given up easily.

Another feeling edged in: a tide of warmth spreading from where their bodies pressed together. Shamed by his lust for a helpless foe, he loosened his hold and shifted to take his weight off of her.

Carmen, a flashing bundle of fury, hurtled across the bed and latched onto his back. Her momentum propelled everyone off the bed and onto the floor.

Hank rolled across the floor and came to his knees, the kid still clinging to his back. First an exhausted and terrified woman attacking him despite the weapon he held on her, and now a mere slip of a girl. What kind of people were these? Reaching back over his shoulders, he grasped the child with both hands and tried to lift her over his head.

Clinging with her legs around his waist, Carmen hissed like an enraged cat. Her arms snaked around his head. Fingernails dug furrows in his cheek.

By jerking her upward and forward over his head, he dislodged her. He stood her in front of him and spun her so she faced away and could no longer reach his face.

When Carmen's momentum drove them all onto the floor, the target had landed on her back. Now, audibly gasping for air, she struggled to her feet and zombie-shuffled to the pistol on the bed. As Hank, holding Carmen with one hand, got to his feet and started toward her, she pointed the weapon at him.

He froze. "The kid—careful with that thing."

She steadied the pistol with both hands. "Put her down."

"You put the weapon down. Just drop it on the bed."

"I'll shoot you. I'm good with guns."

"Is that right?" If she knew anything about firearms, why was she squinting instead of drawing a bead on him? And she had not assumed a shooter's stance. The way the heavy semiautomatic shook as she held it at arm's length, everything on his side of the room had an equal chance of being hit if she fired. Whether or not she had killed the three men her contact profile claimed, he guessed she'd never held a firearm before. "Good with semiautomatics, maybe," he said, testing her. "I'll bet that's the first revolver you've held."

"I learned to shoot with my father's revolver. It was just like this one."

He gave her an A for courage even though she was an abysmal failure as a liar. "You're holding a semiautomatic." He set Carmen on the floor and reached for the weapon.

"Stay there!" The target backed until her legs bumped the bed. He kept moving, and her finger flexed on the trigger. She looked shocked when nothing happened.

Before she could try again, he wrenched the weapon from her.

Gripping her handcuffed wrist, he pulled it down and clipped the other cuff to the bed frame. "Next time, be sure the safety's off." Still holding the pistol, he looked at Carmen and touched his cheek, feeling the liquid warmth of oozing blood. "She ripped my face open."

"She's just a baby," the target cried. "Don't hurt her. Please don't hurt her."

He glanced at the pistol in his hand and looked back at the target. Her eyes reflected terror. Not for her fate, he realized, but for what might happen to her sister. "You think I'd . . . ?" Yes, she thought him capable of killing the little girl. Why would she expect a paid killer to have qualms about his victim's age or circumstances?

"I made a terrible mistake," the target cried. With her free hand, she reached out to him. "You have the power. You can be merciful."

Carmen eased around him, crawled onto the bed, and crab-walked across the mattress, keeping her eyes on him. As she pressed close to her big sister, her thin little body vibrated like a tuning fork, but the only sound she made was heavy breathing.

"I'm not a baby killer, so you can put that out of your mind." Hank touched his fingers to the wound on his cheek and winced. "Those nails are deadly weapons, sprout. Stay on the bed with your sister."

He backed into the bathroom, leaving the door open so he could see them. At the sink, he cupped water in his palm and rinsed his cheek. With a damp towel pressed to the wounds, he walked back into the bedroom and sat on the couch, across the room from them. This should have been a simple job, but his halfhearted approach was screwing it up. He glared at the target.

She glared back. The look of a frightened rabbit was gone now.

She must have believed him about not hurting Carmen. With her untethered arm around the kid, she rocked to and fro. "You've terrified her."

He pulled the towel away and inspected it. "She's scared? How do you think I felt when she came at me like a banshee?" He pressed the towel back against his cheek.

"You need ice. To stop the bleeding."

"This is getting it." He needed antiseptic, though. Bandages. Probably needed a tetanus booster, and he was going to have scars. "I'll have to go out, but we've gotta have an understanding."

"I made a mistake," she said again, her voice that of an adult trying to calm an overexcited child—or maybe a sane person trying to sooth a maniac. "I shouldn't have attacked you."

He walked over and extended a hand to Carmen but backed off when she cringed away. Never before had a child been afraid of him, and he didn't like the feeling. Putting calm in his voice, he said, "I'm not going to hurt you, sprout." He shifted his gaze to the target. "Wars get started, whole populations killed off, because people misunderstand each other. Because they don't believe what they're told." He checked the towel and pressed it back against his face. "You both have to listen to me."

She nodded. "We're listening."

The first thing he had to do was wring some of the fright out of the little girl. He needed the target's help to do that. "Sprout, you don't have to be afraid of me. I won't hurt either of you. I don't know why your sister attacked me." He shot a challenging look at the target. "You explain it."

Her arm tightened around Carmen. She seemed to be processing his challenge, deciding whether or not to join in a conspiracy against her sister. A barely perceptible change in her expression told him she had made a decision.

"Hank is protecting us, sweetheart. He fastened me to the bed because he's afraid I'll go out where the bad people can see me."

Carmen spoke in a near-whisper: "You mean Lois?"

Lois? Hank perked up. Hadn't Shelby—*the target,* he reminded himself—didn't the target say the woman who wanted her dead was called Krystal?

"I mean bad men who work for the same people Lois does," the target said. "Hank is afraid they'll try to hurt me, and he's right. We shouldn't have fought him. We mustn't do anything like that again. He's our friend."

Carmen kept her face tucked against her big sister's side. "I hurt his face. Is he mad at me?"

"No, sprout," Hank said. "I'm not angry." He touched her hair, and she didn't shy away. "We need to be nice to each other."

Peeking out, she looked at him. "I'm not a sprout."

"Of course you aren't. You're a very pretty, very sweet young lady. I won't call you that again."

"Are you mad at Shelby?"

"Not the least bit. She's one of my favorite people." He pulled the towel away from his cheek and looked at it: no fresh blood. "I have to go out, get something to put on this. I'll need you to go with me."

Carmen didn't budge until Shelby—until the target—said, "Go with him, honey," and gave her a gentle push.

She slid off the bed and looked up at Hank. "Why can't Shelby come?"

He opened his mouth but closed it again when he realized he had no idea what to say. The target rescued him by forcing a smile and saying, "We can't risk having the bad people see me."

Carmen studied Hank for a moment. "Does she have to stay fastened to the bed?"

"Well, yeah. She needs . . ." He shrugged and looked at the target. She was better at this than he was. "Why don't you tell her?"

"I want him to keep me this way, honey. So I won't be tempted to go outside. It's safer."

Carmen looked dubious, but she let Hank take her hand and lead her outside. Halfway to the car, she said, "I forgot Snaggly."

They went back inside for the stuffed clown, and Carmen apparently decided to take her big sister's word as gospel. "Can I sit up front?" she asked as they approached the car.

"Of course." Hank opened the door for her.

She climbed in and waited for him to fasten her seat belt. "You're supposed to use yours, too," she said when he started to drive off. "It isn't safe."

"Right." He pulled the belt across his lap.

"I'm sorry about your face," she said as he pulled onto the road.

"You thought you were protecting your sister. That's a good thing." Reaching across, he caressed her head, tensing with worry that she would flinch. She didn't, and a flood of emotion warmed him.

What the hell was wrong with him? he wondered as he cruised in search of a pharmacy. At that shopping center, he had looked into the target's eyes and hesitated to use his stun gun. He'd almost waited too long, pressing the button only when she pulled that snub-nosed .38 from her bag. Another second and she'd have gotten the drop on him. He didn't know her, didn't want to know her, so why had his protective instincts kicked in? Why had he worried about giving her too much of the anesthetic when she had only a short time left anyway?

It had come close to costing him everything. In the motel

room, he'd barely avoided having his balls squashed by her knee, and she would have blown him away if she'd known how to fire a semiautomatic.

She had demonstrated the instincts of a killer. It gave credence to the statement in her contact profile that she'd iced three men. Why not go ahead with the hit, earn the additional twenty-four grand? The neat, simple way to do it was another injection like the one he'd given her at the shopping center, a massive overdose this time. She wouldn't even feel it. Her heart would just stop.

Carmen was a major complication. A really nice kid. Brave as a seasoned combat soldier, the way she'd stood up to him, trying to protect her big sister. He wasn't a kid killer, but that didn't mean he had to adopt her. He could just drop her off with the librarian in the morning, complete his contract, and go on to Vegas.

Yeah, he decided. *That's what I'll do.*

In the Walgreens, he bought cotton balls, sterile swabs, topical antiseptic, a tube of anesthetizing ointment, and a box of palm-sized gauze bandages. Standing in the checkout line with Carmen, he rested a hand lightly on her shoulder.

The clerk at the register eyed his purchases, then his face. "You had a tetanus booster?" she asked.

"I'll check with my doctor in the morning," he said, smiling at her. A popcorn machine near the store's exit enticed Carmen with its aroma, and she asked him for a box, promising to wait and eat it after dinner. They pulled in at a drive-through fast-food place, where he read the menu aloud and let her pick their meal: cheeseburgers and French fries.

At the UPS office in Flagstaff, Arizona, Vlad picked up the parcel he had shipped to himself to circumvent airline security procedures. Back in his rental car, he inspected the contents: a model 75B, nine-millimeter Luger semiautomatic in a nylon holster, a noise suppressor for the Luger, a long-barreled .357 Smith & Wesson revolver with a laser sight, ammunition for both, a razor-edged hunting knife in a soft leather scabbard, and his electronics kit. With his weapons and tools back where they belonged, he felt more secure. At a Radio Shack outlet, he picked up a universal garage door opener, a voltammeter, and a canvas tool bag. He transferred several miniaturized transmitters from his electronics kit to the tool bag and dropped in the voltammeter. Following a city map, he drove to the home of the woman who had been Shelby Cervosier's classmate in graduate school: Barbara Rogers, wife to the Reverend Frederick Rogers. On the way, he clicked through local stations on the car's radio, looking for cool jazz.

As he approached his destination, the neighborhood changed. Split-level and two-story brick homes with two- and three-car garages gave way to newer and smaller, balloon-frame houses with carports, and free-standing garages or on-street parking. Sidewalks ended. Instead of wide boulevards bordered by sculpted lawns and mature shade trees, he traversed narrow streets between yards with haphazard landscaping. Graveled shoulders with drainage ditches supplanted concrete curbs with storm-water grates. With particular satisfaction, he noted that there were no streetlights. Pickup trucks in driveways or parked on the shoulder sported political slogans and environmental messages. His favorite, he decided, was DON'T CALIFORNICATE ARIZONA.

A stunted oak, the only mature tree on the Rogerses' block, shaded a portion of the shoulder occupied by a pickup truck and an aging SUV. Vlad backed his rental car between them. The SUV blocked his view, forcing him to slide over to the passenger side.

The Rogerses' home sported an attached two-car garage, one of the few on the block. Glass inserts adorned the garage door just above eye level. Vlad grunted his approval and slouched in the car seat, waiting for a light to come on inside the garage. When it did, he aimed his universal garage door opener, pressed the button twice, and held it down until whoever was inside opened the door. His door opener's LED blinked as its digital scanner captured the code that tripped the door.

A man he assumed to be the Reverend Frederick Rogers backed an ancient Volvo sedan into the street. The driver waved at the house, and the Volvo pulled away.

Vlad waited another twenty minutes. Then, wearing clean but faded serviceman's coveralls and a blond wig, carrying the canvas tool bag and whistling a show tune from the vintage musical *Oklahoma*, he sauntered to the house and rang the doorbell.

The woman who answered wore an ankle-length, pink chenille housecoat. She had brushed her hair but let it hang loose. Pretty but plain, she wore no makeup.

"Telephone company," he said, blessing her with his most engaging smile and flashing his wallet with a photo ID. "May I speak with the man of the house?"

She hesitated, probably wondering whether or not to tell him she was the only adult at home. "The reverend stepped out for a minute. Can I help you?"

"Well, shucks." Vlad twisted his face into a little-boy pout. "We've got a phone glitch somewhere on the block. I've narrowed it to this side of the street. Got to be downtown in an hour, but I could drive back out here." He put his smile back on. "I'm supposed to take my son to little league practice. Guess he'll have to miss."

"What is it that you need?"

He shifted his expression from shy little boy to handsome young man. "I have to check the impedance on your phones. It would only take a minute, but I don't want to intrude."

"Impedance? I don't understand."

He tweaked his smile a smidgen toward flirtatious but kept it mostly friendly. "It's a measure of opposition to current flow, ma'am. We need to keep the impedance of the load equal to that of the source of power. Takes just a minute to check, and it'll solve your neighbors' problem. I don't suppose you'd let me . . . ?"

"What do you have to do?"

He pulled the voltammeter from his tool bag. "Just run this little fellow by your phones. A matter of five or ten seconds on each receiver, and I'll be on my way. Sorry to disturb you."

Her posture, her expression, radiated reluctance. Would she blow the scam by calling the phone company? Nope, she unlatched the screen door and stepped back.

Vlad cranked up the amperage of his smile and pulled the screen door open. Damn, he was good. "Thank you so much, ma'am. This'll get my boy to ball practice on time."

With the voltammeter's dangling wires clipped to the first telephone, he unscrewed its mouthpiece and inserted a miniature transmitter, reassembled the mouthpiece, listened, and gave a grunt of satisfaction. He wiped the receiver to eliminate fingerprints and dropped it back onto its cradle. "No problem here," he said after bugging each of the household's three phones. "Must be the trans- former. That means we'll have to dig up your street. Sorry."

"That's all right. I'm sorry you didn't find the problem."

"You've been most gracious, ma'am. If you don't mind, I'll

check your junction box on my way out." She looked puzzled, and he treated her to his toothpaste-ad smile. "The outside gizmo where the phone wires come in. You know which side of the house it's on?"

She shrugged. "Ditzy housewife, right?"

"Don't worry about it. I'll just circle around and check on my way out. You have a real good day."

He found the outside junction box, noted obstacles in the yard that he might stumble over in the dark and the wire he would need to cut to disable their phones, and strolled back to his rental car. With a receiver plugged into the cigarette lighter, he cruised the neighborhood while monitoring the Rogerses' calls. If Cervosier showed up, he could take her before she got to the house. If not, they had no intruder alarm system, and he had easy access through the garage with his door opener.

CHAPTER SIX

THE MOMENT HANK AND Carmen left the motel room in search of bandages and food, Shelby jerked on her handcuff and pulled at the bedpost. Hopeless, no way to escape. She had blown her only chance. He would be on guard now, ready to kill at a moment's notice. Why hadn't she moved faster? Hit harder? Her fate was sealed; she was going to die. But he seemed committed to getting Carmen to Elizabeth. There was consolation in that.

Gradually, her attention shifted from her predicament to her overfull bladder. Remarkable how a simple biological function could push aside everything else. Life or death, she had to pee.

But maybe something more insidious was at work: a psychic shift. Like termites destroying a building's foundation, the corrosive essence of submission could be undermining her will to survive.

And why shouldn't it? The certainty of death was suffocating but at the same time liberating. Acceptance narrowed her focus to how she could convince Hank to deliver Carmen into Elizabeth's protection. No more escape attempts. Another failed rebellion would condemn her sister.

"I have to go," she said the moment Hank, trailing after Carmen and lugging a shopping bag in each hand, stepped back into the motel room. They had been away no more than half an hour, but the pressure of her bladder made it seem longer. "The bathroom."

Hank set his shopping bags down, locked the door, and stepped close. Speaking low so Carmen could not hear, he said, "You want the cuffs off so you can take another shot?"

"If I do it here, you'll smell it all night."

"Carmen, let's sit on the couch and find a TV program." He picked up his overnight bag and, sitting by Carmen with one arm along the back of the couch, handed her the TV remote. While she fiddled with it, he pulled something out of the bag—the stun gun he had used to put Shelby on the floor in the shopping center. Keeping it behind Carmen, he raised his hand enough for Shelby to see the hideous thing. He tossed the handcuff key to within her reach on the bed. "Leave the bathroom door open."

Defying his order, she closed the door far enough for a modicum of privacy. When she had finished and returned to the bed, she fumbled with the handcuffs, trying to shackle herself to the post.

"Shift across," he said. "Fasten your other arm."

She unlocked the cuff from the post, scooted to the other side of the bed, and shackled her left wrist. Her right, raw and bruised from the metal cuff, throbbed. "Thank you." She tossed him the key.

He sat on the edge of the bed. "Let's see that wrist." From his pharmacy shopping bag he pulled a tube of anesthetizing ointment. He smoothed the cream on her abused wrist.

It felt cool and soothing, and somehow comforting. "Thank you," she said again.

"Got some serious bruising. You try to pull loose?"

"It didn't work, obviously."

He finished applying the cream and carried the pharmacy bag into the bathroom, leaving the door ajar. She watched him use cotton balls and hydrogen peroxide to clean the trenches Carmen's nails had dug in his cheek. He smeared them with what Shelby guessed was an antibacterial salve and covered the clawed area with a palm-sized bandage.

Carmen eased off the couch. Craning her neck to see Hank, she tiptoed to the bed and climbed up by Shelby. She lifted Shelby's bruised wrist and rubbed lightly. "We brought you some food." She rested her head against Shelby's breast.

Shelby wrapped her free arm around her sister's shoulders. "I love you," she murmured.

"We found a drive-through fast-food joint," Hank said from the bathroom. "Burgers and fries." Back in the room, he arranged sandwiches, soft drinks, and a cardboard tub filled with popcorn on the coffee table. He shifted a burger, a bag of fries, and a Coke to the bedside table for Shelby. "Junk food pig-out."

Perching with her legs dangling off the bed, Carmen unwrapped Shelby's cheeseburger, spread the paper wrapper on the bedspread, and dumped the fries on it. Using her teeth, she tore open ketchup packets and squeezed the red goop over the fries.

Shelby's stomach rebelled at the odor of grilled meat and deep-fry grease. But she welcomed the Coke's sugar and moisture.

Carmen sidled back to the coffee table. Eyeing the food with obvious relish, she eased down onto the carpet and leaned back against the couch. At Shelby's prompting, she devoured a cheese-burger with ketchup-smothered fries.

On the opposite end of the couch, Hank toyed with a burger. He seemed more interested in watching Carmen eat than in finishing his own food. After she had swallowed her last bite and began licking ketchup from greasy, red-streaked fingers, he dampened a towel in the bathroom and sat by her. "You're a mess," he said, wiping her face and hands. He finished and tossed the towel back into the bathroom. "You like your burger?"

"A little bit."

"Yeah, I thought so." He slipped off his shoes, plopped down on the carpet before the television, and held the popcorn tub out to her.

She took it from him and climbed back onto the bed, spilling popcorn on the spread. She cuddled against Shelby and held the tub for her.

Shelby forced herself to eat several kernels. Watching Hank as he lay on his stomach on the carpet, the television casting flickering light on his features, she wondered how a killer-for-hire could be so forgiving of her attempt to turn the tables and so concerned with a child's welfare. He defied her preconceptions about men who murdered for money. He was full of surprises, though. Who would have thought a middle-aged man would have such quick reflexes, could recover so quickly from her surprise attack?

He pushed off the floor and sat on the foot of the bed. "Lonely down there by myself." He handed Carmen her soft drink and the TV remote.

They munched popcorn and watched the tube, Carmen selecting the programs and channel surfing during commercials. She fell asleep clutching the remote.

Hank slipped off her shoes and socks, turned back the cover, and lifted her so she lay beside Shelby with her head on a pillow. "You need another bathroom break?" At Shelby's nod, he pulled the stun gun from his bag and, pointing it at her, tossed her the handcuff key.

As she shuffled into the bathroom, he reminded her to leave the door open. As before, she closed it partway and he didn't object. Back on the bed, she cuffed her wrist to the post.

Hank pulled the telephone line from his pocket. With one end plugged into the wall outlet and the other into his computer, he worked for several minutes. Then he coiled the line back into his pocket, unlaced and removed Shelby's sneakers, and turned back the bedcover so she could push her legs under. He found a spare blanket and pillow in a closet and stretched out on the sofa.

Lying on her back in the quiet, dark room with her cuffed arm stretched above her head, Shelby reminded herself that death was an inevitable part of living. And it was not a stranger. It had sat on her shoulder during those horrendous moments in Haiti when she hid in a closet while a government death squad gunned down her students, again when she slipped out of the country one jump ahead of her pursuers.

The rationalizing didn't work. No matter how she played it, life seemed more precious as its end loomed.

Light from a turning automobile flooded through the room's flimsy window drapes. A toilet flushed next door. Voices and laughter leaked in from outside. The sounds of life surging and churning around her made her feel isolated, and lost, and so very alone. She welcomed even the presence of her executioner as an antidote.

"I'm afraid," she said.

"It will be quick." Hank's voice, coming from outside her range of vision, seemed disembodied. "You won't feel it."

"It isn't the pain. It's extinction. The finality of it." She stared at the ceiling, and the room seemed to grow lighter. Time became dimensionless, empty. The feeling of isolation grew intolerable. Better to hear his voice than to suffer this silence. "Thank you for sticking with the arrangement for Carmen."

"What'd you expect? Think I'm a monster?"

"Doesn't it bother you at all, killing people for money?"

"Your profile says you've killed. Three men. Says you're a menace to society."

Did knowing she had taken lives make it easier for him? "The only person who feels threatened by me is Krystal. She's afraid I'll tell someone what she did."

Talking had pushed back Shelby's incipient panic. As silence stretched between them, it returned and threatened to suffocate her. To cut through it, she said the first thing that came to mind. "Have you been doing this a long time? Killing people for money?"

"What difference does it make?"

"Please talk to me. It . . . it helps."

Another long silence. "I've not been doing it long."

"What did you do before?"

"Military. Navy SEAL."

"A seal?"

"It means sea, air, and land. Naval commandos."

"So, you killed for your government, learned your trade, then went into business for yourself?"

"Something like that."

She lapsed into silence until it began closing in on her again. To keep him talking and prolong the illusion of human contact, she asked, "How many?"

"What?"

"How many people have you killed? For money, I mean."

"Look, I don't . . . not many."

"How many?" She didn't really want to know, but she needed to hear his voice. "If I'm dying tomorrow, it can't hurt to tell me."

Another audible sigh. "Counting you, one."

Had she understood him correctly? "I'm your first victim?"

"You're not a victim. You're a casualty in a war between killers."

"I don't understand."

"You've snuffed three guys. You tried to kill me."

"Those men I killed? The first one was holding me prisoner, beating and raping me over and over. The second tried the same thing. The third, a rogue immigration agent, planned to kill me."

"Rapists and crooked cops. Hard to fault you for that."

His voice sounded softer. Was she sick to feel comforted by it? "I didn't want to kill them. Don't want to kill anyone."

"You pointed my Beretta at me and pulled the trigger. I'd be dead if you'd known about safeties and trigger locks."

"I was scared out of my wits. I didn't know what else to do."

"Neither do I. The navy taught me to kill. Nothing else."

"You were doing it for your country, protecting it from its enemies. I'm nobody's enemy. No threat to anyone."

"Tell that to the guys you iced. To their wives and children."

"I explained about that."

"One version. Maybe they saw it differently."

Did he think she was lying, trying to justify cold-blooded murder? "How many ways are there to see violent rape? Attempted murder?"

He didn't answer, so she said, "Do you really think I'm a menace to society? That killing me will make the world a safer place?"

"I don't know."

"But you're going to kill me anyway?"

"Talk isn't getting us anywhere. Won't make this easier for either of us." He got off the couch and looked across the room at her in the dim light. After a moment, he left her field of vision, and cushions squished on the couch.

She drifted into sleep, napping in fits and starts. Sometime during the night, Hank got up, and she jerked awake. He took a pill, washing it down with tap water. He woke her a second time by getting up to use the bathroom. The third time, he simply walked around the room, silent in sock-clad feet. He pulled a window drape aside and looked out, walked some more, looked out the window again. He stared down at Carmen.

The bedside clock said three a.m. "Trouble sleeping?" Shelby asked.

"A little antsy. No sense you lying there fretting or scheming."

"I have an excuse for being awake. What about you? Conscience?"

"You figure you've found an angle? Gonna talk me out of honoring my contract?"

That seemed hopeless, but it was the only chance she had left. "You could return the money, explain that you can't go through with it."

"It'd be the last job anybody offered. I've got responsibilities."

"There must be another way to earn a living."

"Go back to sleep." He twisted the television so it faced away from the bed and watched it without the audio. The flashing screen turned his face a pulsating, pale blue.

Shelby digested the inevitable with an awful clarity of thought. *He's going to kill me in a matter of hours. There it is.* She studied her executioner's face in the television's ghostly light: square jaw, flesh still firm but signaling an imminent loosening and sagging, sandy brown hair thinning without receding. Except for a trim waist and tapered torso, nothing to distinguish him from the legion of middle-aged functionaries who trudge to offices every day to turn the wheels of commerce.

He clicked off the television, and the room's only light came from red neon filtering through the window drapes. She watched him as he sat staring at the drapes until gray morning light appeared.

He made another trip to the bathroom, and the sound awakened Carmen. "Lois?" she said. Sitting up in the bed, she called again, "Lois."

Shelby rubbed her sister's forehead. "You're with me, honey."

"I had a scary dream."

"Do you remember it?"

"No, but it was scary. I have to go to the bathroom." She slid off the bed and returned minutes later. "I'm hungry."

"We'll get some food," Hank said. "You watch TV while I fix myself up." He checked Shelby's handcuff and carried his overnight bag into the bathroom. As before, he left the door open. Shelby watched his reflection in the bathroom mirror while he stripped to his underwear and washed himself, shaved, brushed his teeth, and changed the bandage on his face. He dressed, packed away his toiletries, and brought the bag out of the bathroom. Wearing khaki slacks and a knit pullover, he sat on the edge of the bed and pulled on a pair of argyle socks. He slipped on brown loafers and handed Shelby the handcuff key. "Take it off the bedpost, fasten your wrists together. You can freshen up." He sat on the couch, his hand in the bag that held his weapons.

She tethered her wrists together, struggling awkwardly to close the second cuff, and stumbled into the bathroom. Her last dawn. She yearned to step outside and watch the sun come up. She would never again see it reflect off the water as it rose over her homeland. Never watch it set in a blaze of orange light.

In her youth she had discussed death with other girls, her classmates and playmates. They agreed that there were things they would not do to save their lives. She remembered swearing that she would fight to the death to avoid rape. Yet, when it became clear he would beat her to death if she didn't, she had cooperated with her rapist until she found a way to strike back. Would she have accepted that degradation, she wondered, had she known it would lead to this bizarre end?

Her hands shook as she squeezed toothpaste onto her brush; she missed on the first squeeze. Why bother, anyway? How clean did she need to be when he cut her throat or put a bullet through her head?

She knew the answer, of course. Carmen had to think this was just another day, no worse than yesterday. That meant sticking with routine. She brushed her teeth, washed her body as best she could with her wrists cuffed, and worked on her hair.

"You about finished?" Hank asked, raising his voice from outside the bathroom.

"I need—" her voice broke. She started over. "I need to help Carmen."

To Carmen he said, "Shelby's going to help you spruce up. Then we'll eat. What's your favorite breakfast?"

"Pancakes."

"Pancakes it is. All you can eat."

He paced just outside the bathroom door until Carmen was dressed. Then he tossed Shelby the handcuff key. Her hands trembled so that she had trouble fitting the tiny key into the slot. She freed a wrist and cuffed the other to the bedpost.

He hung the DO NOT DISTURB sign on the door and turned back to Carmen. "Let's go find those pancakes."

"Why can't Shelby come?"

"We'll bring her something." He reached for Carmen's hand.

She backed away and looked at Shelby.

"Be nice," Shelby said. Struggling to accept what she knew the day held for her, she willed herself to feel nothing. For Carmen's sake, she had to show nothing. The title of a book and movie drummed in her head as Carmen followed Hank out the door, her hand hanging limply from his: *Dead Man Walking.*

How would dying feel? she wondered as she waited for their return. Would it be something other than a descending of silence and stillness and nothingness? As a teenager, she had abandoned Catholicism and surrendered her childhood belief in an afterlife. She suspected death to be a simple fading away of identity, an unraveling and disappearing of memory and experience and awareness. She had expected it to claim her after she had loved a husband and raised a family. She would have been ready then to embrace it as life's terminal experience. But this ending, so abrupt, so . . . so banal. Would Hank expect her to kneel while he executed her? Could she face those final seconds without breaking, without crying, without begging?

CHAPTER SEVEN

A SCRAPING NOISE AT the door pulled Shelby's attention back to her surroundings. The door opened, and Carmen dashed inside ahead of Hank. "We brought you apple pancakes," she chirped.

A final meal? The pancakes' smell nauseated her. "That's great, sweetheart. But I need to go to the bathroom."

"No problem." Hank tossed her the handcuff key. "Carmen, how about if we set up your sister's breakfast?" He stood close to Carmen, one hand in the bag that held his weapons. "Leave the key on the bed," he ordered after Shelby had freed her wrist. "Lock your wrists together, and leave the door open."

"Why does the door have to stay open?" Carmen asked.

"It sticks," Hank said. "We wouldn't want her trapped in there."

He hadn't objected before when Shelby pushed the door half-way shut to give herself some privacy. She did it again and, sitting on the toilet, let her mind freewheel in search of a last-minute ploy, some way to foil or delay him.

He seemed reluctant but apparently felt obligated to fulfill his contract. If she had more time, she might be able to . . . but no, time had run out.

Glancing around the bathroom, she looked for a makeshift weapon. The aluminum shower rod, maybe. Too light to use as a club, but what if she crimped its end to fashion a crude spear? Or the plastic shower curtain. Could she toss it over his head and hug him until he used up his oxygen? Did she dare try and risk having him kill Carmen in retribution?

He pushed the bathroom door farther open, and she saw his reflection as he watched her in the mirror over the sink. He pointed first at Carmen, then at her, and held up two fingers: a warning. She turned her back on him before patting herself with tissue and pulling up her jeans. She returned to where she had left the handcuff key on the bed, unlocked one cuff, and, struggling with the awkward maneuver, snapped it to the bedpost.

"Pitch the key over here." He pocketed it and walked over to inspect the cuff. Carmen had set up Shelby's breakfast on the coffee table. "It will be better to serve her in bed," Hank said. "She isn't feeling well."

Carmen moved the food to the bedside table. "What's wrong, Shelby?"

"Queasy stomach, baby. Don't worry."

Carmen turned her attention to morning cartoons on TV, and Hank peeled the top from Shelby's Styrofoam coffee cup. "You going to be able to eat?"

Fearing that her voice would quiver, that she couldn't suppress the hysteria hovering just under its surface, she merely shook her head.

"Drink some coffee. It's loaded with sugar." He pressed the lukewarm cup into her free hand and held it until she controlled its shaking. "You owe your sister," he whispered. "Don't fall apart on her."

"I'm trying." She lifted the cup to her lips, gagged at the smell, and set it aside. "It's hard. I didn't . . ." her voice broke again. She took a deep breath. "I didn't think it would be this hard."

He started to say something but snapped his mouth shut and paced their cramped quarters, looking at the floor and then the ceiling. Standing in the middle of the room, he studied her. His gaze shifted to Carmen, then back to her. "I called your librarian friend. She has a cast on her leg."

"Your booby trap. Are you proud of yourself?"

"Point is, it'll be a couple weeks 'til she can get around on crutches."

That meant she couldn't take Carmen. The tears Shelby had been controlling welled up, clouding her vision. She had come so close to keeping her sister safe. Would he dump her and let them send her back to Haiti? What if he decided to keep things tidy by killing them both?

He stepped into the bathroom and returned with facial tissues. "Here."

Shelby blotted her cheeks and eyes and blew her nose. "She has her whole life ahead of her," she said when she saw Hank studying Carmen. "She deserves a chance."

"I've got an associate out west who'll watch her for a couple weeks. Then he'll send her back down here, turn her over to your friend. That's if you don't give me any trouble."

A flood of gratitude washed over Shelby. Having seen for a brief, horrifying moment that death wasn't the absolute worst that could happen, the prospect of not witnessing another sunset numbed her less than it had five minutes earlier. "Don't let her know what happened to me."

"Better push that back, too."

"Push it back?"

"I'll need you to keep her in line during the trip."

A reprieve? He had her at his mercy, yet he was putting off his payday, exposing himself to additional risk? She'd been right about his internal conflict. He was still wrestling with the dilemma, and the longer he put it off, the harder it would be for him.

"Shelby," Carmen called from across the room. "Why are you crying?"

"Hank gave me good news, sweetie. I'm crying from happiness."

"What did he tell you?"

"We're going on a trip."

Shelby rode with her wrist shackled to the seat control rod until her hunched-over posture became intolerably painful. Grimacing, she twisted about, trying to find a comfortable position.

"There a problem?" Hank asked.

"Muscle cramps."

He pulled off the road and, keeping Carmen in the car with him, let Shelby get out and stretch. When she returned to the car, he had used his switchblade to burrow through the seat's fabric and foam rubber padding, exposing the metal framework and springs. He fastened the handcuff to the frame so she could rest her cuffed hand between her legs on the seat.

"You've ruined the upholstery," she said.

"Car's a wreck anyway. You need to be comfortable. Long trip."

"Thank you."

Traveling west on I-40, they crossed Arkansas and Oklahoma. Hank restricted bathroom breaks to isolated rest areas or stands of bushes along the roadway. When they stopped for food, he took Carmen with him and bought takeout to eat in the car. Despite his vocational choice, he seemed to have a code of honor, and Shelby believed his promise to send Carmen to safety with Elizabeth. She had several opportunities to hail people in nearby cars during refueling stops but feared he would kill her on the spot and abandon Carmen. If that happened, the child would end up back in Haiti. Unless a clear-cut opportunity presented itself, Shelby didn't dare challenge him.

When Carmen was not demanding her attention, Shelby talked with Hank, trying to make him see her as a person instead of a mere target. If he had definitely decided to kill her, he would have done so already, so there was a chance.

At a truck stop where they refueled, he bought crayons, coloring books, and several picture- and storybooks for Carmen. Shelby read the stories to her and entertained her with a game of counting big trucks and a contest to see who could spot roadside signs first. When the monotony of Great Plains topography and the car's gentle rocking lulled Carmen to sleep, she drifted off also. A bump in the pavement jarred her awake, and she caught Hank studying her. "Will you tell me where we're going?" she asked.

"You'll see when we get there."

"I've kept my promise. Haven't given you an ounce of trouble."

He nodded, keeping his eyes on the road. "That's why you're still breathing."

"You aren't as unfeeling as you like to pretend."

He turned the rearview mirror so he could see her face in it. "You don't think so?"

"You've been kind. In spite of what you plan to do, I find myself liking you."

"I like you, too. There's nothing personal in this."

"What if it became personal? If we got, you know, involved? Would you still murder me?"

Their gazes met in the mirror, and he raised an eyebrow. "You propositioning me?"

"I'm trying to figure out what kind of man you are."

"I'm the kind that doesn't get involved with his targets. A guy that does his work, collects his fee, and moves on."

Finally, she had him talking about himself. "You're not a loner if you have a friend who will care for Carmen."

"An associate. It'll be a commercial transaction."

"You're going to all this trouble and expense to keep her safe. That shows feelings, compassion."

He shook his head. "I dumped that crap a long time ago."

He was lying to himself, Shelby decided. He wouldn't have made such elaborate arrangements for Carmen if he were too calloused, too morally bankrupt, to be touched by compassion. "You don't feel anything?"

"When I'm hungry, I eat. Tired, I rest. I get horny, I fuck." He scowled. "What's your point?"

"Earlier, you pointed out that I've killed the same as you. But I haven't dismissed my emotions."

"Maybe that's why your boss wants you dead. No killer instinct."

"You think it's a weakness, being able to feel?"

"Know it."

"Then I'm sorry for you."

He laughed, but it didn't sound genuine. "When you're history, I'll have a payday. And you feel sorry for me?"

"I think you're going to remember us for a long time."

"A few days from now, I won't even remember—Carmen's waking up."

Sometime after dark, they turned off the interstate and traveled north on a two-lane highway. They spent the night in a run-down motel in Clayton, New Mexico. Back in the car at sunup, they rode in silence. Shelby drifted in and out of sleep until a change in the car's noise pulled her awake. They were back on an interstate, and the engine sounded labored. "We're climbing," she said.

"Raton Pass." Hank pushed a button, and warm air spewed from vents. "Getting chilly. High altitude."

Minutes later, Shelby saw a sign welcoming them to Colorado. They passed through Colorado Springs at midmorning. Shortly before noon, traffic congestion signaled their approach to Denver.

"I called my associate when we gassed up," Hank said. "You want to explain the program to Carmen?"

Explain that her big sister was abandoning her? That she had to spend two weeks with thugs and killers before flying into the unknown in small-town Arkansas? Shelby doubted that she could keep a straight face and a steady voice. Her stomach knotting, she twisted about in the seat and looked into Carmen's eyes. "Sweetheart, I'm going away for a while. You'll need to stay with Elizabeth until I return."

"Why can't I go with you?"

"Children don't belong there. It isn't a nice place."

"If it isn't nice, you shouldn't go, either."

Shelby rubbed her little sister's cheek. "You like Elizabeth. She'll take good care of you."

"But Hank said she's hurt."

"That's a problem, sweetie. It will be a few days before you can go to her house."

"So, I'll stay with you until then?"

Shelby swallowed a lump that wouldn't stay down. "I have to

leave right away. Hank's friends will take care of you."

"I don't know his friends."

"It's just for a few days. Until Elizabeth is better."

"No!"

With her head turned away, Shelby knuckled tears from her eyes. "We have to do it this way. I can't—" Hank braked the car, and she turned to see why.

He pulled into a roadside rest area and parked in front of a vintage Volkswagen camper. "This is it," he said.

Pushing back at the dread that tried to disable her, Shelby caressed Carmen's cheek again. "I'm sorry, baby. I love you."

Carmen signaled her acceptance by leaning between the divided seats and hugging Shelby. Returning the hug with her free arm, Shelby quit trying to control her tears.

Hank cleared his throat. "We have to get on with this." He lifted Shelby's overnight bag from the rear seat and opened it. Making a pretense of the need, Shelby rummaged through it and pulled out her skimpy belongings.

Holding the bag with one hand and Carmen's fingers with the other, Hank led her to the camper. Shelby watched him open a door, toss the bag inside, and lift Carmen in after it. He walked back to the Skylark and turned its side-mounted rearview mirror downward. "I'm about to invite my associate over for a chat. It would be stupid to screw things up by trying to get a look at him."

Shelby stared rigidly ahead. Shoes crunched on gravel—someone approaching.

"I want to give you these instructions where my traveling companion can hear them," Hank said to the unseen person. "That way, there'll be no question about what I've told you. The little girl's name is Carmen. Treat her like a princess. After two weeks, if everything goes according to plan, call the Arkansas librarian and tell her Carmen's coming for a visit. Then put the kid on a plane."

"Got it."

"That's if there are no glitches. You'll get an e-mail from me every day with the code word I gave you earlier. If you get the wrong code word, you'll know it's someone else or I'm being forced. If that happens, or if I miss a day, don't ask for the correct word or wait for a catch-up message. Take the kid to Denver and leave her in the lobby of Immigration and Customs Enforcement."

Shelby's breathing became abruptly labored. "You wouldn't do that. She'll die back home. You wouldn't."

"I won't like it," the man said, speaking with a slow drawl, "but I'll do what Hank says."

"I don't like it, either," Hank said. "But if you screw things up, it's what has to be done. One other thing. Tell my traveling companion what I know about where you live."

"He knows it's somewhere west of Boulder," the man said. "We always meet like this so neither knows exactly where the other lives."

Hank stood by the door while the man returned to his camper and the ancient vehicle chugged away with Carmen staring through a window, her hands pressed against the glass. Only then did he circle the Skylark, slide behind the wheel, and crank the engine.

As he guided the car back onto the freeway and nursed it to cruising speed, Shelby heard him speaking but had no idea what he said. She didn't see the countryside, didn't feel the road under them. She saw only that last glimpse of her sister's face twisted into an expression of pleading that would burn in her memory for the brief time she had left on earth.

She had thought she was making progress, that Hank had become conflicted about killing her and would not harm Carmen.

She'd been wrong. Whatever his motive for keeping her alive this long, it was not compassion. His instructions to the man in the camper had made that clear.

He raised his voice, cutting into her thoughts. "You need a bathroom break?"

"Why am I still alive?"

"Because I haven't killed you yet."

"You said you'd do it as soon as you made arrangements for Carmen. That's done."

"Don't be in such a hurry to die."

"You've fixed it so there's nothing to do but wait for a bullet. I'd just as soon get it over with."

"Does your sister's genetic heritage bother you?"

"What?" *We're discussing my death, and his mind is on genetics?* "What do you mean?"

"With her hair and skin color, she's obviously part African."

Shelby didn't want to grant him the courtesy of conversation. If she offended him, however, he might retaliate by reneging on his promise to keep Carmen safe. "I told you, we have the same father but different mothers."

"So, you have an Anglo mother but an African stepmother?"

"Carmen's mother is Creole, and she isn't my stepmother. She's our head housekeeper's daughter."

"The kid's illegitimate, but you think of her as your sister?"

He's bored, she decided. *He hasn't slept much. Running on coffee and those pills, maybe he needs to talk to stay awake.* "Carmen lives, she did live, with her grandmother in the servant's wing of our house. She stayed in my suite more than her own quarters."

"Your loyalty to her is impressive. Most people would sacrifice their own offspring to breathe another hour."

"Not everyone is like you."

"There are more like me than there are like you."

While she mulled over his comment, he pulled in at a roadside restaurant. Leaning across, he opened the handcuff. "We don't need this anymore, do we?"

An easy question. Unless she learned his accomplice's e-mail address and the code word they had agreed upon, she dared not disrupt the daily message that would keep Carmen safe. She rubbed her wrist and noticed his face drawn into a pained grimace. "Something wrong?"

"Old age catching up with me." He tossed the handcuffs into the car's glove compartment. "Let's get some lunch."

Is he sick? Sidelong glances as they walked into the restaurant revealed a grim set to his jaw and an exaggerated squint, as if he expected a jolt of something unpleasant.

"Order for me," he said after a hostess had shown them to a booth. He headed for the men's room.

Shelby had seen that he guzzled coffee, so she ordered iced tea for herself and coffee for him. He had not returned when the server brought the drinks, so she ordered bacon, lettuce, and tomato sandwiches. She wondered why the server stared so, until she realized he had seen her wrist. She clasped her hands in her lap to hide the bruised and raw flesh from the handcuffs.

CHAPTER EIGHT

IN THE RESTROOM, HANK washed down two pain pills with water from the faucet, captured in his cupped palms. He splashed cold water on his face, blotted it with paper towels, and studied his reflection in the mirror over the sink. *What the hell are you doing? Don't you have enough problems without taking on other people's?*

He'd known since their late-night talk in that Arkansas motel room that he couldn't kill her. For a while after they fell silent, he had beat up on himself for his loss of resolve. Then his mind wrestled with the problem of what to do with her. Just walking away, leaving her and Carmen in the room, would have sealed their fate as surely as if he snuffed them himself. The dilemma kept him awake for what was left of the night.

The next morning, he'd contacted the broker on the Internet and reported no trace of Shelby. He reminded the broker of the pending contract in Las Vegas and suggested cutting his Arkansas surveillance short by one day. The broker's response startled him:

Hang in there for another day and earn yourself the surveillance fee. After that, it's open season on the target, and you're authorized to take whatever steps you deem appropriate to get information from the librarian. The target should be easy to spot—she's traveling with a kid. The girl is seven but looks five or six. Mixed African and Anglo, pretty as a pinup, and she has a Caribbean accent that makes her English sound like poetry. Those markers, plus what you get out of the librarian, will make your job simple. The only tough part will be getting to her ahead of the other contractor.

Hank agreed to watch the librarian's house for another day, promised to keep the broker posted, and signed off. By then, Carmen was ready to go for pancakes. He talked with her, pretending excitement over the food and the sights she pointed out, but all the while he racked his brain for a way to cut Shelby free yet keep her safe from other contract killers.

Carmen was the major problem. Her size, her looks, and her accent were beacons that would guide hunters to Shelby. He decided to solve the problem by separating them. Lying about Shelby's friend being laid up for a couple of weeks had done the job.

Staring at himself in the mirror over the sink, he chuckled at the memory of Jason, who loved children more than life itself, pretending to be a tough guy who wouldn't mind turning Carmen over to the government to be deported. Now, the challenge was to keep moving Shelby around, create an ever-lengthening trail for anyone who tried to track her. And he had to do it without trying to explain, since she had no reason to trust him. He ran a pocket comb through his hair and returned to the dining room.

"I guessed our diet of pancakes, pizza, and burgers was in deference to Carmen," Shelby said when he slid into the booth across from her. "If you don't like BLTs, we can change the order."

With the medication kicking in, the pain in his arm had become less intense, but it still bothered him. "I'm not a picky eater," he said, trying not to let his discomfort show.

"You sure you're all right?" she asked.

"I'm touched by your concern."

"I want you to be able to send those e-mails."

"BLTs are fine." He sipped his coffee and began a discourse on Rocky Mountain flora. Under the circumstances, he knew his monologue seemed surreal to her. So must sharing a casual meal with a man she thought would be her executioner.

Back in the car, he did not mention the handcuffs. The pills had finally dampened his pain to a nagging but tolerable discomfort, permitting him to relax.

Shelby rubbed her chafed wrist in silence as he accelerated up the freeway entry ramp. "You never answered my question," she said once they were on the freeway.

"What question is that?"

"Why you're keeping me alive."

"This idle curiosity?"

"I'd like to know how much time I have."

To keep her manageable, he had to pretend he was going through with the hit, but pushing back the time would give her some comfort. "Your contract came in so quickly they left details to be worked out. We have to settle on the method of completion, how I'm to be paid, and so on."

"How can you do that while we're traveling?"

"My broker will handle it."

"A broker? Like in the stock market?"

"More like real estate. He matches clients with contractors. He's off-shore." Hank smiled at her and shifted his eyes back to the road. "Where there's no extradition treaty with the United States"

"I never realized murder was such an organized business. How did you meet this broker?"

"It isn't an interesting story."

"Will you kill whoever he says?"

She needed to talk, he decided. Needed human contact, even if it had to be with a killer. "I plan to specialize in targets that deserve their fate."

"For example?"

"Crime bosses. Leaders of terrorist cells. Rapists and killers with sharp lawyers that get them off."

"I'm none of those, no threat to anybody."

"You've admitted killing three people. The cops want you."

"I told you why those men died, and I think you believe me. So how does killing me fit your plan?"

"Somebody's gonna do the job, and another contractor might not worry about Carmen." He concentrated on weaving between big trucks that hogged both lanes on an uphill grade but glanced across and caught her studying him. "Besides, I made a commitment, accepted a retainer."

"How long until they give you the details?"

He pulled a time out of the air. "The broker said maybe a week."

"A week." She pursed her lips and frowned. "Where are we going to spend the week?"

"On the road. Our first stop is Las Vegas. Ever been there?"

"I spent two years at school in Arizona. That's the only place I've been in the American West."

He nodded and fiddled with the car's radio. She must have decided she had all the information he was going to give her, because she slumped in her seat and closed her eyes. Plotting strategy, no doubt. Waiting for him to let his guard down so she could torture him into telling her how to get her sister back.

In Flagstaff, Arizona, Vlad finished his second day of monitoring the Reverend Frederick Rogers's telephone without hearing anything about Shelby Cervosier. But he learned that the reverend kept regular weekday hours, leaving home at nine a.m. and returning at four p.m. Vlad supposed the pattern would differ on Sundays, with morning and evening worship services, and on Wednesdays, since he'd learned the church had a midweek service, as well. The preacher called his wife several times each day. They sounded like teenagers, sighing and cooing their love to each other.

If Cervosier didn't show at one of the stakeouts by the end of the third day, the broker had said he would declare open season. She'd had plenty of time already; if she were going to show up here, she would already have done so. *I'm gonna track her down, so why give her an extra day's head start?*

On his way to dinner, he stopped at an Ace Hardware store for needle-nosed pliers and two rolls of duct tape. He swung by a variety store to pick up surgical gloves, a sponge, and spray cleaner. After an early meal, he returned to his motel and caught the news on CNN before stretching out for a six-hour nap.

His bedside alarm awakened him at midnight. He spent an hour in the bathroom shaving off all body hair except his eyelashes and brows and scrubbing away loose skin as a precaution against leaving DNA evidence. He brushed his brows and lashes to dislodge loose hair and devoted ten minutes to scouring the bath. Over the toilet, he cut and filed his already-short fingernails and flushed the trimmings. He packed his belongings and, wearing his new surgical gloves and using the sponge and spray cleaner, scrubbed every surface in the room. Before using a stolen credit card on the motel's express checkout system, he glanced a final time at the bedside clock. Two a.m., time to go to work.

At the Rogerses' home, he pulled onto the shoulder across the street, parking under the sole shade tree so the quarter-moon would not illuminate his rental car. Most of the lights were out on the block, he noted as he screwed the sound suppressor onto his Luger. The few that still glowed were probably night lights.

Using a penlight and pliers, he snipped the wires leading out of the telephone junction box that Mrs. Reverend had so accommodatingly let him pinpoint. His universal garage door opener worked like a charm. Inside their garage, he stood where he could not be seen from the street and pushed the button to close the door. The underpowered electric motor whined as the rollers screeched on their ungreased track. Counting on the noise to awaken the house's occupants, he flattened himself against the wall by the door that led inside.

A light clicked on. Seconds later, the door opened. The Reverend Rogers, wearing pajama bottoms but no top, looked out.

The butt of Vlad's Luger caught the preacher on the side of his head. It sent him reeling backward to crash against a kitchen cabinet. A second blow sat him on his ass on the floor. Vlad slapped duct tape over the man's mouth and rolled him onto his stomach to duct-tape his hands behind his back. Gloved fingers in the man's hair jerked him to his feet.

"Fred," a woman's voice called. It came from what Vlad's telephone-bugging foray had revealed was the master bedroom. Pushing the trussed preacher before him, he headed there.

The wife, wearing the top part of the preacher's pajamas, met them in the bedroom doorway. Vlad shoved her husband into her, sending her staggering back into the bedroom. With his fingers still wrapped in the preacher's hair, he slammed a foot against the back of the man's knee.

The preacher went down on his face.

Vlad dashed to the wife and drove a fist into her stomach. It silenced her after one brief, confused shriek. Duct tape sealed her mouth and secured her wrists.

As Vlad finished the chore, the preacher's shoulder slammed into his back. He whirled and cracked the man on the temple with his Luger. The preacher collapsed on the carpet. "Stubborn bastard," Vlad murmured.

An interior hallway led from the master bedroom past two other doors to the living room. The hallway had doors at each end and no windows. Vlad herded his captives there so the light would not make neighbors curious. One of the doors, he remembered from his visit as a telephone repairman, led to the preacher's study. From that room he pulled a swivel chair with rollers and padded arms.

The wife's legs had given way. She sat on the hallway floor with her husband squatting by her side. Vlad taped her ankles together, leaving enough slack to permit six-inch steps. He helped her to her feet and leaned her against a wall. Gripping her shoulders with both hands, he absorbed the trembling of her body while his eyes sucked in her terror, and a warm glow suffused him. "I'm going to free your wrists. You try fighting me, try pulling the tape off your mouth, I'll slice you open. You understand me?"

Wide-eyed, she nodded.

"Turn around." He jerked the tape off her wrists. Hair on her forearms came off with the tape.

She faced him, frozen, while he lifted her pajama shirt and

dragged his knife back and forth across her stomach. "I don't plan on hurting you. All I want is information. But I don't mind slaughtering both of you if it comes to that." Locking gazes with the preacher, he motioned to the roller-equipped chair with his knife. "Rev, take a seat."

When the husband had settled in the chair, Vlad dug a roll of duct tape from his pocket and handed it to the wife. "Tape his ankles to the chair legs. Loop the tape around each ankle three times. Keep it tight." Looking at the preacher, he said, "Slide forward so your ankles touch the chair legs."

With his ankles taped to the chair, the preacher sat forward with his buttocks hanging over the front edge. His awkward position rendered him helpless. "Spread your knees," Vlad ordered. "Wider."

The man's knees opened so that his thighs pressed against the chair arms, and Vlad ordered the wife to tape them there. "You're doing good, sweet meat. Now, pull the tape off his wrists and tape them to the chair arms."

She finished, and Vlad helped her sit on the floor. He cut the tape that hobbled her and used fresh strips to tape her wrists to her ankles with her elbows between her knees. Then he turned his attention to the preacher, looping additional strands of tape around the man's thighs so he could not pull loose when panic gave him superhuman strength, and around his neck to fasten it to the chair's back.

He admired his work for a moment and said, "You're probably wondering why I called this meeting. I'm looking for a friend of ours. You tell me where to find her, and I'm outta here. That seem fair?"

The preacher nodded. His wife glared.

Vlad decided the husband would be easiest to break. "Here's how it works. I know the answers to most of the questions I'll be asking. When you lie, and I know you're lying, I exact a penalty." He pulled Shelby's digitized photo from his pocket and showed it first to the wife and then the husband. He stepped back so he could see both their faces. "You guys know her?"

The wife shook her head. The husband hesitated and followed her lead.

"That's your first lie." Vlad flashed his needle-nosed pliers and loomed over the wife. Staring at the husband, he smiled. "First her nips, then her clit. Everything gets twisted off."

Wriggling in his chair and grunting frantically, the reverend nodded.

Vlad pulled the picture out again, shook it. "You know her name?"

The preacher shot his wife a glance, refocused on Vlad, and nodded again.

"We're going to get along just fine." Vlad patted the preacher's shoulder. "I'm pulling the tape off your mouth. You shout or scream, you'll have a mutilated wife. You understand?" At another nod, Vlad ripped away the tape and patted the man's shoulder again. "You're doing what a devoted husband should, Rev. Protecting your wife. Have either of you talked with Cervosier recently?"

"She called us," the preacher gasped.

"When?"

"Six weeks back. Maybe seven, I'm not sure."

"Where was she?"

"Arkansas. Some little town."

"What did you talk about?"

"She needed documents. Identity documents. Please, Barb needs air."

"You keep answering my questions, no more lies, and she'll be all right. Where'd you send the documents?"

"Care of a librarian. Public library. That's all I know. Please."

"How'd you send it? Mail? UPS?"

"FedEx. Overnight."

"Where do you keep your receipts?"

"Drawer. Kitchen."

Vlad rolled the man's chair into the kitchen. "Which drawer?" The preacher nodded at one, and Vlad pulled the drawer from the cabinet, then wheeled the chair back into the hallway. After dumping the drawer's contents on the floor, he rifled through the pile until he found a Federal Express shipping receipt: "Elizabeth Fontaine, care of Clanal County Public Library, 437 Commerce Street, Perryville, Arkansas."

"That wasn't so hard, was it, Rev?" Vlad shoved the receipt into his pocket, tore off a fresh strip of duct tape, and plastered it over the preacher's mouth. "You're an intelligent man. You must know I can't leave witnesses."

CHAPTER NINE

SHELBY DOZED UNTIL THE car's deceleration awakened her. They coasted down a freeway exit ramp and pulled in at a Marriott hotel. "Where are we?"

"Utah. Near Salina." Hank's voice had the intensity, his face the grim look, that she associated with his need for those pills.

After he registered, she followed him to an elevator and along a hallway to what proved to be a suite: a sitting room, a kitchenette, and a bedroom with a king-sized bed. He dropped his overnight bag and computer on a luggage rack.

She looked at the bed and back at him. "One bed?"

"It's what they had." He fiddled with the room's thermostat and headed for the minibar in the front room. "Relax. I'm a killer, not a rapist. Something to drink?"

What choice did she have but to trust him? "A Chablis would be nice," she said with a fatalistic shrug.

He poured wine into a plastic glass, passed it to her, and poured himself a club soda. "Want dibs on the bath?"

"You go. I'll be outside until the room cools off." A sliding glass door led to a tiny balcony overlooking the parking lot. Shelby stepped out, but the moment the bathroom door clicked shut behind him, she bee-lined for the minibar, where he had set his pills.

"Tramadol," she read from the label. "Take one every four

to six hours as needed for pain." The prescription, for Robert Townsend, had been filled by a pharmacy in Seattle. She pulled out the telephone directory and dialed a local Walgreens. A pharmacy technician explained that Tramadol was a non-narcotic medicine for moderately severe pain.

Non-narcotic; he wasn't an addict. Maybe he'd been injured.

Her attention shifted again to the single, king-sized bed. She mumbled Hank's comment—"I'm a killer, not a rapist"—and rubbed scar tissue where her supposed protector in that Arkansas safe house had scalded her hand before beating and raping her.

They had fought. She broke his nose and loosened his tooth, but he won by threatening to pour boiling water in Carmen's face. "Hold out your hand," he ordered, standing by Shelby with the steaming kettle after she surrendered. He grasped her wrist and poured the water over the back of her hand. Shrieking, she had tried to jerk the hand away, but he held her with bruising force.

"Great shower," Hank said, emerging from the bathroom in a billow of steam. The tension lines in his face seemed less drawn. He wore a white terry-cloth bathrobe that sported the Marriott logo. A fresh bandage covered the furrows Carmen's nails had left on his cheek. "It has one of those adjustable showerheads. Everything from mist to massage."

Shelby locked herself in the bathroom and let the shower thump pulses of hot water on her neck and back for a long time, trying to wash away the lingering flashback to that time in Arkansas. She could have avoided the torture by cooperating with her rapist. Had she learned anything from that, or would she fight Hank if he decided to force himself on her, knowing he could win the same way Tucker had: by threatening to harm her little sister?

But he'd said he wouldn't do that, and he had seemed honest

so far. She pulled on her last pair of clean underwear, a T-shirt, and her only remaining jeans, and walked back into the suite's front room. "I need to do laundry."

Hank, fully dressed, sat in a chair sipping a fresh club soda. "We'll be in Vegas tomorrow. You can do it there." He set his drink aside. "Want to take a chance on the restaurant downstairs? We can go out if you prefer."

"Downstairs is fine. I'm not at all hungry."

Shelby's gaze darted around the Marriott's dining room as she and Hank followed the hostess. Only a few tables were occupied, most by one or two men. Probably traveling salesmen. She spotted three women: one sitting by herself, another with a man, a third with two preteen children and a stone-faced man. Hank seemed in high spirits as the hostess seated them and a waiter took their dinner order.

"How far are we from Las Vegas?" Shelby asked as they waited for their food.

"Five or six hours. We'll be there in time to go shopping, get you a decent outfit."

He was going to buy her clothing? "If I only have a few days left, why do I need a wardrobe?"

"You look great in jeans, but they're not the uniform of the day in casinos."

A compliment, however oblique. Was it a personality quirk, or was her campaign to make him see her as a person bearing fruit? "I'm confused. Am I about to be erased, or entertained?"

"We'll be spending a couple days in Vegas. Since it's your first time, I thought we'd look around. Let you see what a weird place it is."

That did not sound like an executioner's plan for his victim. "I doubt you'll find me good company. I don't exactly feel like partying."

The waiter arrived with their food, and they fell silent. "When you're in life's end game," Hank said after the young man departed, "even when you know how it will turn out and you can't do anything about it, you still have choices."

"A bit limited, though."

"Choices, nonetheless. You can race full-throttle to the end, savoring every second, or you can quit and be as good as dead while you're still breathing. Life is too precious to waste."

"Since the incident that launched me on this surreal venture, I guess I've accepted that my time is winding down. I just . . . I worry about what will happen to Carmen."

"You don't believe my promise? Don't think I'll ship her to your friend in Arkansas?"

"I believe you, but . . ."

"The kid weighs what? Maybe forty pounds? And her head barely reaches my belt buckle. Yet she jumped me, tried to rip my face off. How many adults would have the guts to do that? I admire her, and I want her to be okay. I sincerely hope you don't make that impossible."

"Elizabeth won't know what to do. She'll take care of Carmen for a while, expecting me to show up. When I don't . . ."

"What do you anticipate she'll do?"

"I have no idea. That's why I worry."

Hank pursed his lips. "Write a letter. Be circumspect, but let her know she has Carmen long-term. I'll see she gets it."

Shelby studied him across the table. "You will let me make final arrangements, so to speak?"

"If you're careful what you say. I'll e-mail it to my colleague, ask him to pass it on."

"You're concerned about Carmen's welfare, yet you would let that man turn her over to the authorities?"

"When I gave him those instructions, I didn't consider it a serious prospect. I'd gotten a pretty good read on you, figured you wouldn't gamble with her life. I still see it that way."

"When should I write the letter?" The unasked question—when did he intend to kill her?—hung silently between them. She held her breath and waited for his answer.

"You've got some time. Mull it over, think about what you want to say."

"And you won't . . . I'll have a chance to finish it?"

"You have my word on that."

As they strolled across the lobby on the way back to their suite, Shelby realized with a start that she had enjoyed the meal. At first she had been tense and alert, looking around for she knew not what, registering details as if the dining room were a potential battlefield. But she pretended to relax, and reality followed the charade. She recalled a lecture by a visiting psychologist in college. Over the short term, he explained, our bodies' chemical responses govern the way we feel. Over a longer period, we choose our emotions by how we act. Given this body/mind nexus, he had argued, why not act, and therefore eventually feel, the way that gets you what you want?

Back in their suite, no longer fearing a replay of the rape she had suffered in Arkansas, she borrowed a T-shirt to use as a nightgown. She laid out her toothbrush in the bathroom and started flossing but paused. If she had only a few days to live, wasn't it ludicrous to worry about healthy teeth and gums? That she was sticking with activities that had only long-range payoffs told her she still harbored hope. Over the last three days, she had gone from imminent death to death in three days to death in a week or so. If he was looking for excuses to put it off, what was to keep him from doing so indefinitely?

She finished, rinsed her mouth, and emerged from the bathroom barefooted, wearing the hotel's white terry-cloth robe over her borrowed T-shirt. Accepting her lack of control over how this would end was liberating, she realized. Her remaining days might be limited, but Hank's comment at dinner had been on target: why quit living while you're still breathing? She smiled at him and asked, "May I have another Chablis?"

"No problem." He squatted to rummage through the minibar.

"You don't mind running up your hotel bill? It cuts into your profit."

He poured the wine and handed her the plastic glass. "Nice thing about my business, the margins are so hefty you don't sweat minor expenses. I'm gonna hit the shower again."

The night had turned cool. Shelby walked onto the balcony, stretched out on a chaise lounge, and studied the lights on a distant hillside while sipping her wine. She marveled at the calm that had settled over her. The weeks of uncertainty, of dreading what might happen, were behind her. As distasteful as her limited options were, at least she no longer had to struggle.

Hank joined her, wearing a hotel robe. He had removed the facial bandage, and Carmen's livid fingernail tracks looked startling on his tanned cheek. Holding a drink in one hand, he used the other to rub his wet hair with a towel. He pulled the only chair around to face her. "What's on your mind?"

"An old movie they showed us in college: *The Band Played On*."

"A musical?"

"No, it was . . . it had a musical dimension. The protagonist was a composer and director. But the movie was about dying."

"You need to get your mind off that."

"When you tell me it's going to happen in a matter of days? That's impossible. Anyway, the movie was about accepting one's fate."

"The protagonist dies?"

"Of natural causes. But he knows it's coming, knows it won't be long. Refusing to accept his fate, he goes to other specialists and gets the same bad news. He boils with resentment: at doctors for the prognosis, at his friends for being healthy while he's dying, at the world for going on pretty much as if he didn't exist. His anger threatens to destroy the relationships that make life worthwhile. He lapses into a deep melancholia that seems worse than death. He considers suicide."

"What happens?"

"He comes to terms with his predicament, accepts that he's dying and there's nothing he can do about it. His days grow richer, fuller than before he knew they were winding down. He doesn't waste time on idle pursuits or petty goals."

Hank looked thoughtful for several moments. "Can you do that?"

"I'll try, if you'll make me another promise."

"Promise you what?"

"When it's time, will you tell me?"

He tossed his damp towel into their suite and turned back to her. "You sure you'll want to know?"

"I have to. Otherwise, every time you look my way I'll wonder if you're about to put a bullet in my head."

"Shelby, you need to—" He clamped his jaw shut. "I check each morning for word from the broker."

"Promise me, then. Whenever you check, tell me if I have another twenty-four hours. Don't make me wonder all day if I'm going to see the sun go down."

He stood and gazed for a moment at distant lights. Then he faced her, leaning against the balcony rail. "I can tell you right now, unless you decide to sacrifice Carmen and force the issue, it won't happen before we reach my home."

"Your home?" Was this another stretching out of her execution date? She willed her heart to settle down. "Why there?"

"The client doesn't want a body turning up. I can handle that easier where I live. The other reason . . ." He turned his chair around so it faced away from her and straddled it with his forearms on its back, bringing their faces close. "If you don't force my hand by acting stupid, you won't die before Carmen is with your librarian friend in Arkansas."

He had told his associate in Colorado to keep Carmen for two weeks before sending her to Elizabeth. That doubled the time she had in which to find a way out of this maze. "Are you saying this to make me easier to handle?"

"I don't have to. You won't do anything to put your sister at risk."

She studied his face and decided he was sincere, that he needed the time to sort out conflicting emotions and decide whether or not he wanted to honor his contract. "I believe you."

"Good, because I want you to make me a promise."

He was going to ask her not to try escaping. She would lie, and he'd know she was lying. "Something reasonable, I hope."

"Promise not to talk about this while we're on the road."

For the first time, he had expressed a personal need. Her heart raced as it had when he extended her stay of execution, and she reminded herself not to overdose on optimism. "Pretend we're just tourists?"

"Why not? You know how I make my living. I know you'll escape, or kill me, if you get the chance and can find a way to save Carmen. It'll be on my mind as well as yours. But we don't have to talk about it."

"Fair enough."

They finished their drinks, and Hank yawned. They stood as if making a joint decision.

"You've spent two nights on couches," she said. "It's my turn."

"One more won't hurt me." He pulled a blanket and pillow from a closet and shut the bedroom door on his way to the sitting room.

She climbed into bed, turned off the light, and pondered their latest exchange. Less than twelve hours had elapsed since he had turned Carmen over to that man. The glimpses of humanity Hank had shown since did not fit her concept of a killer. She was making progress in her campaign to have him see her as someone he would not want to harm.

They arose early, breakfasted, and headed for Las Vegas as the sun's first rays burned over the mountains. "You're in for a treat," Hank said when they were back on the interstate. "Everyone should see Vegas at least once."

"Before they die, you mean?"

"Thought we had an agreement."

Don't bait him! "You're right, sorry."

"We're staying at the Aladdin. It has a day spa, so I booked you for the works. That all right?"

A day spa. Would he do that for someone he was just ware-housing until he found a convenient disposal site? Maybe so; he was a strange man. Shelby imagined the expressions on the faces of the luxury hotel's workers when Hank turned his decrepit old Buick Skylark over to valet parking. "That will be nice. Thank you."

"You'll finish with plenty of time for shopping."

"You're really going to buy me clothes?"

"I'm not showing you Vegas in those wrinkled jeans."

Shelby had not slept well, and drowsiness induced by the Skylark's gentle swaying clouded her initial image of Las Vegas. She regis-tered only harsh sunlight, tall buildings, heavy traffic, and—when they got out of the car—searing heat and a multitude on the side-walk, an equal number, it seemed, heading in both directions.

A shower revived her, and they descended in the hotel elevator for the promised day spa and shopping trip. She floated through a massage, facial, manicure, and pedicure. Then the attendant led her to the spa's hairdressing saloon. Shelby started to explain how she wanted her hair done, but the hairdresser said, "Your gentle-man told me what to do."

"It isn't my gentleman's hair."

"He was very specific. Rather adamant."

"Why don't we skip it?" Maybe she couldn't keep him from kill-ing her, but she could decide how she would look when it happened. She reached back to pull loose the Velcro strip on the protective cloth the hairdresser had draped around her.

The woman's hand on the strip stopped her. "Your friend's in the juice bar. Will you wait while I get him? Please?" At Shelby's nod, the hairdresser almost ran from the room. She returned with Hank. "I'll leave you two alone," she said, and disappeared again.

"There a problem?" Hank asked.

Shelby's anger ratcheted higher. "You told her how to do my hair? Yes, that's a problem."

He rubbed the back of his neck. "Sorry. I'm not good at these things."

"While I'm still breathing, I'll decide what happens to my body."

"We need to change your appearance, make you less identifiable." He looked around as if to satisfy himself that they were alone. "My contract called for a three-day stakeout in Arkansas. The time has expired, and the broker says it's open season on you."

"Open season?"

"They had other places staked out. Those contractors are now free to track you. There's a sizeable bounty for whoever makes the kill."

Other hit men were looking for her? That meant Hank hadn't told the broker he'd captured her. Would he keep it a secret, chance having one of the others take her from him and get the bounty, if he intended to complete the contract? "Send the hairdresser back in."

CHAPTER TEN

SHELBY'S HAIR, SHOULDER LENGTH for as long as she could remember, was now short enough for a wig to fit comfortably, and she missed the hair's weight, missed the feel of it swishing across her neck and shoulders when she turned her head. Hank bought her three wigs in different styles and colors. Their next stop was a clothing boutique in a basement level of the hotel, and she learned something new about herself.

"I have a gown I want you to try," the boutique owner said after studying Shelby's face and figure. "Please reserve judgment until you see yourself wearing it. You'll be surprised." She brought out a shimmering emerald garment. "It's the same color as your eyes."

The gown had a high neckline but swept low in the back. "I'm not sure I want to expose that much of my body," Shelby said. "Anyway, how does one wear a bra with nothing to cover the straps?"

"It doesn't need a bra; it has stays. It's designed for someone like you, with breasts that need little support."

The gown's silk lining caressed Shelby's skin. The fabric hugged her torso so that even her navel's indentation cast a shadow when she viewed herself in the dressing room's three-sided mirror under overhead spots. She turned, twisted, flexed a buttock and then a leg. The fabric moved with her, creating rippling highlights. Ankle length and split on both sides to just above the knee, the skirt limited her movement. She took experimental steps and learned that most of the action had to be in her lower legs, accentuating the shifting of her hips and causing the material to shimmer.

She unsnapped the neckband and peeled the fabric down over her hips but hesitated before stepping out of the glistening circle. No one she knew would see her wearing it, and though she and Hank had established a relationship of sorts, he might yet decide to kill her. Or another hit man might find her. She had always refused to wear this kind of gown but admired them on more adventurous women. With life so uncertain, why not be daring? Vanity, perhaps, but so what? The urge, the personality defect if that's what it was, existed whether or not she gave vent to it.

Wriggling and tugging to fit the fabric to her body's contours, she pulled the gown back up, refastened the neck snap, and stepped out of the dressing room. She twirled for the boutique owner, who waited just outside.

The woman's jaw dropped, her mouth forming an oval. "It's exactly right for you. I figured it would bring out the color and shape of your eyes. I never dreamed it would do that to your body."

"Is it too revealing?"

"It's perfect. You're tall and slender, but not a bone shows anywhere. The dress whispers that perfection. It invites the world to pause and admire."

Together they walked to where Hank lounged in an upholstered chair near the front of the boutique. Shelby turned before him. "Will this be all right?"

He studied her for a long time, his face blank but his Adam's apple pumping. "It will do," he said. "And you need a bathing suit, sandals, and a beach robe for tomorrow."

Shamed by her delight with the gown, her decision to wear

something so daring, she did penance by insisting on a conservative bathing suit, a modest two-piece, white spandex affair. As a cover, she selected a white knit smock with sleeves that reached her elbows and with a mid-thigh hemline. White rubber flip-flops and Dior sunglasses completed the ensemble.

"Our host this evening will insist on drinks before dinner," Hank said as the proprietor rung up their purchases. "Let's grab a snack to sop up the alcohol." He asked that everything be delivered to their hotel suite, and they detoured to a street-level coffee shop.

Shelby got her first nighttime view of Las Vegas when they walked out of their hotel to catch a cab to the Imperial Palace for dinner. Her brain adjusted and began filtering out the noise, a mélange of voices, vehicles, and music that blended into a frenzied cacophony. But the light! In all colors of the spectrum, coming from stationary and animated sources, it melded into a crude brilliance that blanked out the night sky and assaulted her eyes. The dry air, still hot but noticeably cooler than when they entered the hotel, made her throat ache. How did people live in a place with no silence, no night, no moisture?

The dining room, apparently one of several in the Imperial Palace, seemed a sea of tranquility after the press of pedestrians on the street and in the lobby and compared to the casino crowd they'd fought their way through to reach the elevator. Hank introduced their hosts as Silvia and John Jefferies. Shelby learned that John, short, rotund, and balding, was a lawyer who specialized in entertainment contracts. Silvia, an ex-showgirl, stood several inches taller than her husband and still had her chorus-line figure. Her platinum blond hair, Shelby decided after a few minutes of conversation, covered a head filled mostly with hot, desert air.

A glass of wine before dinner relaxed Shelby. The band, playing romantic tunes from another era, further mellowed her. Wearing a tightly curled, reddish-brown wig, with her eyes highlighted by a touch of liner and her body luminescent in the second-skin, emerald green gown, she looked like an entirely different person. She felt different, too. The old, conservative Shelby Cervosier had given way to a glittery creature living on the edge.

Hank asked her to dance. As they moved with the music, she rested her head on his shoulder and inhaled the subtle musk of his cologne. She caught herself and stiffened.

He looked down at her. "What?"

"Just remembering who I am. Who I'm with."

"I've lived twenty years longer than you, kiddo. A lot faster and harder, I suspect. I've learned some lessons that could stand you in good stead."

"You're about to give me advice?"

"Grab life by the scruff and shake it. Whatever's there, get on with it while you can."

"Could you do that if your days were numbered?"

He took a long time to answer. Had she upset him by breaking her promise not to talk about death?

"If I knew I had just a little time left," he said, "I'd try to experience everything as intensely as possible. When the end came, I'd want to know I'd seen it all, felt and done everything worthwhile." They danced in silence for several moments, and he said, "I've often thought about the end of my life. About what I haven't done. The regrets I'll have for putting things off."

"Me, too." Shelby's response surprised her. How sick was it to discuss her feelings about dying with the man who might yet kill her?

"What have you not done that you'll regret most?" he asked. "Maybe we can cover it."

"I regret not having given birth."

"Don't think we can squeeze that in."

She chuckled. Realizing how ghoulish it sounded, she turned pensive.

"You laughed," he said. "That's the first time I've heard you laugh."

They returned to the table, and Silvia leaned close. "Honey, John says I should invite you to the powder room. That means they're gonna talk about stuff we ain't supposed to hear." Chattering nonstop, she led Shelby through the casino crowd, parting the throng with nudges and an occasional shove. They spent ten minutes fussing with hair and makeup, and Silvia complimented Shelby on having snagged Hank. "He's a hunk," the ex-showgirl said, slurring the words through lips pursed to receive fresh lipstick.

The description made Shelby smile. "He might have been a hunk once. He's just a middle-aged businessman now."

"Hah!" Silvia rolled the lipstick back into its bronze sleeve and blotted her lips with a tissue. "Monkey business, maybe." She sprayed perfume toward the ceiling and stepped into the descending mist. "His eyes. That icy stare makes me itch all over."

"Itch?"

"You know." Silvia dropped the lipstick and perfume back into her purse. "If John wasn't here, you and me'd probably have a cat fight over him." She checked her watch. "John said half an hour."

They wandered around the casino until the thirty minutes were up. Back in the dining room, John asked what Shelby thought of Las Vegas.

"Do you want the abridged version?" she asked. "Or shall I monopolize the rest of the evening?"

He laughed. "Sum it up. One word."

That's easy, she thought: *vulgar*. "One word? Unique."

They made small talk for several more minutes. Then Hank said, "Tomorrow's going to be a long day. We need to get some rest." He stood and offered his arm to Shelby.

During the cab ride back to their hotel, he sat with his shoulders hunched. His face had the drawn look she associated with his need for pain medication. "Shouldn't you carry them with you?" she asked.

"What?" He rested a hand on hers. "Sorry, I didn't mean to snap. What'd you say?"

"Your pills. Shouldn't you carry a few with you?"

"Forgot. Stupid of me." He smiled. "You have a good time?"

She thought about it. "I did. I guess I'm starting to do what you suggested, concentrating on cramming in pleasant experiences. Relaxing music, great food."

"You have any idea how good you look? In that dress you . . ." He licked his lips. "Every man there envied me. Jefferies included."

For the brief remainder of the cab ride, he left his hand on hers. She considered pulling hers away, but that would have left his palm on her thigh. Besides, she found the contact comforting.

In their suite, Hank washed one of his pills down with water from the bathroom faucet and stretched out on a reclining chair. "Give me ten minutes. I'll be human again."

Shelby bathed and slipped on the T-shirt she had borrowed from him the previous night. The Aladdin's robes were noticeably finer than the Marriott's. Wearing one of the two she found hanging in the bathroom, she walked to where Hank lay stretched out with his eyes shut. "Can I get you anything?"

"A club soda would be great. No ice."

She carried the glass to his chair. "Feeling better?"

"Hundred percent. Thanks."

She dug through his bag, careful to avoid touching the pistol or the stun gun, and found the medication he had bought for the wounds on his face. "Let's take care of those scratches." She eased the bandage off, cleaned the fingernail marks with hydrogen peroxide, and smeared them with antiseptic. "We should leave the bandage off. Let the wounds air-dry."

"Thanks." He sat up and sipped his drink. "Were you being straight about having a good time tonight?"

"Yes, I was. It's been a long time since I enjoyed an evening out."

They lapsed into silence, and the night closed around them. After several minutes Hank said, "Do you think there's anything left of us when we die?"

He wanted to talk about death again, after extracting a promise from her not to? "You mean an afterlife?"

"Not the Christian heaven and hell thing. I never did buy that."

"What, then?" Shelby asked.

"I wonder if we merge with a universal consciousness, become a part of some collective will. Something like that. It's hard to accept that we're just a set of complex electrical circuits. That it's all over when the power goes off."

"I guess there's only one way to find out."

He shifted in the recliner, making it squeak. "You're Catholic, aren't you?"

"Lapsed."

"So, you no longer believe in absolution? What about the therapeutic benefits of confession?"

"That works without the religious trappings. It's a matter of talking to a sympathetic listener. It never hurts. Sometimes it helps."

The suite had twin beds. They had been in them with the lights off for a quarter-hour when Hank's voice drifted across the twenty or so inches of space between them. "You called yourself a lapsed Catholic. If you were still practicing and went to a priest for confession, would there be things you'd want to get off your chest?"

"Of course."

"What sort of things?"

It seemed bizarre to think that unloading on a killer would lighten her load, but hadn't she said earlier that it never hurts? That it sometimes helps? Certainly, the ghosts that haunted her would give him no advantage he didn't already have. And he had begun opening up to her. "I told you about killing those men."

"You said one raped you and another tried. The third tried to kill you. It troubles you that you defended yourself?"

"I've always opposed capital punishment, yet I appointed myself their executioner. I'd do it again under the same circumstances, but I'm not certain I would do some of the other things."

"For example?"

"Working for the CBTF, I lured a man to a place where he could be assassinated."

"Did you know what they planned?"

"Krystal, my handler, said they were going to capture him and put him on trial. I should have known better, though."

"Did you have a choice?"

"If I hadn't agreed, I would have been indicted for manslaughter.

My sister and other illegal immigrants would have been deported. Back home, most of them would have been killed or imprisoned."

"Then, didn't you choose the lesser evil, as they say?"

"What they had me do, the mission they sent me on, was pretty much what you do. I didn't pull the trigger, but I may as well have."

Lying on her back and staring at the darkened ceiling, shut off from Las Vegas' twenty-four-hour madness by heavy drapes and high-quality soundproofing, she imagined herself back in the confessional booths of her youth. Hank's invitation to unload about her mission for the CBTF became the priest's intonation, "In what way have you sinned?" She stared at the ceiling and let memories take her back four weeks—it seemed half a lifetime—to when she returned to Haiti at the CBTF's behest, to her first encounter with Haitian authorities since escaping with Carmen.

The Haitian customs officer had accepted her passport with a bored expression. He typed her name into a computer, and his boredom faded. Clutching the passport as if he feared it might squirm away, he nodded to someone behind her.

Shelby steeled herself to avoid looking around. A naïve expatriate returning with her record cleared by the intercession of the U.S. State Department would feel she had nothing to fear.

"Mademoiselle," said a polite but authoritative voice.

She turned and faced two uniformed policemen. They escorted her to a room furnished only with a wooden table and two straight-backed chairs. A man identifiable as an officer by the bar on his collar sat across the table from her. The policemen left, closing the door behind them.

The officer invited her to take the other chair. He opened a manila folder and eyed its contents. "Why have you returned to Haiti?"

"It's my home."

He looked up, locking gazes with her. "You left without authorization."

"A misunderstanding."

Another glance at the folder. "You're the daughter of Rene Julien-Dumarsis de Cervosier?"

"I am, yes."

"Where is your father?"

"I don't know." A fellow refugee had told her that her father, though in poor health, had joined resistance fighters in Haiti's mountains, but she wasn't supposed to know that.

"Where will you be staying?"

"I understand the government has taken possession of my family's estate. I've booked a suite at the Hotel Constanza de Luje."

The officer made notes in the folder. He pulled Shelby's passport from an inside breast pocket and slid it across the table. "You are required to report any change of address within twenty-four hours. You are required to immediately report any contact with your father or with foreign nationals. Welcome home, Mademoiselle Cervosier."

Hank cut into her thoughts: "You asleep?"

"Just thinking."

"About the obvious?"

"About the CBTF sending me back to Haiti. The mission that got me targeted by you."

"They sent you back, and the strongman down there, that colonel who headed the junta, recently died. Was he the target?"

Not a difficult guess. Colonel Burgess's death wouldn't have been big news in America, but it would have been reported. "Yes."

"And you're the only outside witness?"

"If I'm just a target, what difference does it make to you why they hired you?"

He let silence fill the space between them for several moments. "The colonel must have had a bevy of bodyguards. How'd you pull it off?"

"Everything seems to be a commercial transaction with you. I'll tell you how I separated him from his armed retinue, but you have to pay."

"What's your price?"

"A telephone call. I want to speak with Carmen."

"That might upset her. Why chance it?"

"I have to know she's all right. I don't trust you."

He didn't respond. Was he considering it? She remembered her father describing his negotiating technique: "In a clash of wills, whoever speaks first loses."

"Let's compromise," Hank said after a long silence. "You can e-mail her."

"How will I know it's really she who answers?"

"You're a smart woman. You'll figure something out."

"A chat room, then. The kind they have on Yahoo, where we can exchange messages in real time."

"Instant messages? Sure, I can set that up. So, how'd you lure the Haitian government's top dog away from his human shield?"

"Help came from an unexpected source."

Unexpected, she thought as she gave Hank the details, and ultimately lifesaving. If Chuck Barlow, Fuquay International's corporate pilot and a long-time Cervosier family acquaintance, hadn't tried to pick her up, she wouldn't have reached the junta's chairman so quickly. And if Chuck hadn't been scheduled to fly to America without passengers, she would not have gotten out of Haiti alive.

Like Shelby, he had been staying at the Hotel Constanza de Luje.

He spotted her in the dining room and approached with a drink in his hand and a smile on his face. Her unaccompanied status at dinner had garnered disapproving glowers from matrons and flirtatious stares from several men. It made her pleased to see Chuck.

"I spotted you from the bar," he said. "Mind if I sit?" He took the chair closest to hers. "Can't tell you how good it is to see a friendly face."

"Haitians have always liked Americans."

He chuckled. "My job, when I'm not flying, is to attend official parties and receptions and be friendly. Lately, I've not had much luck with the friendly part."

They asked each other innocuous questions while Shelby finished her meal. Chuck invited her to join him for a cocktail, for a carriage ride, for a stroll. She politely demurred, thanked him for keeping her company, and said good night. He walked her to the stairwell and shook her hand. "Your government has appointed a new minister of industry and commerce," he said. "There's a reception for him on Friday, and I have to attend. I don't suppose I could interest you?"

The reception was a black-tie affair. Shelby wore an ankle-length, baby-blue silk gown. She danced with Chuck and with another American who stopped by their table. On each circle of the dance floor, she looked for Colonel Burgess. As the most politically influential man in Haiti, he would have been invited, and he would attend unless military or statecraft issues got in the way. She would have no trouble recognizing him, because his face had been a daily feature on local television and in the newspaper before she fled the country. A tall, light-complexioned, movie-star handsome mulatto, he would be hard to miss even if he wore civilian clothing.

She did not see him in the ballroom, but she spotted his wife. Eight years older than Shelby, Mrs. Burgess had been a supporting actress in European theater and had bit parts in several Italian movies before marrying the colonel. Gossipmongers reported that she had been seen with bruises and had on several occasions been treated for injuries improbably attributed to accidents. She never appeared in public without the colonel.

From attending affairs of state with her father, Shelby remembered a smoking lounge in a ballroom annex beyond the restrooms. She excused herself to her escort and headed for the powder room but walked past it and barged, head down, into the men-only lounge. Colonel Burgess sat there, holding court with a group of hangers-on.

"Oh!" Shelby forced her voice to a shriek of distress. "Sorry, I'm looking for the . . . please forgive me. Terribly sorry."

She turned to leave and bumped into a mountain of a man in uniform. "Off-limits," he snapped.

"I know, I . . . mistake. Please, let me by."

With another man almost as large, he hustled her into the hallway and ran his hands over her. "Name," he demanded.

"Shelby Cervosier. Please, sir. The powder room."

Pawing through her purse, he found the Haitian passport the CBTF had provided. "Your address?"

She gave him the address of her family's estate. "But I'm not living there at the moment. I'm at the hotel Constanza de Luge."

"You were invited to the reception?"

"My escort was. Please, I have to go to the powder room." She no longer pretended. Tension weighed on her bladder so that she feared an accident.

"I'll handle it," said a fresh voice from just outside the smoking lounge door. The two burly men snapped to attention, and Shelby faced Colonel Burgess. He inspected her at length. "You look familiar. Have we met?"

"No, sir. May I go to the powder room?"

"You recognize the breach of decorum here?"

"Yes, sir. I was looking for the . . . the facility, and went through the wrong door. If I could just . . ."

"You can't wait?"

She shifted from foot to foot. "Colonel, I need to go."

"Come on." He marched her to the women's room and stepped inside with her. "Wait in the hallway," he ordered the female attendant. "See that no one enters."

"I would very much like privacy," Shelby said.

The colonel chuckled. "A woman taking a piss is neither a novelty nor a matter of particular interest to me." With crossed arms, he leaned against a textured, floral-patterned wall. "It would, however, interest my men. Would you prefer them?"

Having gotten in much deeper than she intended, she stiffened and put as much dignity in her voice as she could muster. "Thank you, no."

She chose the stall farthest from him, but he shifted and stood just beyond the partition. Despite her physical distress, release proved nearly impossible. She finally managed a trickle, and it sounded embarrassingly loud in the otherwise quiet room.

The flow stopped abruptly when Colonel Burgess spoke to her through the partition: "Are you related to Rene Julien-Dumarsis de Cervosier?"

"He's my father."

"Hmmm."

She straightened her gown and came out of the stall, her face flaming. After rinsing her hands and drying them on a towel from the attendant's stand, she blotted her face with a tissue and inspected her makeup. She turned to the handsome colonel, who still leaned against the wall, his face impassive, his arms crossed on his chest. "Your men have my purse. My makeup."

He muscled off the wall, stepped outside, and returned with the purse. "You're a professor at the university, I believe."

"I was. I got into trouble."

"Yes. Sorry about your father. He bet on the wrong horse."

Using a fresh tissue, Shelby wiped errant eyeliner. "He's old. Change is hard for the elderly." She dug lipstick from her purse and touched up her lips. Turning to the door, she found the colonel blocking her path. "Will you please excuse me?"

He escorted her to the end of the hallway and raised her hand to his lips. "We will see more of each other."

Shelby wondered if Hank had fallen asleep while she recounted her experience. She had spoken in a deliberate monotone to control the emotion building inside her.

"Your Colonel Burgess sounds like a real stand-up guy," he said.

"I thought you were sleeping."

"In the middle of this saga? Not likely. Having seen this evening what you do to a gown, I'd guess Burgess didn't wait long to make his move."

"Two days. His aide-de-camp accosted me as I headed for the elevator after breakfast. He said the colonel had reserved a private dining room at the Metropolitan Officers' Club. A staff car would pick me up at eight p.m."

"He made the arrangements assuming you would be available?"

"This was the most powerful man in Haiti. He could order executions, unlimited detention, barbarous interrogations. He wasn't accustomed to being refused."

"You were supposed to lure him to an isolated location? A club in Port-au-Prince hardly filled the bill."

"The dinner turned out to be an audition for the main event. He used it to explain his expectations—and my options."

Colonel Burgess had been all charm and manners when he met her in the doorway of a private dining room in the Metropolitan Officers' Club. He murmured his pleasure at seeing her again, and a fawning headwaiter led them to a dining room large enough to accommodate a small banquet but furnished with a single table and two chairs. The cavernous, dimly lit space emphasized the table with its white linen and its burnished flatware, sparkling crystal, and silver candelabra. A magnum of champagne in a bucket of ice rested on a small cart within arm's reach of the table.

"I took the liberty of selecting our wine," Burgess said as he held her chair. "If you have a contrary preference, the steward will accommodate you."

"Countermand your order? Colonel, I wouldn't dare."

He sat across from her and poured the champagne. "As chairman of the governing council, I welcome you back to Haiti. Even as the biblical prodigal son's father welcomed him home."

"I appreciate the government's tolerance."

"Within limits, a young woman's hysteria must be accommodated."

"Hysteria?"

He chuckled. "I have a report on the events leading to your flight."

"You mean the massacre of my students?"

"The students were meeting illegally." His hand gripped her knee under the table. "In America, I understand you were taught the wisdom of acceding to male dominion."

He was referring, she supposed, to the beating and rape in Arkansas. Her face flamed. She felt the heat but hoped it was not obvious in the candlelight.

The hand on her knee slid upward. "You left Haiti as a naïve innocent and returned as a worldly-wise courtesan."

She pushed his hand away. "Being raped does not make one a courtesan."

"No, but accepting it speaks volumes about your character."

"What do these volumes tell you, Colonel?"

The hand that had been on her leg now grasped the stem of his champagne flute. "They tell me you have a healthy survival instinct. That you are not given to self-destructive behavior in the face of the inevitable."

"Are you still alluding to the past?"

"I am alluding, as you say, to what I expect from you."

"I'm a simple woman. You need to be straightforward."

He chuckled. "You were an honor student as an undergraduate. You hold a doctorate from that American university in—where is it? Arizona, I believe. You were a university professor until your flawed judgment brought the house of Cervosier tumbling down. And you would have me believe you don't understand?"

"Given my flawed judgment, can you accept the possibility?"

He set his champagne flute on the table and leaned back. "Since your return to Haiti, you've made inquiries about reclaiming your ancestral estate and gaining access to your family's bank accounts. You've made no progress, and your resources are meager."

"I'm impressed with your ability to collect information. But its relevance escapes me."

"You will soon be destitute. Your hotel will evict you. Your acquaintances, after visits from Internal Security, will pretend they don't remember you."

"You have a low opinion of my resourcefulness."

"Perhaps you anticipate becoming the whore of your American pilot friend. But a word from me will get Mister Barlow expelled from Haiti."

Shelby pushed back her chair and stood. "I wish to return to the hotel."

Colonel Burgess's face took on a frightening hardness. His voice became tempered steel. "Sit down."

She sat.

"At all times, you will conduct yourself in public as a lady."

His proprietary air told her she had succeeded in the first phase of her mission. She was unsure how she felt about that. "And in private?"

"You will learn to anticipate my expectations, my whims."

Eyes downcast. She had to convince him to leave his bodyguards behind, to be alone with her. "I have social position, an impeccable reputation. Do you intend to destroy me?"

"To protect your treasured reputation, you will avoid any future contact with the American pilot."

"The scandal of associating with an American pales in comparison to being seen alone with you."

"Which explains why I had you brought here in a separate staff car. Why we're dining in a private room and why you will remain

for a period after I leave." The colonel sipped champagne and re-
filled his flute. "Having survived a childhood in Port-au-Prince's
worst slum and climbed out over the bodies of the upper class, it
pleases me to own the daughter of a man who came within a hairs-
breadth of the presidency. It will amuse me to see you lording it
over the starched ladies of our capital city yet groveling at my feet
in private."

"You intend to make me grovel?"

Another chuckle. "It is women's nature to grovel."

She should look at the floor and slump her shoulders submis-
sively. She knew that, but she couldn't do it. She locked gazes with
him. "And if I choose to defy this nature?"

"I will teach you the folly of your ways."

The icy cruelty in his eyes forced her to glance away. Unable to
eat, she pushed her filet of sole around with her fork. The colonel
insisted that she have a second flute of champagne. The waiter removed their main course, served strawberry crepes, and withdrew.

Colonel Burgess tasted the crepes and said, "I have a villa in the
foothills, about an hour's drive from the city."

Lead him to the decision you want. She looked into his eyes and
quickly down. "Your pied-a-terre is notorious, Colonel. The entire
city takes note when a caravan departs with your paramour of the
moment."

"Caravan?"

"Your fleet of armored sedans filled with thuggish bodyguards. The
women who accompany you are branded as being without virtue."

"You think me incapable of discretion?"

She wouldn't get a better opening. If she failed, the mission
would collapse and she would be at his mercy. "Then take me there
alone. If you will protect my reputation, I will strive to become in

private what you want me to be."

He guffawed. "Women never cease to amuse me. They are whores by nature, yet they worry about what other whores think of them." He took another bite of his crepes and spoke with his mouth stuffed. "Not to worry. I will preserve your precious reputation."

"You actually talked him into leaving his personal army at home?" Hank sounded incredulous.

"Not exactly. A week later, on a Friday afternoon, I walked into the hotel and found his driver waiting in the lobby. He had instructions to escort me to the colonel's villa. My orders were to pack toiletries and clothing for the weekend."

"Where was the colonel?"

"That's what I asked the driver. He pointed out that enlisted men don't keep track of officers. They merely follow orders."

"And he expected you to do the same? To obey like an enlisted man?"

"Apparently so. He gave me no chance to use one of the message drops the CBTF had set up, to tell them about the development. I had to trust that they were shadowing me and would see us leaving the hotel."

"Did they?"

"I don't know. But they had someone inside the villa. Colonel Burgess didn't get out alive."

"Are you going to tell me how it went down?"

"I've earned my Internet hookup with Carmen. If you're an honorable assassin, you'll set it up as promised."

"We need to get some sleep anyway," Hank said. "Busy day tomorrow. You like boating?"

"We're going on a boat?"

"A yacht. Big party on Lake Mead."

"That's what you and John talked about? Are he and Silvia going to be there?"

"Yeah."

"Are you planning to kill someone at this party?"

"Good night, Shelby."

CHAPTER ELEVEN

WHAT KIND OF WOMAN is sharing my hotel room? Hank asked himself as he lay in his bed staring at the darkened ceiling. That she had killed three men in self-defense was impressive enough, even intimidating. But her tale of putting herself in harm's way to gain freedom for her sister and a group of illegal aliens would have been unbelievable if he had not learned so much about her already. Apparently reared as a child of wealth and privilege, she had a PhD in history and had been a university professor. How had that background equipped her to survive rape and torture, execute her abusers, and collaborate to assassinate a head of state?

His thoughts shifted to tomorrow. Completing a contract in a confined space with no avenue of retreat was dicey, but Jefferies had convinced him there was no alternative. The target, hard to find and always surrounded by bodyguards, would be more vulnerable on the yacht than at any other time or place.

Hank planned to gain the target's trust so the guy would make himself easily accessible. Complete the contract when they returned to the dock but before they disembarked, stow the body on the boat, and put some distance between them before anyone found the corpse. Jefferies had warned that guests were checked with a metal detector as they boarded, so he would have to use his garrote, a strand of nylon he carried threaded into his belt. Chemically treated, the strand was as stiff and strong as piano wire. Wrap its ends around something to serve as makeshift handles, loop it around the target's neck from behind, and jerk. It would cut off sound, air, and blood circulation.

Shelby was both an asset and a major complication. He needed a date for the party, but Jefferies could easily arrange that with a play-for-pay escort. He toyed with the idea of handling it that way and leaving Shelby in the hotel, but what if something went wrong and he wasn't able to come back for her? What would she do, alone in a strange city and with no idea how to find her little sister? Yet, if he left her with money and told her how to get to Carmen, she wouldn't wait for him. Alone with Carmen in an alien environment, she would be easy prey for other contractors.

The least risky alternative was to take her with him. If things fell apart, there would be no reason for anyone to suspect she was other than a date he had picked up in one of the casinos. With the decision made, he concentrated on blanking his mind so he could get some sleep.

Disgruntled over the airline's choice of equipment, Vlad settled in his seat for the flight from Arizona to Arkansas: three hours of confinement in what felt like a third-world airplane. He preferred wide-bodied jets, the difference between a ship and a rowboat. If you folded its wings, Northwest Flight 1753 out of Phoenix would fit into a wide-body's baggage compartment.

A heavy-thighed, thirtyish flight attendant ruled the plane's first-class cabin. Fat and old was a better description, Vlad decided. Even so, it wouldn't hurt to charm her. Good practice. Her name tag identified her as A. Flores. When she offered to take his beverage order, he flashed his Hollywood smile. "What do your friends call you, honey?"

"Ms. Flores. What would you like to drink, sir?"

Her comeback made him feel like a pimply kid. He ordered a vodka martini, specifying Finlandia. As the attendant walked away, he fantasized doing her the way he had that preacher's wife.

The mental image of her blood oozing after he impaled her, of life gradually fading from her terror-stricken eyes, brightened his mood for a moment, but he sank back into brooding. Net of the broker's commission, his six-grand payday for the Arizona stakeout would barely cover his first-class airline tickets and his hotel and car rental bills. He would need another car to get from Little Rock to the burg in southeast Arkansas where the preacher had sent Cervosier's package in care of a librarian. That would put him in the red. To turn a profit, he had to find the target before another contractor took her out. The pleasure of dispatching her would be a bonus.

In Little Rock, to avoid leaving a trail back to his flight, he took a cab from the airport to a downtown hotel. Thumbing through a copy of *USA Today* while waiting for his rental car, he spotted a blurb about the double homicide in Arizona: "A spokesperson for Flagstaff's Department of Public Safety says the method, slow and painful death by impalement, fits the pattern of a series of gruesome murders in and around Chicago last summer."

"What's the world coming to?" Vlad murmured as he tossed the paper aside. He claimed his rental car and headed south out of Little Rock. Ten hours after boarding the predawn flight from Phoenix, he parked across the street from the Clanal County Public Library in Perryville. Wearing a wig and fake mustache, he flirted with a part-time, teenage library worker and learned that Elizabeth

Fontaine, the head librarian, usually left around six p.m. He came back at five and waited outside for her.

She left the library an hour behind schedule and drove off in an old Volvo sedan. Vlad tailed her to a supermarket in a neighborhood shopping center, where she spent half an hour. Dozing at the wheel, he almost missed her when she loaded her purchases and drove away.

The sun had dropped behind a nearby tree line when she parked in front of a modest wood-frame bungalow on a street with few houses. Lights were on in the other houses, but the librarian's place was dark until she entered—no one waiting for her. He parked half a block away and watched. Three hours later, satisfied that she lived alone, he drove back to the highway and booked a motel room. His weapons would arrive the next day by UPS, and he would go to work.

CHAPTER TWELVE

SHELBY AND HANK SLEPT late on their first morning in Las Vegas. They ate a leisurely breakfast and headed for Lake Mead shortly before noon. "What about my instant messaging session with Carmen?" Shelby asked as Hank nursed his old Buick Skylark through a traffic snarl. "You promised."

"We'll get back late, so I left a message for Jason to check his e-mail after nine and be prepared to get her out of bed."

Jason. The Colorado man's name was Jason, he lived somewhere west of Boulder, Colorado, and Hank knew his phone number and Internet address. "Couldn't we have done it this morning?"

"When we got up, he'd already left for work. He won't check his e-mail until he gets home."

"This work—does he also kill people for a living?"

"No, he's a . . . he has a regular job."

They headed southeast out of Las Vegas on U.S. 95 and turned northeast on a secondary road at a town called Henderson. The road meandered over terrain that looked too barren to sustain life. Lake Mead remained hidden until they reached the village of Echo Bay, but Shelby smelled the water long before she saw it. They topped a rise, and the lake stretched like a sparkling jewel across the arid landscape.

It took her breath away. "It's a miracle. A seemingly endless stretch of desolate land, then a gleaming inland sea."

"An engineering marvel." Hank wheeled the Skylark into a marina, where a fleet of small boats bobbed near yachts like ladies-in-waiting surrounding royalty. "They dammed the Colorado River back in the nineteen-thirties. Middle of the so-called Great Depression. To put men to work, the government went on a building spree."

"The artistry of it," Shelby said. "Blue-green water lapping at red rocks. It's as if God dropped a giant turquoise into the desert. But I expected more people. Towns along the shore."

"Government owns the shoreline. They've restricted development, holding the land for recreation and conservation." Hank pointed to the largest yacht. "There's our boat."

"Good lord. It belongs on the ocean."

"Rankin isn't known for subtlety." Hank pulled the keys from the Skylark's ignition and twisted to face her. "You're not gonna like this guy, but you need to be tolerant. Try to overlook his attitude."

"What's wrong with his attitude?"

"According to Jefferies, he's obsessed with women. They're like dope to him."

"That doesn't sound bad. If you shared his obsession, my life would be less hazardous." A silent glare reminded her of their agreement to keep that topic off the table. "Sorry," she mumbled.

He nodded. "Like most addicts, Rankin resents the objects of his addiction. I'd have left you at the hotel, but I'm supposed to have a date, and—" A white Lincoln Town Car pulled up, and he opened his door. "There's John, right on time."

They greeted Silvia and John Jefferies, and the four of them approached the yacht, the *Bad Girl*. A blond, crew-cut, and suntanned young man, his overdeveloped physique showcased in tight jeans and a body-hugging T-shirt, stood at the foot of the gangway.

"The Jefferies party," John said. "Mister Rankin is expecting us."

The muscular gatekeeper punched a button on his cell phone and repeated Jefferies's name. He flipped the phone's lid closed and said, "Welcome aboard."

At the top of the gangway, a duplicate of the muscleman stood with a handheld metal detector. He ran the wand over them and rummaged through their beach bags. The precaution eased Shelby's suspicion that Hank planned to kill someone. No gun or knife could be smuggled on board.

"John," said a narrow-shouldered, elderly man in white pants and sky-blue polo shirt. His arms and legs were thin, but the shirt stretched over a gut that made him look eight months pregnant. Shelby guessed him to be in his late sixties or early seventies. Wearing the barest trace of a smile, he shook Jefferies's hand.

Jefferies made the introductions, addressing their host as Mister Rankin but using everyone else's first names. Rankin nodded to Hank but did not offer his hand. When Jefferies introduced the women, Rankin acknowledged them with inspections as if they were merchandise on display. "Cocktails on the aft deck as soon as we clear the harbor," he said, and turned to one of the husky twins who had guarded the gangway. "Show our guests to their quarters."

As they went below, the yacht began to vibrate. Three steps led down to a narrow, carpeted passageway. They walked past two doors, and their escort opened a third, the one nearest the end. "We're underway. Mister Rankin will meet you on the aft deck in fifteen minutes. For the ladies, bathing attire is appropriate."

Shelby wore her new bathing suit under her jeans and pullover shirt. Hank carried a beach bag that held everything she normally kept in her purse, plus sunglasses, sunblock, and her flip-flops. He tossed the bag onto the stateroom's bed, plopped down on the couch, and pointed at a door across from the entry. "That's got to be the john. You ladies want dibs, I'd guess."

"Yeah," Silvia Jefferies said. "Gotta get naked." She dug through a beach bag similar to Hank's and came up with two wisps of black cloth. Looking at Shelby, she said, "You coming?"

"You go ahead." Shelby sat on the couch by Hank. His expression told her that he needed his medication. "You brought them this time, I trust."

"In the bag."

"I'll get water." The wet bar held a selection of beverages but no ice. She opened a bottle of mineral water, half-filled a plastic tumbler, and rummaged through their beach bag for his medicine.

"Thanks." He tapped a pill into his palm and passed the vial back to her. "Migraine," he said, glancing at Jefferies.

"Silvia gets 'em," Jefferies said. "They're a bitch."

Silvia stepped out of the lavatory and posed in the doorway wearing the bits of black fabric. "Ta-da! Cool, huh?"

She might as well have been naked. The top barely covered her nipples. A narrow band of matching fabric circled her waist and looped between her thighs. She must have removed every trace of body hair. Shelby wondered how much it had hurt.

"You look good, Silvia," said Jefferies. "Rankin's gonna love it."

"Fuck Rankin." Silvia pirouetted before Hank and faced him with her pelvis thrust forward. "What do you think?"

"Hot. More than that. Sizzling."

She grinned at Shelby. "John's all yours, honey." She pointed to the lavatory. "That one, not my hubby."

In the lavatory, Shelby slipped off her jeans and shirt, tugged at the bathing suit where it had ridden up, and checked her wig. If she went into the water, she would come out with different hair. Back in the cabin, she slipped on the knitted cover she had bought with the bathing suit, exchanged her canvas boat shoes for the rubber flip-flops, and sat by Hank again. "Feeling better?"

"Feel great." He made a trip to the lavatory and then stood by the door to the passageway. "We'd better make our grand entrance."

Shelby glanced from him to Jefferies. Both men still wore their traveling clothes: Hank in khakis and a pullover shirt, Jefferies in linen slacks and a short-sleeved Hawaiian shirt. "You guys not swimming?"

"Nobody swims," Jefferies said. "On Rankin's boat, that's the uniform for women." He shrugged.

"He's a goddamn lech," Silvia said, her voice thick with contempt. "This is as naked as he can get us, starting out."

They found Rankin on the aft deck with the twin bodybuilders and four women who wore thongs much like Barbara's. Shelby supposed there must be a crew, but they were not evident.

An upholstered bench spanned the rear of the deck. Rankin sprawled there with his legs outstretched, clasping a drink in one hand and the flesh of a woman's inner thigh in the other. He got to his feet. "There you are."

The yacht's speed created a breeze across the deck. "Air feels good," Jefferies said.

"We'll drop anchor in the shade. It'll be cool." Rankin fixed his gaze on Hank. "Your name again?"

"Hank."

In a louder voice, and pointing to them in turn, Rankin announced to the deck, "This is Hank and John." He jabbed a thumb at the blond twins. "Edward and Hamilton." Nodding toward two women at the rear of the deck, the one he had been mauling and another nearby, he said, "My bitches." He aimed his thumb and finger like a gun at the other two women, standing by a wet bar. "Couple whores I picked up for my boys. Have a drink. Everybody get comfortable."

"I see what you mean about attitude," Shelby whispered to Hank. She introduced herself to the women Rankin had referred to as whores. They shook hands, and one offered her a glass of white wine, which she carried across the deck to the women Rankin had called his bitches. The one Rankin had been pawing—thirtysome-thing, tall, big-busted, and wide hipped—introduced herself and her companion, a smaller and much younger woman with short, curly blond hair and a spray of pale freckles across her nose.

Rankin and Jefferies, drinks in hand, huddled on one side of the deck by themselves. Rankin's twin sidekicks shifted their atten-tion to their dates. Hank and Silvia joined Shelby and Rankin's two women at the rear of the yacht and watched its wake. Silvia nodded toward Rankin. "Real charmer, ain't he?"

"Are you and John friends with Mister Rankin?" Shelby asked.

"He's John's client. We've partied together a few times."

"He has a really nice boat."

Silvia laughed. "A goddamned floating palace. He's big cheese in the rackets."

"Rackets? You mean criminal activity?"

"The Mob, honey. What government mucky-mucks call orga-nized crime."

"And John works for him?"

"Tries to keep him out of jail. John says nothing goes down in

Vegas without Rankin getting a piece of it."

Shelby excused herself and pulled Hank away. "I'm confused by the dynamics here," she said, speaking in a low voice.

"Rankin has some differences with one of John's other clients," Hank said. "John's trying to iron it out."

"How do we fit in? Are we here for our entertainment value?"

"Rankin goes nowhere without his muscle." Hank glanced across the deck, where the twins, Edward and Hamilton, talked with their dates and ran exploratory hands over them. "John thought it prudent to have a little heft of his own."

"You're here as his bodyguard?"

"It pays well, and it requires no effort." Hank waved a hand to take in the yacht. "Can't complain about the perks."

"Silvia said Rankin is a gangster. Will there be trouble?"

"His beef's with the client, not with John."

The yacht came to rest under the shade of a towering cliff, and Shelby saw her first crew member, a uniformed woman who came on deck with hors d'oeuvres and fresh ice. Music spilled from hidden speakers, and Edward and Hamilton danced with their dates. Rankin's two women leaned against the bar, talking with their heads close together. A few minutes later, the twins took their dates below. "Silvia," Jefferies called across the deck from where he stood with Rankin, "come over here."

"Oh, shit," Silvia mumbled. She crossed the deck on obviously reluctant legs and nodded when Jefferies said something to her. Rankin slid an arm around her, talked with Jefferies for several more minutes, and headed for the hatch, pushing Silvia ahead of him. Jefferies walked back to Hank and Shelby. "I've got some work to do. Dinner's at seven." He went below.

"What do you suppose is going on down there?" Shelby asked.

Hank shrugged. "Exactly what you suspect, I imagine."

"John doesn't seem upset about it. Nether do Rankin's women."

Hank's gaze followed Shelby's to where the two women were conversing softly, standing so close their bodies almost touched. "The women are probably happy to have some time off."

Crew members—the woman Shelby had seen earlier and a man who appeared for the first time—served dinner on a table set up on the foredeck. Rankin, ignoring Jefferies and the other diners, made small talk with Hank. Between courses, he gestured at Shelby with a fork. "Known her long?"

"Awhile," Hank said.

"What you think of my bitches?"

"The ladies seem very nice."

"You ever do any sharing? Swapping?"

Hank winked at Shelby. "I think of women kind of like toothbrushes. Not something I'd want to use after somebody else."

"Toothbrushes." Rankin's laughter seemed ripped from his throat. "You guys hear that?" he called to his bodyguards. Sitting with their dates near the end of the table, they looked his way when his laughter erupted. "Sluts are like toothbrushes." Rankin's attention swung back to Hank. "A sense of humor. I like you."

"I'm flattered."

"No, I mean it. You ever need work, you look me up."

"I'll keep that in mind."

Crew members cleared the table and set up a bar. Night had fallen with no moon, so indirect lighting close to the deck provided the only illumination. Music flooded through speakers again, and the twins and their dates resumed dancing. John and Silvia Jefferies also danced, leaving Shelby and Hank at the table with Rankin and his two women. Rankin watched the dancing for a couple minutes and then turned to Hank. "You been with Jefferies a long time?"

"Not so long."

"I know most of the muscle out here."

"I don't . . ." Hank seemed to search for words. "I don't work for John. He asked me to come along."

"Afraid I'll cut his nuts off? Goddamn lawyers." Rankin watched the dancing for another minute. "If I wanted to hurt him, you figure you could stop me?"

"Why would you want to hurt him? He's just a go-between."

"Good answer. You don't cave, but you're not a wise-guy wannabe. I could use a boy like you."

"In what capacity?"

"We'll talk about that." Rankin tapped a spoon against his cocktail glass to get attention. "Edward, it's time for the whores to go home."

The male crew member lowered a motor launch that hung from a small crane at the rear of the yacht. The twins' dates clambered on board, and the launch sped away with a twin whom Shelby assumed was Edward—she couldn't tell them apart—at the controls. "Nobody left but family," Rankin said as the launch's sound faded. "You all get a chance to meet my bitches?" He beckoned to them. "Come here, girls."

The two women walked over. The older, heavier one—she had introduced herself as Rosie—led. The young blonde followed on leaden feet. Shelby strained to remember her name: Pearl. A couple inches shorter than Shelby and equally trim, she looked barely past the age of consent. And she looked as if she would prefer to be anywhere on earth other than standing before Rankin.

Rankin gripped Rosie's arm, and her face registered discomfort. "I found this one about a year ago, working in a titty bar." He glanced at Pearl and shifted his eyes back to Rosie. "She brought the young cunt on board a couple days back. They figure I'm stupid. Think I don't know what's going on."

Rosie touched the hand that squeezed her arm. "Honey, let's just—"

He released her and backhanded the side of her head, knocking her to the deck. "Stay there."

Shelby jumped to her feet and started toward Rosie, but Hank grabbed her wrist. He shook his head almost imperceptibly, frowning. Shelby's muscles bunched and jerked, but she held her position.

Rankin massaged the knuckles of the hand that had decked Rosie. "They got a real hot routine they do on each other. Pretend it's a show for me. They think I can't see they're gettin' off on it."

Rage sliced through Shelby: at Rankin for mistreating Rosie, at Hank for letting it happen, at herself for being so docile. She jerked her wrist free of Hank's grasp. "I'm going to the cabin."

Pearl knelt by the older woman and whispered to her as Shelby headed for the stairs. Rosie pushed the small blonde away and shouted, "The dyke picked me up, honey. I thought you'd like it."

CHAPTER THIRTEEN

ANGER BOILED IN SHELBY as she raced down the steps of Rankin's yacht and along the passageway to the stateroom she shared with Hank and the Jefferies. Inside, she pulled on her jeans over her bathing suit, slipped on her boat shoes, and paced the tiny room, fuming at her helplessness.

Hank had just stood there when that Neanderthal knocked Rosie to the deck. But why not? Why would a man who murdered for money care if a woman got beaten up? Not that he could have done much, afloat on an isolated waterway with Rankin's bodyguard standing by and crew members only a shout away. Still, he could have shown disapproval.

Was she any better, though? She could have said something, given Rosie moral support. Instead, she'd let Hank shush her the way a child might acquiesce to a parent. She flung herself facedown across the bed. Hank was a killer and these were his people. She ought to have expected animalistic behavior.

A knock on the stateroom door startled her. Hank walked in, and she scrambled to her feet. "Why aren't you on deck helping that animal kick women around?"

"I don't like it any better than you. Not much I can do about it."

"You could have said something."

"Toward what end? Rankin's goons are armed. We're isolated

out here."

Masculine laughter from the passageway seeped through the stateroom walls, and Shelby strained to hear. A door slammed in the adjacent stateroom, the one she had learned belonged to Edward and Hamilton. A moment later, something hit the wall between the rooms. Pearl's voice stabbed through, screaming obscenities and yelping in pain.

Shelby lunged for the door. Hank pulled her back and, before she could protest, slipped into the passageway. She followed him to the other stateroom.

Pearl crouched in a corner, naked, her mouth and nose bloody. She seemed unaware of her surroundings.

One of the twin musclemen towered over her. He scowled at Hank and Shelby. "Get the fuck outta here!"

Hank stepped close, dipped his knees, and straightened them as he brought the heel of his hand up under the man's chin. It snapped the thug's head back. With a lightning shift of his body, Hank karate-chopped the exposed larynx.

The muscleman staggered back and leaned against the wall, holding his throat with both hands. An inhuman rasping sound issued from his mouth as he slid down the wall. Hank assumed a football punter's stance and looked ready to swing the toe of his shoe at the man's head, when the stateroom door opened.

"You do her, Ham?" Rankin called as the door swung wide. "Fix the bi—" He stopped, openmouthed. Hank's fist plowed into his bulging gut, and he doubled forward with a low-pitched, "Woof." On his knees, his hands folded against his stomach, he struggled to inhale.

"Hank," Shelby screamed. "Behind you!" The bodyguard—Hamilton, apparently—was back on his feet, a switchblade in his hand.

Hank whirled about. Backpedaling, he kicked a chair into Hamilton's path.

The bodyguard sidestepped the chair and dropped into a crouch, his knife blade glistening in the overhead light. Moving around Hank in a slow circle, he held the knife underhanded and low, the blade's sharp side up, and slashed the air inches from Hank's stomach.

Frantic to help, Shelby looked for something to use as a weapon. *The telephone.* She grabbed its base and jerked it free from its wire tether. Not heavy, but at least it was hard and blunt-edged. If she could get behind the knife wielder, bring it down on the back of his head, maybe—

Rankin, still wheezing, and moving slowly, pulled up the cuff of his trousers. He jerked a palm-sized pistol from an ankle holster.

Shelby slammed the phone's base against his temple. She hit him again, and the pot-gutted mobster dropped back onto his knees, supporting himself with both hands. A third blow with the phone base put him on his side on the carpet. She took the pistol from his slack hand. Except for its size, it looked identical to the one she had taken from the fake nanny in Florida. Unlike Hank's complicated semiautomatic, the nanny's had fired when Shelby pulled the trigger. She pointed this one at Hamilton and shouted, "Stop!"

The combatants ignored her. Hamilton had backed Hank into a corner, where he could no longer maneuver. The knife fighter feinted and slashed. His knife sliced through Hank's T-shirt and left a bloody trail across his stomach.

Before Hamilton could slash again, Shelby pointed the revolver at his back and squeezed the trigger. The shot sounded like dynamite exploding in the cabin.

Hamilton twisted to face her, still holding the knife.

Shelby's legs turned rubbery. She dropped to her knees on the carpet but, using both hands, centered the revolver on the muscleman's chest. She squeezed off another round, then another.

Hamilton lost his grip on the knife. He leaned against the desk, touched his hand to one of the wounds in his chest, and studied the blood. He looked at Shelby again, lost his balance, and collapsed.

Rankin, back on his feet, bear-hugged Shelby from behind.

Twisting, trying to free herself, she fell on her side, taking him with her. Struggling in his arms, she was vaguely aware of Hank picking up Hamilton's knife.

Hank fisted Rankin's hair and jerked the man's head back. With a single, quick slash, he cut the yacht owner's throat.

A long, drawn-out sound, like air escaping from a punctured tire, hissed from Rankin. He collapsed onto the carpet.

Hank folded the knife's blade into its handle and stuck it in his pocket. He offered Shelby his hand.

She waved him away and pushed to her feet. Staring at him, she digested what she had just seen. He'd killed in cold blood, efficiently, ruthlessly. Was that how he planned to dispatch her?

"You've been cut," she said, pushing the thought away. "How bad?"

"Nothing's hanging out. Are you hurt?"

Instead of answering, Shelby turned to Pearl. "You okay?" she asked.

Still in a corner, the young woman squatted with her hands clasped around her ankles. Her forehead rested on her knees.

"Pearl," Shelby snapped. "Pearl! Look at me."

Pearl raised her head, but her eyes were closed. "No more. Please don't hurt me."

"Nobody's going to hurt you. We have to get off the boat."

"Don't hurt me," she said again.

Shelby slapped her lightly. "Listen to me. We have to get off the boat."

Hank stepped between them. Grasping Pearl's shoulders, he pulled her to her feet and leaned her against the wall.

"Oh, wow," she gasped. "Dizzy."

"Take it slow." Hank steadied her as she took a tentative step, then another. "Good girl. You can do this." He released her, and she staggered but steadied herself.

Hank took the revolver from Shelby. He shoved it under his belt. Grasping Pearl's hand, he pulled her into the passageway.

Shelby realized that only seconds had passed as she followed them to the deck, but everything seemed to be happening in slow motion. On deck, they paused just outside the hatch as the uniformed duo who had served dinner appeared. The woman held a handgun, the man a rifle.

"In there," Hank shouted, pointing to the hatch. "Sounded like it came from the last cabin."

The couple rushed inside, and Hank dragged Pearl to the deck railing. "You can swim, right?" Without waiting for a response, he tossed her overboard.

Shelby jumped. As she sank into the water and fought her way back up, thoughts warred for dominance: Hank was wounded and might not be able to swim, the gunmen would come on deck and shoot them, she didn't know which direction was closest to land.

Her head broke the surface. She gulped air and went back under to slip off her shoes. On the surface again. No gunshots. Had Hank jumped? Where was Pearl? There, two dark blobs in the water.

Noise—the yacht's engines. The vessel began moving. It swung around, and its engines cranked higher, raising the prow out of the water. Heading for port, and if they called the authorities, police in swift patrol boats would find the swimmers easily. If Silvia was right about Rankin being a mobster, though, would they want to involve the police?

The yacht had been anchored no more than fifty yards offshore to get afternoon shade from a towering cliff, but the cliff looked impossible to climb. No place at water level to rest. Shelby remembered seeing land on the other side of the yacht but guessed it was half a mile away.

Hank and Pearl were swimming toward the far shore, so they must have drawn the same conclusion about the cliff. For Shelby the distance would be a cinch, but how good a swimmer was Pearl? How much strength could the young woman marshal after being beaten? Hank was twenty years Shelby's senior and had a knife wound in his stomach. Was he still losing blood?

The yacht became no more than a set of running lights, heading back the way it had come. Then it disappeared.

Shelby concentrated on her stroke but kept an eye on the other two swimmers. She guessed they were about midway to the far shore when Hank started wheezing. Remembering a survival technique from an article she'd read about shipwrecks, Shelby unsnapped her jeans and opened the zipper. She took a deep breath and sank underwater while struggling to get her legs out of the wet denim. Back on the surface, she knotted the pant legs near the bottoms and tossed them to Pearl, who treaded water at her side. "Capture air," she said. "Help you float." She turned to suggest the same thing to Hank and did not see him. Panic surged, but it dissipated when he surfaced with his trousers in his hands.

"Smart," he gasped. "Lifesaver."

The makeshift airbags helped. The trio made steady though slow progress for several minutes, until Hank quit swimming. He didn't say anything; he just stopped.

Shelby reached him with three overhand strokes and found him lying facedown in the water, held on the surface by the partially inflated legs of his trousers. Treading water, she lifted his face to the surface by pulling on his hair. "Swim, dammit." She swallowed water, coughed, pulled at his head again. "Don't . . . you . . . quit . . . on . . . me."

Pearl had proven to be a strong swimmer. She treaded water just in front of them. "Is he conscious?"

Most of the air had escaped from his makeshift float. Shelby tried to inflate the waterlogged trouser legs once more by waving them above the surface, but her exhausted arms and shoulders wouldn't cooperate. With Pearl's help, she pulled Hank until his chin rested in the crotch of the jeans the two women had been sharing as a float. They began towing him.

Shelby didn't remember reaching land. Sunlight warming her face awakened her, but she didn't want to move. Hank, stretched out on the gravelly shore on his stomach no more than three feet away, wore only his underwear. Pearl, wearing nothing, sat on the other side of him, hugging her knees and watching them with a worried frown.

Her gaze met Shelby's, and she expelled a big gulp of air. "Thought you'd both died on me."

Both died? Fear dragged its fingers across Shelby's heart. Hank wasn't a young man, and he was wounded. Had he cheated death in the water only to have the stress trigger a heart attack or stroke? Had he bled to death? She stretched out a hand and shook him. "Hank? Hank!"

He groaned, moved a shoulder, groaned again. "Everything hurts."

She sat up. "Big crybaby." Worried about the knife wound on his stomach, she said, "Don't try to sit. Just roll over." Remembering how beaten Pearl had been the night before, she studied the young woman.

Sporting a split lip and a shiner that almost closed one eye, Pearl flashed a broad smile. "Stomach's growling. Got any cash on you?"

The question reminded Shelby that she wore only her bathing suit. She looked for the trousers she had stripped off and used for flotation. "Seen my jeans?"

Pearl shrugged. "No pockets, no pesos, huh?"

"Hunger is the least of our worries." The lakefront looked deserted. Even if they were able to walk to a populated area, what then? Naked and near-naked partygoers wandering up from the lake, one with a bruised face and battered body—someone would call the police. They would demand identification.

"Relax," Pearl said. "It's uncomfortable, going to be embarrassing. Beats dying, though."

"It's more complicated than that," Shelby said as she rolled up Hank's T-shirt and inspected his stomach wound. Twisting onto his back had reopened the cut, and it seeped blood, but it was only about three inches long and didn't look deep. "You're lucky," she said. "He didn't get much of you."

"Don't feel lucky." Hank labored to a sitting position. The bandage had come off his face, and the scratches from Carmen's fingernails—the wounds were bright pink, almost red, but they had closed—seemed to glow in the morning light. He groaned again. "Need a bottle. A week in bed."

"Let's think this through," Shelby said. "We need to find a road or hail a boat. Is there someone you can call to get help?"

Hank snorted. "In Nevada? Not hardly."

"What about John Jefferies? You guys acted like pals."

"After what just went down? He wouldn't take kindly to hearing from me."

"I have friends," Pearl said in a soft voice.

Hank smiled at her. "I don't remember your name."

"Pearl."

Shelby cast a wary glance at Hank. "What you saw on the boat, Pearl. Is that going to be a problem?"

"The son of a bitch sicced his muscle on me," Pearl said. "He let that slimy bastard work me over. Told him to rape me."

"Still," Hank said, "you're a witness."

Pearl grinned. "Some guy picked me up at a casino. I can't recall his name. I had too much to drink, fell off his boat. That's all I remember."

"She helped me pull you ashore," Shelby said, fearing for Pearl's life. "You wouldn't have made it without her."

Pearl jumped to her feet. "What? You think he's going to kill me? I've had the shit kicked out of me, barely missed being raped. That's enough, goddamnit!"

Hank spoke in as friendly a voice as Shelby had heard him use. "Pearl, is there someone you can call? They'll come get us, no questions asked?"

"No problem."

Shelby stood. "We can't walk far on these rocks with bare feet.

If we stay put, what's the chance of getting a boater's attention?"

A shrug from Hank. "It's a weekend. Looks like we're on the main channel, but powerboaters won't hear us shouting. See us wave, maybe."

Hank gave Pearl his T-shirt as a cover, and they talked quietly, waiting for rescue. Glancing at Hank's shirtless torso, Shelby was struck by his muscularity. Only a small roll of loose skin at his waist signaled the onset of his middle years. She wrestled with competing images: his cold efficiency in slicing Rankin's throat, her stab of concern when it looked as if he might drown. She needed to keep him alive to assure Carmen's safety, but that thought hadn't motivated her when she saved him—at least not consciously. Pearl's voice pulled her away from the disturbing thought that she had simply wanted the contract killer to live.

"Rankin was right about me," Pearl said. "I do like girls."

"So do I," Hank said. "Nobody slaps me around because of it."

Pearl laughed. "I had a thing going with my English lit professor at Wellesley, but she dumped me and I dropped out. Daddy—he's a big-time cardiac surgeon—put me on an allowance and forbade me to come home until I'm ready to be committed."

"Committed to what?" Shelby asked.

"His friend's psychiatric lockup."

"He thinks you're crazy?"

"He figures all lesbians are nuts. Until I see it his way, I'm exiled from New England. I've been out here six months. What about you guys?"

"Shelby's a schoolteacher," Hank said. "I met her at a casino. It surprised me that she'd go out with an old guy."

"That's how it works in Vegas," Pearl said. "The chicks hang with rich geezers; the young studs squire loaded old broads."

Hank shook his head. "I'm just a working stiff. A salesman."

"Selling what?"

"Bibles."

Pearl's laughter rolled across the deserted lakeshore. "You're selling bullshit. Selling me a load of it."

Worried about Hank's reaction, Shelby said, "Sometimes, Pearl, it's better not to look too far under the surface."

Pearl looked thoughtful. "Bibles. They're out there, so somebody must be selling them. I wonder if—you hear that?"

Laughter, a shout, beyond a hillock on their left. Hank labored to his feet. "Let's check it out." Wincing with each step, he hobbled across the rocks.

Shelby and Pearl got to their feet and started to follow, but a voice from nearby scrub brush stopped them: "You guys are overdressed."

They faced a man who wore a baseball cap and shoes and nothing else. He held a can of Budweiser.

"I'd kill for a slug of that," Pearl said.

The naked guy handed her the can. "No clothes allowed on Indecent Inlet."

"Indecent Inlet?" Hank said.

"Unofficial nude beach. The park rangers leave us alone; we keep the area clean. No dope, no fighting." He reached for his beer and saw that Pearl wasn't going to give it back. "No clothes."

"How about cell phones?" Pearl asked. She passed the beer to Shelby. "Those allowed?"

The naked man chuckled. "Standard equipment."

"We need to borrow one. We're stranded."

No more than a big gulp of beer remained. Shelby offered it to Hank, downed it when he waved it off. She handed the empty can to the naked guy. "You suppose one of your friends would have mercy? Let us make a call?"

"You'll have to take your clothes off."

"No problem," Pearl said. She stripped off the T-shirt.

Shelby hesitated and then wriggled out of her bathing suit. She looked away when Hank shrugged and stripped off his skivvies but glanced over and caught him studying her. Trying not to be obvious about it, she turned her back on him. Pearl was younger, more curvaceous; why hadn't he been staring at her?

The naked guy pointed at Hank's stomach. "Nasty wound, man."

"Cut it on rocks when we swam ashore."

The man led them to a cove peopled by a couple dozen nudists. He borrowed a cell phone, and Pearl made her call. Their hosts plied them with beer, sandwiches, music, and jokes until Pearl's friends called back, then gave them a speedboat ride across the lake to where two men and a woman much like Pearl—young, friendly, seemingly carefree—waited in a Chevy Tahoe with a Goodwill bag of used but clean clothing. The woman asked how they had gotten stranded with nothing to wear.

Pearl said, "Honey, you don't want to know." She turned to Hank and Shelby, who, dressed in ill-fitting pants and pullover shirts from the Goodwill bag, sat in the Tahoe's rear seat sorting through battered running shoes. "Where can we drop you guys?"

Shelby started to give the name of their hotel, but Hank stopped her by resting a hand on her thigh. "Our problem seems to be compounding," he said. "My wallet and keys are at the bottom of the lake. Shelby's, too. We can't rent a place until we get replacements."

Pearl flashed her impish grin. "Let's go to my pad. We'll rest up, work this out. My debt to you guys is way short of repaid."

"Your girlfriend know where you live?"

"My girlfri—the bitch who turned on me? We only met a couple weeks ago. We always used her place, and I drove myself."

"You in the phone book?"

"The apartment is Daddy's. Unlisted number."

"Does Rosie know your father?"

Pearl shook her head, looking sad. "I've been careful about that. His medical practice is back East, but he's well known out here. It would humiliate him if people learned his only child is a dyke."

Pearl lived near the top of a high-rise apartment building in downtown Las Vegas, just off Sahara Avenue. The building had underground parking and a concierge. A glass wall and a covered balcony afforded a view of the strip. Pearl showed them to a guest bedroom with its own bath and a sliding glass door to the balcony. "It's yours for as long as you want. I can front you some cash for clothes and stuff." She pulled a first-aid kit from a closet and handed it to Hank. "You need stitches on that cut."

Shelby took the kit from Hank and insisted that he lie on the bed while she put antibiotic on the wound and taped it shut. With the day more than half over, she worried about the e-mail he owed to Carmen's keeper. She pulled his shirt down over the taped wound and turned to Pearl. "Do you have an Internet connection? Hank needs to send a message."

"Sure. Come on, Hank. I'll show you."

Hank followed her, and Shelby, after reminding him to reschedule her chat-room session with Carmen, headed for the bath. She swooned over the big tub's pliable, heated lining and whirlpool jets with steamy water. When she came out, her tingling body wrapped in a borrowed robe, she learned that Hank had driven somewhere in Pearl's car.

"He sent some e-mails and deleted the files," Pearl said. "He even emptied the Windows Recycle Bin. He's a careful fellow."

Shelby worried about how careful. Because Pearl had witnessed the killings, would Hank consider her a threat to be neutralized? "It was kind of you to take us in."

Pearl's smile disappeared. "I've never been so hurt, so scared. If you hadn't helped, I'd probably be dead now."

"You'd have done the same if you saw another woman being treated like that."

Pearl shook her head. "I'd feel awful, but I'm way too cowardly to do what you did."

"What I did, what Hank did, is something you shouldn't mention, Pearl. Not to anybody."

"Don't worry. Besides not wanting to hurt you guys, it would be the last straw for Daddy. He'd boot my tail, put me on the street."

"You may be misjudging him."

"Anyway"—Pearl dragged a finger and thumb across her lips in a zipping motion. "I called my doctor. She wants me to come over right away."

"Did Hank say when he would be back?"

"No, but he has a key card. I logged you guys at the security desk as Hank and Shelby Jones, so you can come and go. I'll grab a cab."

Four days had elapsed since Shelby missed her meeting with Elizabeth Fontaine at that Arkansas shopping mall; Elizabeth would be worried sick. Shelby decided to reassure her and prepare her for Carmen's arrival. She asked Pearl's permission to use her Internet connection.

"Help yourself." Pearl showed her how to log on and gave her the password.

"One other thing, Pearl. I'll be in big trouble if Hank learns I sent a message."

A conspiratorial wink. "We girls have to stick together. Make yourself at home while I'm out."

Shelby pulled up a search engine and found the Clanal County Public Library's home page. It listed Elizabeth Fontaine as the head librarian and gave an e-mail address. Shelby sent a message apologizing for the missed rendezvous at Perryville's River Center Mall. She told Elizabeth to expect someone to call about Carmen and implored her to arrange for the child to stay with her indefinitely. "I don't know whether or not I will be able to reclaim her." She signed off with a promise to send another message if the opportunity presented itself.

Pearl had laid out fresh pajamas on the guest bed. Wearing the borrowed pj's, Shelby climbed between the sheets and promptly fell asleep.

CHAPTER FOURTEEN

IN THE LOBBY OF the Aladdin Hotel, Hank loitered by a row of slot machines and considered how to proceed. He needed to get into his and Shelby's room to wipe it clean of fingerprints and to reclaim his cash and weapons and any personal items that might give clues to their identities, but with no ID, how could he convince the desk clerk to give him a replacement key card? He would have to break in, he decided. The room was sandwiched between fire stairs and an alcove that held refreshments and ice vending machines. He'd been annoyed when the apologetic desk clerk explained that it was the only two-bed suite available. Now, the relative isolation at the end of a hallway was a blessing.

The hallway, which turned at ninety degrees between his room and the elevators, was deserted as far as he could see. He walked the fifty or so feet to where it turned and found a housekeeper in the other wing. A cleaning cart blocked an open door where she worked in a room. "Excuse me," he said, inspecting the cart, "I just need a couple glasses." Nothing there he could use to jimmy the door lock, so he lifted two plastic tumblers from the stock on the cart and held them up for the housekeeper to see.

She nodded and smiled, said something in Spanish, and went back to making the bed.

Back in his hallway, Hank split one of the plastic tumblers apart with his shoe heel and slid a sliver between the doorjamb and the lock. A nearby door opened, and he bent farther down, pretending to pick something off the floor.

A woman came out the door holding an ice bucket. To give her time to pass, Hank straightened, put an imaginary retrieved object in his pocket, and studied an abstract watercolor on the wall at the end of the hallway.

The woman turned into the refreshment alcove. Moments later, a harsh grinding noise preceded a resounding *thunk*, as if the ice machine resented parting with its cubes.

The woman returned to her room, and Hank went back to work. When forced into the crevice between the door and the jamb, his makeshift plastic tool snapped off. He split apart the second tumbler and tried again, with the same result. Five sweaty minutes later, he knew he was a failure as a break-in artist. Deciding on brute force, he waited until another hotel guest, a man wearing flip-flops and a robe, entered the refreshment alcove with an ice bucket. The moment the ice machine began grinding, Hank positioned himself. Coincident with the predictable *thunk* from the machine, he slammed his foot against the door in the vicinity of its lock. The door sprang open. He dashed inside and closed the door but then opened it a crack and peeked out.

The robe-clad man stuck his head out of the refreshment alcove and looked in both directions. Hank opened his door wider and stuck his head out. He looked up and down the hallway, then at the man. "You hear something?"

"Sounded like an explosion," the man said. "Gunshot, maybe."

"More like splintering wood," Hank said. "And a god-awful grinding noise."

"That was the ice machine." The man lofted his bucket of ice.

"I thought it was gonna take off like a rocket, maybe melt down."

"Could that be what we heard?" Hank said, and put a doubting frown on his face. "Can't imagine an ice machine making a racket like that."

"Naw," the man said, "it wasn't the machine. Sounded like it came from down your way."

"Guess that's why it sounded so loud to me." Hank wrinkled his brow again. "I'll call the desk. Hate the hassle of talking with their maintenance guys, but it could be something important." He raised his eyebrows as if suddenly possessed of a superior idea. "Hey, why don't you call? I'm kinda busy here."

The man shook his head. "I'm, ah, having a party. Don't want to, you know, slow things down."

"I guess its up to me, then. Goddamnit."

The man shuffled away, his arms cradling his bucket of ice, and Hank closed the door. Working frantically, praying that no one else got curious, he pulled his weapons and cash out of the room's safe, threw his and Shelby's belongings into their overnight cases, and wiped the room for fingerprints. Downstairs, gripping the bags so hard his forearms ached, he forced himself to stroll across the lobby. He should have changed out of his Goodwill clothing, he realized. Wearing them, he didn't look as if he belonged in a luxury hotel, but people dressed casually in Vegas, so maybe . . .

Don't rush, he reminded himself over and over as he approached the exit. Expecting security men to accost him any minute, he maintained a relaxed gait. As he sauntered through sliding doors that opened automatically upon his approach, the blast of hot, dry, outside air seemed a breath of freedom.

"I'll take those," said a heavy male voice at his side.

Hank whirled to face an overweight doorman sweating in a

uniform that made him look like a comic-opera field marshal. "No problem. They're light."

"Need a cab?"

"My limo's around the corner. I came out the wrong door."

"Thanks for staying at the Aladdin." The doorman gave him a salute. "Have a great day, sir."

As he drove back to Pearl's apartment, Hank plotted his next move. He couldn't keep dragging Shelby around the country, pretending he planned to kill her, but how would she take it if he leveled with her? Not yet, he decided, recalling how she had unhesitatingly pumped bullets into the bodyguard on the yacht. If she learned Carmen was in no danger, she might end up taking him out.

With his mind in turmoil, he longed for the familiarity of home. He had told Shelby he was taking her there, so why not do it? She was smart, fast, and strong for her size, but she would have no chance against a professional killer. At the farm, he could teach her how to defend herself.

His problem was how to convince her to hang around once she learned Carmen was safe. He couldn't think that through at the moment. Not with his near-exhaustion and the pain racking his arm. He'd left his medication on the yacht. By now, the Mob would be calling the Seattle pharmacy whose number was on the label, trying to get a lead on Robert Townsend, in whose name the prescription had been written.

Okay, too tired, and hurting too much, to think clearly. What, then? Stop at a storefront doctor's office, have them sew up his stomach wound and see if he could get some pain medication. Then crash in Pearl's apartment. When his mental fog lifted and he could think again, decide what to tell Shelby.

In Perryville, Arkansas, at three, a.m., Vlad parked his rental car near the librarian's residence. Wearing latex gloves, he gained entry with no sound other than a faint scratching as he cut a circle of glass from the patio door. A suction cup kept the cut-out segment from falling. He laid it aside and reached through the hole to flip the catch and slide the door open.

The night before, by watching until her lights went out, he had pinpointed her bedroom. As he headed there on kitten-soft feet, a creaking floorboard and a flicker of movement in the shadows made him hit the floor.

Something slammed into the wall where his head had been. A shadowy figure cocked a club again.

Pushing with his feet, Vlad scooted across the floor on his back to put distance between them. With hammering heart and shaky hands, he pointed his silenced Luger.

A muted click, and light flooded the room. Wearing pajamas, the librarian loomed over him with a baseball bat. She looked ready to take another swing but froze with her gaze fixed on the pistol.

Vlad adjusted his aim. "You move or make a sound, you're history."

Looking more angry than scared, she glared at him.

"Drop the bat." He scooted farther away and got to his feet. Several deep, slow breaths helped him settle down. "Face the wall and put your hands behind you." No, he needed her to use her hands. "Clasp them in front, at your waist."

Standing behind her, he reached around and taped her wrists together in front. Marvelous stuff, duct tape. It solved so many of life's problems. He turned off the light—no need alerting neighbors that the librarian was up at an unusual hour. "I don't want to hurt you, but I will if you act up. Show me your telephone."

A piece of luck: her phone had caller ID. Using his penlight for illumination, he had her retrieve all the numbers stored in the system. "Print the name of the caller by each number that has an out-of-town area code. I'll call them during business hours, and if you've lied to me about even one, you won't see the sun go down."

He scanned her handwritten list: nothing from Cervosier. "Let's have a look at your e-mail."

She booted her computer and opened her e-mail account. Chafing at her clumsy progress, he took control of the mouse and began scrolling through the stored messages.

Shifting abruptly from near-comatose to live wire, she slipped out of her chair and dashed for the kitchen. At the kitchen door, she struggled to open the dead bolt, an awkward maneuver with her wrists taped together.

He caught her. Grasping her hair, he jerked her backward.

Snarling, she twisted and swung at his face. Her fist connected with the side of his head.

She must have been an athlete in her youth, because the blow jarred him. He staggered back. His Luger, tucked into the waistband of his trousers, clattered to the floor.

He expected her to scream, maybe head for the door again, but she did neither. Instead, she scrambled for the loose weapon. She picked it up and, on her knees, fumbled with her taped hands to flick off the safety.

He stepped forward as if to punt a football, and the toe of his boot slammed into her stomach, doubling her over. A second kick connected with the side of her head.

She fell sideways. The Luger skittered across the linoleum.

He drove a kick into her ribs and then reined in his anger. He needed her functioning. With the Luger tucked back in his waistband, he slapped a piece of duct tape over her mouth. Using a knee to hold her head against the floor, he bent and twisted her fingers, slowly, one at a time, splintering the bones. "See you punch me now, bitch." Gripping her hair with a latex-gloved fist, he dragged her to a sitting position on the floor and pulled her to her feet.

As he marched her back to the computer and forced her into a roller-equipped tilt-and-swivel chair with heavy wooden arms, the noise that came through the tape over her mouth sounded like a growl. He pulled her taped-together hands to the right arm of the chair, pressed them down, and taped her right wrist to the chair's arm. He sliced through the tape that held her wrists together and, grasping her left hand by its misshapen fingers, forced it to the other chair arm. Holding it in place with a knee, he taped it, as well.

Back at the computer, he finished scrolling through her e-mail and clicked on the Windows program's Recycle Bin icon, looking for a contact with Cervosier. Nothing there.

The librarian had grown pale. He touched her forehead and found it cold and clammy. "Your mangled fingers are your own fault. I told you I didn't plan on hurting you. The tape's coming off your mouth. If you make a sound other than answering my questions, I'll cut out your tongue." He stripped away the tape and, following her mumbled instructions, logged onto the public library's computer system and called up her e-mail account there. Scrolling through her saved messages, he hit pay dirt:

Dear Elizabeth, I apologize for missing our meeting. I hope your broken leg is healing all right. A man should be contacting you in a few days about sending Carmen to stay with you. I beg you to accommodate her. She has no one else, and I do not know if I will be able to reclaim her. I will call or e-mail you again if I get the chance. Love, Shelby.

Vlad printed the message, noted with satisfaction that the header and routing information were intact on the hard copy, and deleted it from the computer. He turned back to the librarian. "Somebody named Shelby's worried about your broken leg? You look okay to me."

"I don't know what she's talking about."

He shrugged. "Guess someone lied to her." He gripped one of the librarian's ruined fingers. Smiling and watching her face, he squeezed where the bones were splintered. "Who is she?"

"A friend," the librarian gasped. She breathed like a sprinter at the end of a race. "She's my friend."

"How old is this Carmen?"

"She's seven."

"Is Shelby her mother?"

"No."

He twisted the mutilated finger, and the librarian made a meowing sound, like a frightened kitten. "I swear, she isn't. They're sisters."

"Where are they?"

"Torture me all you want. I only know what you read in the e-mail."

He caressed her cheek. "I believe you, Elizabeth. And I'm sorry you made me hurt you." He plastered fresh duct tape over her mouth.

With her fingers twisted like pretzels, she ought to know her place. But the old cow just glared at him.

"I'm going to conduct an experiment," he said. "Let's see how much pain it takes to make your heart shut down."

CHAPTER FIFTEEN

IN PEARL'S GUEST BEDROOM, Shelby napped until Hank's hand on her shoulder pulled her awake. Groggy, she took a moment to orient herself. "Everything all right?"

"Copasetic." He sat on the edge of the bed.

"Did you see a doctor about your wound?"

"Yeah, got some stitches. And I got our stuff out of the hotel. Wiped the room for prints."

"What if the police inspect the yacht? Our fingerprints are all over it."

"The cops won't get a whiff of what went down on the lake. It's Rankin's people who worry me. I hope Pearl's right about her girl-friend not knowing where she lives." Hank rubbed his eyes. "I can't remember ever being this tired. Feel like a zombie."

Shelby wriggled to one side of the queen-sized mattress and pat-ted the spare pillow. By the time what she had done fully dawned on her, Hank had stripped to his underwear and slid between the sheets. What if he misinterpreted her simple offer to share?

He turned his back on her and nestled his head on the pillow. "Gonna be out for several hours."

"Hank, when we leave here . . ." She wasn't certain how to phrase her concern. "You once said you're careful not to leave any loose ends."

He flipped onto his other side and faced her. "Yeah?"

"Pearl has been a godsend."

"You figure I cover my tracks with a trail of bodies?"

"Even if they find her, she doesn't have a clue about who we are."

"You worry too much." He molded the pillow to his satisfaction and closed his eyes.

Shelby watched him sleep and eventually drifted off once more. When she awakened and slipped out of bed, she checked the time: they had napped for two hours. A shower perked her up, and she returned to the bedroom to get clothes from the bag Hank had retrieved from the hotel. She found him on his back, propped up on pillows.

"Feel better?" he asked.

"Much. How about you?"

"Like a new man. Any hot water left?"

He sounded relaxed, but his face had the drawn look Shelby recognized as pain. She remembered that he'd had his pills on the yacht with him. The physician who treated his wound had probably given him a few, but how long would they last? "I doubt that Pearl ever runs out of hot water."

"Everything courtesy of dear old dad." With a hand on his stomach wound, Hank swung his feet off the bed. "Kid has a soft life."

"Until yesterday."

"She's like you: tough. She'll bounce back." He padded into the bathroom, and Shelby heard the shower start.

He seemed at ease before her in his underwear and unperturbed about sharing the bed. But why shouldn't he be, after spending time naked with her on the lakeshore? Was it prudery that made her feel so awkward?

He'd called her tough. Maybe so, but the toughening had been crammed into a ten-week trauma that, if she escaped this death sentence, would haunt her the rest of her life.

Pearl must have heard them moving about; she knocked on the bedroom door. "You guys want tea?" she asked when Shelby opened it.

"Sounds great, if you're having some."

"I'll put the kettle on. What about Hank? He doesn't strike me as a tea drinker."

"He's in the shower. Let's give him a few minutes. Pearl, do you have any old pain pills around? Something left over from a trip to the dentist, maybe?"

Together they rummaged through a basket that held an assortment of vitamins, out-of-date antibiotics, an almost-empty bottle of cough syrup, and two remnants of prescription analgesics: half a dozen Ultracet tablets and four acetaminophen pills with codeine. Shelby drew half a glass of water from the refrigerator dispenser and knocked on the bathroom door.

Hank opened it wearing a towel and dripping water. He accepted the glass and the pills, read the labels, and said, "You're a lifesaver. Figuratively as well as literally." Ten minutes later, he joined them for tea. "Pearl," he said, "what happens now with you?"

"What do you mean?"

"What they did to you on the boat. You gonna psych out over that?"

She laughed. "I've been knocked around before. Guys learn you're a lesbian, they tend to take it personally."

"I got the impression you and what's-her-name, Rankin's girlfriend, were tight. How do you feel about being ditched?"

She put on a mock sad face. "I've got nobody. Poor me."

Shelby started to worry. "Pearl, Hank needs to know—"

"If I'm likely to rat you out? If he should kill me?"

"He wouldn't do that."

"I've seen what he's capable of. Saw you in action, too." Pearl shrugged. "I brought you home anyway. Guess you could say I'm asking for it."

"Is that what you're doing?" Hank asked, his voice soft and low. "Asking for it?"

Instant tension cramped Shelby's neck and shoulders, but Pearl seemed at ease. "I'd be dead already if Shelby hadn't stood up for me. She saved you twice: in that stateroom, and when you couldn't swim any farther. She won't let you hurt me."

"You figure she calls the shots?"

"Most of the time, no. But I've seen what she's made of. In a clutch, yeah, I figure she'd be the one." Pearl sipped her tea and set the cup back in its saucer. "Anyway, you don't have to worry about me. The day you guys leave, I'll erase all this from my head. I'm a party girl, and that's what I'll do—party."

Hank gave a barely perceptible nod. "That'll be tomorrow. But you need to be more careful who you pick up."

"Tell me about it. You guys feel like hitting the strip tonight? Having a good-bye fling?"

"I think we'll stay in," Hank said. "Be better if you did, too."

Pearl laughed, and Shelby held her breath. But Pearl studied Hank's impassive face for a moment and said, "I suspect I'd feel that way if I were you. No problem."

They had Chinese takeout delivered for dinner. Afterward, Hank e-mailed Jason and arranged for a real-time exchange of messages between Shelby and Carmen in a Yahoo chat room. Jason informed Shelby that he would be typing for Carmen and reading the scroll to her.

To make certain they weren't scamming her, Shelby asked questions about family and friends in Haiti that only Carmen would know. Carmen said she was happy and well cared for, that she had playmates. But the intermediary of the written word, particularly with an unknown adult typing and reading for the child, left Shelby with nagging doubt.

With Pearl and Hank, she sipped wine and watched DVD movies until almost midnight. Apparently assuming they slept together, Pearl did not offer separate accommodations. After slipping back into her borrowed pajamas, Shelby stared at the bed for a moment and shrugged. They had shared it for a nap, a threshold of sorts. She climbed in and scooted to one side.

Hank joined her a minute later, wearing his skivvies. "You feeling all right?" he said, facing her with his head on his pillow.

He might not have meant it that way, but to her the question sounded condescending. "You're holding my sister hostage, forcing me to follow you around while you decide whether or not to kill me. You engineered a situation where I had to shoot a man to keep you alive. You barely made a last-minute decision not to kill that sweet girl in the other room. How would you feel if you were me?"

"What makes you think I won't terminate Pearl in the morning, when we're ready to leave?"

"You'd have done it already, to eliminate the risk that she'll start worrying about you overnight."

"She's right about you," Hank said. "In a clutch, you're inclined to take charge."

"I want to talk with Carmen."

"You think that wasn't her on the Internet?"

"Your friend censored the exchange. She might have said something entirely different from what he typed. I want to hear her voice. Want her to hear mine."

Hank pursed his lips. "You bargained with me, made that Internet chat the cost of learning something about you. I want to know the rest of it."

"In exchange for a telephone call?"

He nodded. "How did you end up in an Arkansas shopping mall with a price on your head?"

"I told you about my dinner with Colonel Burgess, the chairman of Haiti's governing council. Told you he sent a staff car to take me to his villa. You want the sordid details?"

"I want to know you. So, yeah, tell me what happened."

She twisted onto her back. Staring at the darkened ceiling, she let the past overtake her once more.

Chain-link fencing topped with razor wire made the colonel's villa resemble a prison as Shelby, alone in the backseat of the staff car Colonel Burgess had sent for her, approached the compound. Three guards manned the gatehouse. They asked Shelby and her driver to step out of the car. One covered them with a submachine gun while another rummaged through Shelby's overnight bag and purse and ran a metal-detection wand over her. The third searched the car's interior, trunk, and engine compartment. He walked around the vehicle with a mirror on a long pole, inspecting the undercarriage.

A telephone call cleared the way for them to proceed along a meandering, cobblestone drive. "What was that all about?" Shelby asked, shaken by the guards' menacing actions.

"Security breach," her driver said. "Terrorist in the rocks above the villa."

Had they spotted one of the men who were supposed to capture the lecherous colonel on his way to the villa? A sudden light-headedness made Shelby grateful she was sitting. "Did they capture him?"

"Guards didn't say." The driver pulled to the curb in front of the villa. A mansion-sized structure constructed of native stone, it looked rustic except for a glass wall that flooded the interior with light and connected it with its hilly environment. Carrying Shelby's overnight bag, the driver led her to an inside guard post and spoke briefly with an elderly, uniformed man whom he addressed as Sergeant. Dismissed, the driver nodded to Shelby and left. The sergeant barked orders into a telephone.

A maid came to take Shelby's bag, and Shelby bit her tongue to keep quiet. In Port-au-Prince, the maid had been one of her CBTF contacts. The plan was for CBTF agents to capture Colonel Burgess on his way to the villa. So, why did they need an agent inside? And why had a CBTF agent, if that's who he was, been lurking in the rocks above the villa?

The woman smiled at Shelby with no hint of recognition. "If you will please follow me?" She led Shelby into a carpeted room dominated by a massive bed under ceiling mirrors.

The room also held a couch and two overstuffed chairs, a large coffee table, a massage table, a fireplace, and a compact kitchen. Yet its size kept it from looking cramped. A wheeled table burdened with fruit, cheese, bread, crackers, and an opened bottle of wine stood near the bed. Realizing that the room could be bugged and that there might be hidden video cameras, Shelby stifled an urge to inquire about the fate of the man who had been seen in the hills.

"The bathroom is through that door," the woman said. "Colonel Burgess's instructions are for you to bathe and partake of refreshments. He will join you shortly." She executed a cross between a curtsy and a bow and left the room.

Burgess would join her? That meant the plan to capture him had failed. What would the CBTF people do now? If they did nothing, what would happen to her? Shuddering with the realization that she was at the colonel's mercy, a quality he had demonstrated to be lacking, Shelby prowled the bedroom, feigning mere curiosity but looking for something to use as a weapon. She found only a short, dull-bladed knife intended for spreading soft cheese on crackers. She checked the windows for escape routes but found them sealed. French doors opened onto a walled courtyard. Another door led to an empty closet. A third, the one through which the agent-cum-maid had left, opened to a narrow, tiled hallway that Shelby guessed led to service facilities. She was trapped.

Colonel Burgess, looking debonair in his dress uniform, sauntered into the bedroom and flashed his movie-star smile. "Welcome to my hideaway." He unbuckled his pistol belt and stowed it in a cupboard. After slipping off his jacket and hanging it in the closet, he filled two glasses with wine and handed one to Shelby. "Are you always a harbinger of bad news?"

"Bad news?" Shelby's grip on her wineglass tightened.

"A terrorist in the hills above the villa."

The colonel's eyes, tracking Shelby as she moved, reminded her of a hawk she had once studied in an aviary. Trying to conceal her desperate need for space, she wandered toward the doors leading to the courtyard. "Pretty flowers."

"The landscaping is old hat." The colonel set his wineglass aside and approached her. "My interest is in a fresh source of beauty. Were you not told to prepare yourself?"

"Take a bath, the maid said." A lie wouldn't make her situation any worse. "I did that."

"And put your street clothes back on? Didn't you see the robe in the bathroom?"

Her galloping heart made Shelby's chest hurt. "It's late in the day. I dressed for dinner."

"You think I brought you here for a meal?" He waved at the food-laden table. "There's no reason to leave this room." He made himself comfortable in an overstuffed chair. "Or for you to wear clothing."

"Colonel, can't we get better acquainted first?"

"The acquaintance I desire requires exposure. Undress."

"I . . ." No preliminaries, no flirting? He intended to treat her like a paid whore, there simply to service him? "You want me to take off my clothes?"

The colonel's voice hardened. "Before he lost consciousness, the terrorist admitted to having a confederate inside the compound. A female, he said. You're the only cunt who has not been fully vetted." He retrieved his wineglass and sipped. "My mind goes back to the night we met. To your supposedly accidental intrusion into the smoking lounge."

"I tried to leave."

"You followed me into the toilet. Made only a token objection to pissing in my presence."

"Would it have done any good?"

"Since you didn't try, we'll never know." He appeared to be studying her, though his eyelids drooped so that she found it impossible to read anything in his eyes. "Instead of objecting to my overtures, you asked me to leave the city without my customary security detachment. They have been alerted and will be here shortly, but I wondered why you wanted me here without them."

He set his wineglass on a table and got to his feet, unbuckled his belt, and pulled the heavy leather strap from its loops. "Strip where you're standing." He pointed to a low-backed, upholstered chair. "Climb up there on your knees, facing the rear. Legs open, ass in the air."

Shelby's bladder felt on the cusp of voiding. Her memory flashed to that supposed safe house in Arkansas, where she had been held prisoner after she first fled Haiti and slipped into America, to being beaten until she knew she must grovel or die. "You . . . you're not going to . . ."

"To belt-whip you? Flay the skin off your ass?" He motioned to the chair with a nod. "Tell me why you proved so easy to entice, or get naked and get on the chair."

What to do? Could she absorb the pain without cracking? If she admitted her role in the planned ambush, would that save her from torture? Giving in to weakness in her legs, she fell to her knees. "Won't you have mercy? I'm just a—" A knock at the door sounded loud, almost like miniature explosions. It came from the door that Shelby had guessed led to the servants' quarters.

"Enter," Burgess shouted.

The door opened slowly. A woman in a maid's uniform backed through, pulling a cart. Shelby labored to her feet and recognized the woman who worked for the CBTF, the maid who had shown her to the room.

The woman dipped one knee and nodded her head. "Fresh provisions, sir." The cart held two carafes, one sweating as if it contained cold liquid, and several dishes. She looked toward the table and back at the colonel. "May I?"

"Get on with it."

For several moments, the only sound was a muted tinkle when tongs the woman used to replenish the fruit and bread platters touched the china. Then the loud but dull *thump* of a nearby explosion shattered the quiet. There followed a series of similar explosions in rapid succession, each sounding closer than its predecessor.

"Mortars," Burgess shouted. "Son of a bitch, mortars." He grabbed the telephone and started punching buttons.

Moving so swiftly that Shelby barely registered the action, the maid leaped at his back, brandishing a carving knife.

He whirled and raised an arm. The knife, slashing at his neck, cut into his forearm. He slammed the telephone into the side of the woman's head.

She sagged but held onto the knife. Burgess kicked her in the stomach, and the knife plummeted to the carpet. The woman reeled backward and collapsed in the chair the colonel had designated as Shelby's torture rack.

Momentarily frozen, Shelby shook off her paralysis and dashed to the cupboard where she had seen him stow his sidearm. Reaching into the cupboard, she almost hit a red button with the heel of her hand. Careful to avoid it, she lifted the weapon from its holster and turned back to the room.

Burgess had scooped up the carving knife. Moving leisurely, as if he had all the time in the world, he advanced on the maid, who seemed unable to move.

Shelby held the weapon steady with both hands. "Drop the knife!"

Burgess faced her. He smiled.

"Drop it," she shouted again. Panic made her palms sweaty on the heavy pistol. What if she had to turn it on somehow? Click a switch or twist a lever to make it work?

The colonel let the knife drop to the carpet and raised his hands shoulder high. Blood from his sliced forearm poured down to his elbow and trickled onto the carpet.

What to do? The explosions had stopped, and she couldn't hold him forever. Maybe lock him in the closet?

He took a step toward her. "You shoot me, the noise will bring guards. What do you suppose they'll do to you?"

Her hands shook, but she kept the pistol trained on his chest. "Whatever—" her voice cracked. She cleared her throat. "Whatever they do, you won't be alive to see it."

Hands still shoulder high, but looking relaxed, he took another step. "Best thing you can do is give me the weapon. Take your whipping, and I'll overlook this."

Behind him, the maid struggled to her feet. She picked up the carving knife and advanced on him.

Shelby's gaze flitted between them, and Burgess turned. As he did so, the maid swung the knife in an arcing backhand that sliced through his trachea and carotid artery. Spurting arterial blood hit the woman's face.

The colonel lashed out. His fist caught her on the side of her head. It sent her reeling, and she lost her grip on the knife.

His hand went to his gushing throat wound. He inspected his fingers, crimson and dripping with blood, and tried to speak. An inhuman, snakelike hiss issued from his severed trachea. He sank to his knees, tried to support himself with one hand on the floor, but folded slowly onto the carpet.

Shelby dropped the pistol and leaned against a wall. Bile rose in her throat. She fought it back down. They were short on time and had to plan their escape.

The maid picked up the pistol. She inspected it and thumbed a switch. With a grim expression on her blood-streaked face, she used her other hand to pull a lever on the weapon, causing it to issue a dull, metallic click. "I'm sorry," she said, and aimed the weapon at Shelby's head.

"What?" Slow to react, Shelby perceived her peril. "You're not . . . you're . . ."

"Following orders," the woman said, her voice heavy with sadness. "I'm really sorry."

"Wait," Shelby said, her mind numb at the realization that she was about to be shot. "There's something you need to know." Her legs threatened to betray her. She leaned against the cabinet from which she had drawn the weapon, and her gaze centered on the red button. An alarm? "Something the colonel said." She rested her hand on the button and pressed. "The CBTF will want to know about it."

The woman shook her head. "It's over."

"Don't shoot me in the head." Shelby turned halfway around, then back to face the woman. "Promise you won't shoot my head."

"Okay. Turn around."

The door slammed open. Soldiers dashed in. Shots and the sulfurous stench of gunpowder took Shelby back to her college-professor days in cap-Heitien, to the horrifying moment when internal security troops gunned down her students. She regained her senses and found herself sagging against the wall with her hands over her ears. Blood and bits of the maid's flesh fouled her clothing.

Someone's arm settled around her, supporting her. "It's all right, miss. You're safe now."

The maid lay on the carpet, sprawled on her stomach. With a booted foot, the sergeant who had supervised Shelby's entry to the villa flipped the body over. The woman's sightless eyes stared at the ceiling.

The sergeant squatted by Burgess, feeling for a pulse. He stood and faced Shelby. "Are you hurt?"

His concern registered dimly. "I'm all right. Colonel Burgess?"

"Dead, I'm afraid. We'll get you—" the clatter of an approaching helicopter stopped him. "The quick-reaction team." He turned to one of his men. "Corporal, let Mademoiselle Cervosier clean herself up. Then take her to the silver room."

CHAPTER SIXTEEN

"DON'T LEAVE ME HANGING." To Shelby, Hank's voice seemed a disembodied element floating in the dark bedroom. "How did you get away?"

"They treated me as an innocent bystander. The helicopter flew me to a base on the outskirts of Port-au-Prince, and a driver took me to the internal security service's downtown headquarters. I told an interviewer that the colonel and I had been relaxing when the maid brought in refreshments, that she attacked without warning. The officer reminded me that Colonel Burgess was a family man and the country's most respected statesman. He said I should forget I had ever been to the villa."

"But the CBTF made another stab at taking you out?"

"They were going to. I realized they had never intended to capture Colonel Burgess alive, that they had used me to separate him from his security detachment. And I knew they wouldn't let an outside witness live. But I was too tired, too traumatized to plan. I went back to my hotel room and crashed until a Haitian National Police lieutenant knocked on my door. He said his commander, a longtime friend of my father's, had sent him. Haiti's internal security service, apparently not totally convinced of my innocence, had asked the National Police to track my movements. As a by-product of their surveillance, the National Police spotted three men, notorious gang members, trailing me, as well. Based on the gang's reputation, he said they were probably planning to kill me."

"How did you escape?"

"The lieutenant escorted me out of the hotel, and I appealed to another family friend. He smuggled me out of the country."

"Smuggled you? How?"

"He's a pilot with a company that worked with my father's firm. On a trip to pick up an executive in America, he slipped me into the plane. He faked engine trouble and made an emergency landing to let me out in Florida."

"You helped rid Haiti of its worst dictator since Papa Doc Duvalier. Your countrymen owe you a merit badge."

A sudden, desperate need to dispel her growing sense of intimacy with this man possessed Shelby. "Burgess was no worse than you. He killed for position, power. You do it for money."

"You don't have to remind me." The defensive note in Hank's voice melted immediately. "You landed in Florida. How is it that I found you in an Arkansas shopping mall?"

"Florida was a detour. They were holding Carmen there. You promised me a phone call. Have I earned it?"

"First thing in the morning. Before we check out."

"Where are we going?"

"Home. My home."

The news chilled her. He'd said he wouldn't kill her while they were on the road, because it would be easier to dispose of her body at home. "Does that mean my stay of execution is over?"

"It means I'm tired. I need familiar surroundings."

Not a denial, but not confirmation, either. "Where is home?"

"Let's take it one step at a time."

"Afraid I'll escape and come looking for you?"

He chuckled. "If something happened to Carmen, an accident or crossed signals, and you got away, I have no doubt you'd spend the rest of your life looking for me."

"Why take that chance? Why not return Krystal's blood money and let us go?"

"The broker would just send someone else. I wish you could . . ." He twisted onto his back, taking the bedcover with him. "I live in Colorado. West of the Continental Divide."

She jerked the cover, pulling it back across the bed with unnecessary force. How ludicrous was this? Mortal enemies in bed together, bickering like a longtime married couple. Yet a sense of triumph surged through her for having gotten another snippet of information out of him. "We'll retrace our route, then? Drive back up there?"

"Have to take a bus."

"American buses are filthy. They stink."

"Can't be helped. It takes awhile to get fresh ID and a new driver's license. We can't rent a car or go through airport security."

His failure to engage in a cover war angered her. She recognized the misdirected ire but still wanted to dig at him. "What about the car we left at the lake? It's too old to be a rental. Did you steal it?"

He fluffed his pillow and settled onto his other side, facing away from her. "I bought it back East but didn't change the registration. We'll leave it. Rankin's goons probably have it staked out."

After breakfast the next morning, Hank asked Pearl if they could use her telephone. He dialed a number, talked for a minute, and then handed Shelby the receiver.

"Carmen?"

"Shelby," an excited, childish voice cried. "I've got a kitten. Our mama cat had a whole bunch, and Jason let me pick. Are you coming to live with us?"

"I'm glad you have a pet, sweetheart." Shelby had braced for anger over perceived desertion, or at best a dull acceptance of the unexpected voice-to-voice contact. Her heart melted with relief. "I'll see you eventually, but you have to visit Elizabeth first."

"Why can't I stay here?"

Shelby mopped her eyes with her hand. "It's part of the arrangement."

"But Elizabeth doesn't have kids. Polly and Tupper will miss me."

"Those are playmates? Polly and Tupper?"

"Tupper's older. He pulls us in his wagon. Polly shares her dolls with me. Her dishes, too."

"That's wonderful, sweetie." Shelby glanced at Hank, and he tapped his watch. "I have to go. I'll call again as soon as I can. I love you."

Pearl insisted on driving them to the bus station. Along the way she chatted like a tour director, pointing out Las Vegas landmarks, but Shelby's mind lingered on her conversation with Carmen. Her little sister had sounded happy and secure. Could caregivers who made the child feel that way be capable of doing what Hank had threatened?

But what if she was wrong about them? And if she slipped away from Hank, how would she find them? In any event, did she want to escape and be exposed to Krystal's other hired killers? Hank's response, his tone, when she asked him the night before if her stay of execution was over, had reinforced her suspicion that he did not intend to fulfill his contract. With the disguise and the constant movement, he seemed to be protecting her. But she might have that wrong, as well. She could rely on nothing to be as it seemed.

"It isn't right," Pearl said when they reached the bus depot. "I've spent the most intense two days of my life with you guys, and I'll never see you again."

"You never know," Shelby said. "Life has a way of surprising us." When she bent to hug Pearl, she noted tears swimming in the young woman's eyes.

Compared with the bus Shelby had ridden from Atlanta to Arkansas, the Rocky Mountain Express seemed pristine. Objectively, she realized the coaches were not that different. It was a matter of perception. On the trip to Arkansas, she had been exhausted, scared, confused. Now she was riding an emotional high from her telephone call to Carmen and her growing conviction that Hank had no intention of killing her.

They crossed from Nevada into Utah late in the afternoon, and rock formations east of the interstate, resplendent in the setting sun, poked at the sky like giant, fiery fingers. She tugged Hank's sleeve and pointed. "Look at that."

"Spectacular," he said. "The gorge is limestone and shale, half a mile deep at one point. The color changes with the sun's angle. We're just west of Zion Canyon National Park. I wish I could take you through it."

Farther north along I-15, with twilight descending, high desert and bare mountains loomed to the west in shades of red, silver, brown, and gray. Hank identified the timbered peaks to the east as Fishlake National Forest, hazy green against an indigo sky.

Night wrapped itself around them, and the bus's interior seemed to shrink. The driver faded to a mere outline in the diffused glow from his instrument panel. Tiny spotlights above the seats illuminated several passengers, but they were pinpoint accents rather than intrusions; Shelby and Hank occupied a darkened island alone unto themselves. She reclined her seat and stared at the dimly visible overhead luggage rack.

"You brooding about what happened at the lake?" Hank asked.

His question caught her by surprise. Rankin's bodyguard was the fourth person she had killed, and she had given little thought to his or Rankin's death. She did a mental matchup of that reaction with the agonizing she'd gone through over killing the man who had tortured and raped her. Perhaps her conscience was developing calluses. "What I did on the boat was different from when I did it before."

"Different how?"

"The previous events were matters of self-preservation. And they made the world a better place."

"Let me tell you about Rankin and his bodyguard." All the nearby seats on the bus were empty. If they talked softly, nobody would hear them over the engine's deep growl, yet Hank shifted so his mouth was close to her ear and lowered his voice still more. "Rankin controlled every racket in Vegas except dope, and he was moving in on that by snuffing the competition. The muscle-bound ape you dealt with was an enforcer, like his twin brother. He liked to inflict pain. What he was doing to Pearl is tame compared to some of his exploits."

Hank leaned still closer. "That's the upside of my job," he whispered, his breath teasing her ear. "I can be selective."

"And you selected me as your first contract."

"I told you how that happened. You should have seen their description of you."

"You believe everything you read?"

He sighed, and little puffs of moist, warm breath tickled her ear. "What I believe is that you're a much better person than you realize. High moral standards are your greatest weakness."

Her ear tingled. To eliminate the distraction, she turned her head and found herself nose to nose with him. "You planned to take contracts only on bad guys? Are you justifying your career choice?"

"Explaining it. And you're trying to change the subject."

"What subject is that?"

"You." With their faces almost touching, Hank's breath warmed her lips as he spoke. "When you took your sister away from the CBTF, didn't it occur to you that they would send someone to watch your librarian friend, expecting you to show up there?"

"Elizabeth was going to give me money, so I had to risk it. Anyway, I thought I was ahead of them. You know the rest of that story."

Silence settled around them, but neither moved. They simply lounged, their lips and noses an inch apart, and stared into each other's eyes.

Hank pierced the silence by clearing his throat. "When I decided to take on this line of work, I promised myself I'd remain objective. That I'd never get involved with a target."

"Are we involved, Hank?"

He didn't answer. The silence again hung heavily between them.

"Am I still going to die?"

"Somebody might kill you. It won't be me."

She closed her eyes and let his declaration filter through her. The release of pent-up tension made her light-headed. Gradually, relief shifted to speculation. In Las Vegas, he'd said other gunmen were looking for her, and he'd just said someone else might kill her. The next time, however, she wouldn't be taken so easily.

She opened her eyes and stared into his, only inches away. "If you aren't going to do it, why am I here?"

"I'll explain when I figure it out."

"Will you return Carmen to me? Let us go?"

"If that's what you want."

Was it? She'd grown comfortable with his presence and was convinced he'd been moving her around the country to protect her. She wasn't certain she wanted to be alone again. The one certainty she harbored was her desire to reunite with Carmen. "How soon can I see her?"

"She's in a safe place. You heard how happy she is. I want you to meet some people, and we need to talk this through. Then you can do whatever you want."

Meet people? What did he have in mind? "Why can't we talk it through now? Right here?"

"Because my pills are making me drowsy. I need sleep."

Early-morning Colorado sunlight warmed Grand Junction's streets as Shelby and Hank stepped off the bus. The man who greeted Hank looked ancient, ageless, one of those people who begin drying up somewhere in their middle years and get progressively leaner, more leathery with time. He grasped Hank in a hug that seemed as if it were going to be endless and greeted him in a thick accent that Shelby couldn't place.

Hank pushed him back but held on to his shoulders. "Shelby, this is Patrick, my father-in-law and dear friend. He takes care of me."

His father-in-law? He'd never mentioned a wife, but why shouldn't a hardworking hit man have a family to go home to after a day of killing? Struggling to keep her face blank, she shook the old fellow's hand and murmured pleasantries.

Fractured syntax highlighted Patrick's accent, which Shelby guessed to be eastern European. "To Hank's farm we go," he said. "I take care of you, too, missy." He insisted on carrying their bags: Hank's leather overnighter and a suitcase that held Shelby's clothing from the Las Vegas shopping spree.

Hank opened the door to the backseat of a beat-up Ford Econoline van parked behind the bus station. His hand on Shelby's elbow gave her an unneeded assist.

Patrick slapped Hank's shoulder. "Hank, by George. Healthy you look."

"Feeling good." Hank climbed onto the seat beside Shelby.

Patrick loaded their bags through the van's rear door and slid into the driver's seat. As the old fellow cranked the engine, Hank turned to Shelby. "We need to make a couple stops. Then you'll see some of the most beautiful country imaginable."

Their first stop was at a storefront health clinic. Hank spent thirty minutes inside and came out looking relaxed, almost euphoric. Catching Shelby's questioning look, he said, "Miracle of modern pharmaceuticals. I might drift in and out a bit." They dropped off a prescription at a drive-through pharmacy and turned in at a Walmart to buy more clothing for Shelby. "Your Vegas finery won't do for mountain living," Hank said.

The Walmart purchases—jeans, long-sleeved shirts, and a sturdy pair of hiking boots—told her he planned on keeping her in the mountains for a while. On the way out of town, they stopped at the pharmacy so Hank could pick up his prescription.

They drove south on U.S. 50 for half an hour and then southwest on State Road 141 for an hour through sparse traffic. At a single-street village called Gateway, they turned southeast and had the road to themselves. "It wouldn't be far if we could fly," Hank said. "We're working our way around a national forest."

Was he apologizing for the drive? No need. The scenery—sheer drop-offs, rocky outcroppings, frothing streams, and fir trees that reached for heaven and missed by no more than a handshake—mesmerized Shelby. Southeast of Gateway, they paralleled a white-water river that Hank identified as the Dolores. They crossed it on a bridge that looked like it belonged in a Wild West movie. Half an hour later, they crossed another, equally picturesque bridge. "This is the San Miguel River," he said. "It dumps into the Dolores, which we'll cross one more time."

Shelby began to appreciate his comment about distance when the van negotiated another switchback and traveled northwest. They passed through two more tiny towns, one about the size of Gateway, the other still smaller. At Bedrock, a hamlet with no population sign and, so far as she could see, no people, they began paralleling another waterway. "Spring Creek," Hank said. "Another tributary of the Dolores." They crossed the creek, drove through the dilapidated old mining town of Paradox, and left paved roads behind. The winding gravel trail narrowed. They turned onto a dirt road and stopped at a padlocked, chain-link gate.

"Home," Patrick said. He jumped out with surprising agility and unlocked the gate, drove through, and raced back to lock the gate behind them. Despite his wrinkled face and thin arms and legs, he exuded an aura of strength and vitality.

Beyond the gate, the road became nothing more than twin dirt pathways where vehicle tires had kept weeds at bay. Low-lying vegetation thrived between the paths. The trail looped around a spruce-covered mountainside and dipped into a valley bisected with fenced pastures and accented with the rooftops of a house and two outbuildings.

"A farm?" Shelby asked. "This high in the mountains?"

"Vegetables we have," Patrick said from the front seat. "Also, sheep and swine. Goats we have for milk and chickens for eggs."

"It's kind of primitive," Hank said. "Our tractor powers a generator that recharges storage batteries for a computer and a satellite phone. Butane fuels a stove, refrigerator, and freezer. Everything else is nineteenth century."

The van stopped in front of the farmhouse, where a man and a woman stood waiting. Shelby guessed the woman was Hank's wife. The man's body was twisted, his right leg foreshortened, its knee fused. His right arm, which he held at about a twenty-five-degree angle, ended in a shriveled, clawlike hand. Shelby supposed him to be a stroke victim, until she saw the other side of his face. It looked melted, the ear nothing more than a hole and the eye a thin film of scar tissue.

At her quick intake of breath, Hank rested a hand on her shoulder. "I'll tell you later," he whispered.

"Hank, he bring us a guest," Patrick announced through the van's open window. "Pretty she is, like an orchid."

The woman, a thin-lipped brunette with a lean-muscled body, extended her hand. "Anyone Hank brings home will be treasured, as he is."

Shelby grasped the woman's hand and found it calloused. Watching everyone stare at Hank, she pictured the lord of a medieval manor being greeted by adoring serfs.

"I'm Latica," the woman said. She rested a hand on the disfigured man's shoulder. "This is Leonard. You've been traveling awhile. You must be tired."

"I'm Shelby. We slept on the bus."

"You'll want to freshen up. Let me show you to Hank's quarters." She picked up Shelby's suitcase.

Hank had been hugging the disfigured man. "Latica," he said, "why don't we give Shelby the study? Set up a cot in there?"

Did Latica look disappointed? Shelby did another mental adjustment. Unless they were extremely kinky, the woman was neither Hank's wife nor his lover.

Holding the suitcase, Latica waited while Shelby gathered up her Walmart purchases. "This way," the woman said, and led her inside.

They passed through a simply furnished and timeworn but spotless living room, then moved down a narrow hallway. Latica set Shelby's suitcase on the floor in a book-lined room furnished with a beat-up rolltop desk, a metal filing cabinet, a wooden office chair, and a library table. Shelby noted a computer on the desk and a combination printer/scanner/fax on the table—a room configured for work as well as relaxation.

"We have no guest room," Latica said. "You're our first guest."

"Will I meet Hank's wife later?"

Latica frowned. "His wife?"

"He called Patrick his father-in-law."

"Hank's wife, my sister, died three years ago."

"I'm sorry, I didn't know. How long have you been here?"

"Three years. Leonard will clear out the closet for you. We'll set up a cot, find you a more comfortable chair. It won't be so bad."

"It isn't bad at all, Latica. I'm grateful for your hospitality." Shelby deposited her Walmart bags on the table and thought about the woman's comment: they had been in this mountain hideaway since Hank's wife died, and she was their first guest.

Latica showed her a bathroom equipped with a big claw-footed tub. "It's our only bath. Traffic gets heavy when Hank is at home."

"I'll try to stay out of the way. Is he home often?"

"The farm is his sanctuary." Latica laid out a fresh towel and washcloth. "You will want some time to relax. Would you like to bathe?"

"That would be great."

Latica nodded and headed for the kitchen. Shelby pulled toiletries and her Walmart clothing from her suitcase. She brushed her teeth and turned to the bathtub. No hot water. Did they bathe in cold water even during the Rocky Mountain winter? As she contemplated sitting in a tub filled with the icy water that trickled from the faucet, someone knocked on the door: Latica, with a steaming kettle.

"Water heater's broken," she said. "Patrick has ordered parts." She emptied the kettle into the tub. "Shall I heat more?"

Shelby dismissed her earlier image of soaking in the big tub with steaming water up to her neck. "This will be fine, thank you." She bathed hurriedly, dressed in jeans and a white polo shirt, and brushed her hair, which the wig had plastered to her head. She followed the sound of voices to the front porch.

CHAPTER SEVENTEEN

Totally relaxed for the first time in weeks, Hank sat on the porch between Leonard and Patrick while Latica got Shelby settled in the house. With his chair tilted back, he rested his feet on the porch railing and sipped coffee.

Shelby stepped onto the porch, and the air seemed abruptly clearer, the afternoon sun brighter. Leonard and Patrick, also drinking coffee, set their cups aside and started to stand, but she stopped them. "Please don't get up. If I'm going to be here a while, we should dispense with formalities." The men nodded, and she fixed her gaze on Hank. "Am I, Hank?"

"Are you what?"

"Going to be here a while."

Time to lay my cards on the table. He took a deep breath and dropped his feet off the porch railing, letting his chair's tilted legs bang against the floor. "Let's take a walk." To Leonard and Patrick he said, "Excuse us, guys. We have to straighten something out."

He walked her to the barn and sat with her on a bale of hay. "I told you on the bus you'd be free to go anywhere you like. You have to decide where that is and what you're going to do."

"I pretty much had it worked out until you stepped into the picture."

Maybe leveling with her wasn't such a good idea. Telling her how he felt, how much he wanted to be with her, to love her and protect her, might scare her off. But he had to give her a reason to stick around, even if just for a few days. "By yourself, you can blend into American society. Not with Carmen, though. Those hired guns will be looking for a stunning, green-eyed brunette with a seven-year-old biracial beauty."

"What do you suggest?"

"Leave her where she is for now. She has friends; she's being homeschooled. Let her enjoy being a little girl, and give the jackals time to find other prey."

Shelby appeared to chew on his suggestion. "This last week has been a purgatory of sorts," she said. "If you didn't intend to kill me, why did you put me through that?"

"I took your contract in good faith. The spec sheet listed you as a three-time killer, someone ready to strike again whenever it benefited you."

"You planned to take jobs only where you felt the target deserved to die, but you did no independent investigation?"

"That's why I used the stun gun. I planned to check you out before finishing the contract. You know the rest."

"What about Carmen?"

"What about her?" he said, stalling.

"That man. The e-mails."

This was going to be tough. "The couple she's with, Jason and Sylvia Fox, were born thirty years too late. They're old-fashioned hippies in everything but name, committed to peace and love. And they have children close to Carmen's age."

Anger stewed in Shelby's emerald-green eyes. Her voice turned flinty. "That talk about code words and turning her over to Immigration—you were lying to keep me in line?"

"I told you I'm not a very nice person."

"You're a bastard." She swung at him, a roundhouse right that he had no trouble deflecting. "Bastard!" She lunged, both fists flailing.

Grabbing and twisting, he flattened her on the hay bale, captured her wrists, and pinned her with his body. "This isn't getting us anywhere. If I'd told you I would never deliberately harm either of you, would you have stuck with me?"

Her anger seemed to ebb as abruptly as it had flared. She grew quiescent. "Until I found some way to get her back, certainly."

He understood the seriousness of the moment but couldn't help smiling. "By busting my kneecaps, probably. Torturing me until I told you what you wanted to know."

"I don't understand why you're doing this."

Not wanting to lie, but worried about her reaction if he told her the real reason, he decided to be evasive. "It's a matter of cosmic balancing." The feel of her under him had set off a tingling that enervated his entire being but centered in his groin. He released her arms and waited to see if she would take another swing at him. She didn't, and he said, "Besides, you need to hone your survival skills."

"Survival skills?"

"When you attacked me in that Arkansas motel room, I was stunned. You should have been able to take me." With most of his weight supported on his elbows, she could easily wriggle out from under him or roll him off, but she did neither. *Does the contact feel as good to her as it does to me?* "I can teach you to fight. Show you how to spot and lose a tail. How to shadow someone. How to shoot, if it comes to that."

"Things you learned as a SEAL?"

"Some of it. Some I picked up later, working with a special task force."

"How did you get from the navy to this special force?"

She didn't seem bothered by his erection pressing against her, and there was no way she could be unaware of it. He supposed he should get up, but lying on her felt almost unbearably delicious. "They borrowed me, taught me their way of operating."

"Why did you leave?"

"Same as you. They tried to terminate my employment with prejudice, so to speak. I'll tell you about that another time."

"You feel . . . you're getting heavy."

"Sorry." He sat up.

She sat beside him. "You don't think they'll stop looking for me?"

"My partner and I thought we were safe." He picked hay out of her hair and off her clothes as he talked. "That got people killed."

"Leonard is close to your age. Was he your partner?"

He shook his head. "Latica. Leonard is her husband."

"It got people killed, you said." She began picking hay off him. "If it was just you and Latica, why did they kill others?"

"For the same reason Carmen will die if they find her: to make sure nobody who knows anything goes public." His excitement had abated to a less awkward level; he stood, offered her his hand, and pulled her to her feet. "You're free to leave, but it would be a mistake. So would traveling with Carmen right away or sending her to your friend in Arkansas."

"May I think about this?"

"Take all the time you need. The farm's a great place for thinking things through."

They headed back to the house, walking so close their shoulders occasionally brushed. "I believe you're a good man," she said as they approached the porch.

The compliment both warmed and disturbed him. To cover his discomfort, he put a jocular tone in his voice. "Naw, I'm a cold-blooded killer. But I recognize goodness when I see it."

Vlad disliked modern technology in general and computers in particular. A dedicated professional must master his tools, however, so he had forced himself to learn the software he needed in his work. In a Kansas City motel room, he ran eMailTracker on his laptop to determine the numerical address of the Internet service provider that had sent Cervosier's e-mail message to the Arkansas librarian. Another software package, eMailRouteFinder, pinpointed Las Vegas as the city of origin. The user name, pearlis@easynet.net, told him that Pearl-somebody lived in Vegas and owned the computer from which the message originated.

Eager for closure, he wanted to head for Nevada. But he was almost broke and had been offered another contract. Richard Heber, the majority stockholder and chief executive officer of ANSCOM, Inc., had to die within thirty days under circumstances that could not possibly be construed as suicide. Vlad decided to do Heber and then get back on Cervosier's trail.

Two hours of Internet work convinced him that Heber had ordered his own hit. ANSCOM's stock, a high flyer a year earlier, had dropped into the toilet. Its 10-K filings with the SEC revealed the company was short on cash and burdened with debt, a candidate for bankruptcy. The financial press reported a Justice Department investigation into suspected stock manipulation and insider trading. There were rumors that the fifty-year-old tycoon might be ailing. Vlad would have wagered his hit-man credentials the guy had a multimillion-dollar life insurance policy that would not pay in the event of suicide. It probably included double-indemnity for homicide.

All that was just idle curiosity, of course. The key contract clause was that the death must be unmistakably murder. The job paid twenty-five grand, and there were no other restrictions. The target had a forty-one-year-old wife, his second marriage, and two step-daughters, both in their teens. He did not employ bodyguards. The family lived in Florida year-round, at an estate in Boca Raton.

Salivating at the prospect of taking out the whole family, making it look like a ritual killing, Vlad booked a flight for Palm Beach, an easy drive to Boca.

CHAPTER EIGHTEEN

SHELBY'S SELF-DEFENSE LESSONS BEGAN the morning after her arrival at the farm. They followed a pattern that varied only slightly from day to day. After breakfast she exercised with Leonard, who had been a physical education teacher and high school coach, to build dexterity and strength. Latica taught her hand-to-hand fighting, and Hank instructed her in firearms.

"The way you handled that handgun on Lake Mead," Hank said on the occasion of Shelby's first firearms lesson, "you're a natural. But you didn't know the difference between a semiautomatic and a revolver, so you can't have had much experience."

"Experience?" Shelby laughed. "I'd held a pistol twice before that day. I had fired just one bullet—into a ceiling."

"You've never shot at a target or anything?"

"Never. I saw that man going after you with his knife and did the only thing I could think of—grabbed the gun, pointed, and squeezed. Had there been a safety lock or something, I guess we'd both be dead."

"You did fine. Semiautomatics are more complicated, though. And you need to learn about ammunition. Maintenance, too— cleaning and oiling. Marksmanship, of course."

Patrick met them at the range with an array of handguns. Hank passed the smallest one to Shelby.

"It's almost cute," she said. "Until one thinks about its purpose."

"It's a Walther. Twenty-two caliber. Not much stopping power, but it's useful under special circumstances."

"Special in what way?"

"Close up. You shoot someone in the head with a twenty-two, the slug doesn't exit. It ricochets off the inside of the skull and whizzes around. Scrambles the brain."

"Ugh." Shelby wrinkled her nose. Not knowing what to do with the little pistol, she let it dangle in her hand.

"Point it downrange," Hank said. "Get used to holding it. If it's any consolation, the person you shoot won't feel a thing."

"That's hard to believe."

"Only because you've never been shot. The jolt to the nervous system shuts down pain receptors. It takes maybe half an hour, sometimes longer, for feeling to come back. If you're wounded, that's both good and bad. You might be able to function, take out the shooter, but you won't know how badly you're hurt. Then comes the pain, and you'd better not plan on being operational."

"I take it you've been through that?"

"It isn't just bullet wounds. Any major trauma—a knife, a baseball bat—can have the same effect. It's nature's way of giving us a fighting chance."

Balancing the Walther in her hand, Shelby tested its feel and weight as she thought about when she first entered the country and was beaten and raped. She imagined how different it might have been had she owned the little handgun and known how to use it.

Hank took the weapon from her and held it so she could see him flick a switch on its side. "Trigger lock. There's also a firing pin lock. You deactivate it by pulling back the hammer." He demonstrated by jacking the slide to cock the pistol. "Engaging the slide also pumps a round into the firing chamber. If you already have one there, you can use your thumb." He pulled the hammer back and thumbed the combination safety and decocking lever to return it to its previous position.

"We'll start you on this." He offered her the weapon again. "Then you'll fire these." He touched two of the pistols Patrick had laid on a wooden stand. They looked much like the Walther but were larger. "You need to become familiar with the Beretta, because it's standard issue for the military and most government agencies. I think the Glock will suit you better, though."

"What makes it better?"

He picked up the smaller of the two big semiautomatics. "This one, the model nineteen, is half a pound lighter than a Beretta. Makes a difference when you're packing. It's shorter, thinner, less likely to be noticed. Yet it has the same stopping power."

He laid the Glock aside and hefted a weapon that reminded her of the one she had fired on the yacht at Lake Mead "Snub-nosed revolver. It's actually the same caliber as the Walther, but it uses high-velocity ammo. Eight rounds. You load it with hollow points, it'll make a bigger exit hole than a jacketed nine-millimeter."

"Caliber and millimeters—I don't understand."

"American weapons have traditionally been calibrated based on a bullet of one inch diameter. The twenty-two you're holding actually uses a point-two-two caliber bullet—twenty-two one-hundredths of an inch in diameter. European weapons are calibrated in millimeters."

"That makes sense." She laid the Walther aside and took the snub-nose from him. "Less than a quarter inch across? That's a really small bullet."

"It's your backup weapon."

"*My* backup?"

He nudged the revolver's barrel with a finger. "If you're going to point that, make sure it's downrange."

She realized she had been waving the little pistol as she talked. "Sorry."

"When you leave here, the revolver and the Glock go with you. Before that happens, I want you to become as comfortable with them as a cook is with a spatula. And I'm ordering you a scope-equipped sniper rifle that disassembles and fits in a case. It will be your long-range defense. If the bad guys can't get close, they can't hurt you." The lesson ended with what Hank called dry fire: assuming various stances and clicking empty weapons.

On the second day, Patrick did not join them on the firing range. Shelby, eager to learn, paid close attention to Hank's instructions and looked forward to actually firing the weapons. Before that happened, Hank introduced a new and pleasurable element by stepping behind her to correct her stance with encircling arms. Despite her years of freedom from supervision while studying in America, she was sexually inexperienced. Her only time with a man—the ordeal of torture and rape—had been the antithesis of pleasure, yet Hank's touch made her body tingle.

After firing practice, they sat under a shade tree while he showed her how to disassemble the Glock, clean and oil its parts, and put them back together. He suggested a break, and she stretched out on a bed of clover.

He sat cross-legged at her side. "For a woman who had fired only twice in her life, you're doing exceptionally well."

"Thank you. I have an exceptional teacher."

"Those men you took out—you said a crooked cop, a rapist, and his sidekick—would it bother you to talk about it?"

Would rehashing your worst nightmare bother you? "Not a policeman, an immigration agent. What do you want to know?"

"Obviously, you didn't shoot them."

"I shoved one off a boat. He couldn't swim." Still on her back in the clover, she laid an arm across her eyes so she couldn't see Hank watching her. "The immigration agent—I ran over him with a boat. The propeller . . ."

"Talking about it does upset you."

"I guess. But it also bothered me to tell you about Colonel Burgess, yet I felt better afterward. The lapsed-Catholic confessional thing." She lifted her arm off her eyes and gave him a smile. "Should I call you Father Hank?"

"Oh, lord, please."

"After I pushed that brute overboard, I just sat in the boat and watched him drown. And I might have been able to save the immigration agent. I decided to let him bleed to death."

"You did what you had to. You were in a war, so to speak."

"And taking no prisoners. The first was hardest. The man who raped me."

Hank touched her shoulder. "He deserved it."

"It wasn't revenge. He was holding me prisoner. He threatened Carmen."

"How did it happen? I mean, how did he get his hands on you in the first place?"

"Back home I taught at the university. I met with a group of students off-campus, and internal security agents raided us. I don't know whether it was because of the meeting or if that was just an excuse, a way to strike at my father."

"They were after your dad? Why?"

"He'd served in the old, democratic government, and he was still influential. Anyway, a student pulled a gun, and . . ." The memories still hurt, and she found it hard to tell Hank about it in a calm voice. She took a deep breath and plunged ahead. "They started shooting. Kids screamed, tried to get away. Most of them died."

"Were you arrested?"

"I escaped, but they searched for me. Papa arranged for me to be smuggled out of the country and into America. The smugglers turned us over to some men in Arkansas who were supposed to hide us, help us move on. But that hoodlum, Jerry Lee Tucker, he . . ."

Hank rested his hand on her shoulder.

"Tucker worked with the rogue immigration agent," she said when she had regained her composure. "They sold illegal immigrants as stoop laborers, maids, prostitutes."

"Tucker's the guy who raped you?"

"Over and over. He tortured me. Threatened to sell Carmen."

"So you defended yourself. Protected your sister."

"He used his fists, his belt. He scalded my hand." She put her arm back over her eyes and found it easier to talk when she couldn't see Hank. "Sexually, he did everything I can imagine. It was the second day, and he was so sure he'd broken me that he left me free while he napped. I barricaded him in the cabin and burned it to the ground. Burned him. Burned . . ." She gasped and bit her lip.

Hank's hand still rested on her shoulder. He squeezed gently. "You had no alternative."

"He tried to get out. Through a window."

The cabin fire had sounded like a gigantic windstorm. Or maybe she heard actual wind as the inferno sucked in fresh air at its base and spewed furnace-crisped currents heavenward. Wooden beams exploding from expanded internal gases scattered flaming debris and sent sparks cartwheeling like Fourth of July fireworks. She shied away from the heat but forced herself closer again to guard the bedroom's only window.

In light from the mounting flames, she could see Tucker inside. Naked, and obviously disoriented from booze-fueled sleep, he stood by the blocked door and stared at the broken window. "Goddamn," he shouted, and dashed for the window but jumped back when flames erupted in his path.

Standing outside the window, Shelby held a broken-off tree limb, ready to use its pointed end as a prod to keep him inside. Her hands ached from gripping it.

He circled the flames and stood just inside the window. For what must have been a split second but seemed a slow-motion minute, they stared at each other. "Bitch," he shouted, and tried to climb through.

Holding the slender tree branch like a spear, she jabbed the pointed end at him. He leaped back and tried to grab the branch. She jerked it away and jabbed again.

His skin seemed aglow with orange flames as he used an arm to shield his face from the heat. He shouted again and leaped into the window. His feet landed on the windowsill, and he grasped the pointed end of her tree branch.

His leap and the pressure of his grip on the branch caused her to stumble. The branch's blunt end ploughed into soft dirt behind her. He fell forward through the window, and the pointed end punctured his stomach. As it dug into him, halting his forward momentum, the slender branch shuddered in her hands but did not break.

He stood on the windowsill with both hands wrapped around

the branch where it protruded from his midsection. Mouth open, eyes abnormally wide, he stared at her.

She wanted to drop the branch and run. Instead, she gripped it tighter and lunged forward.

His blood darkened the bark where the branch had impaled him, but he resisted her effort to force him back inside. He screamed something that she could not understand over the crackle of flames and the pounding inside her head.

Gripping the pole with all her might, she leaned into his weight. Abruptly, the counterpressure disappeared as he fell back into the burning room, taking the branch with him. The sudden change cost Shelby her balance. She lost her grip on the branch and fell on her face. The tree branch slid in through the window and moved farther into the room. It was, she realized, still embedded in him and moving with him as he backed away.

Over the fire's roar, he cursed. Then he shrieked. His screams chased her, slicing through her like knives as she raced to where Carmen waited for her by the river.

"Come on, Shelby. Come on, now. Speak to me."

Hank's voice sounded at first as if it came from a great distance. It pulled her back from the cabin, back from the crackle and hiss of flames consuming the ancient, dried timber and the man inside the bedroom, back from his curses as he tried to escape and his shrieks as the inferno claimed him.

Hank cradled her in his arms and rocked her. "That's it," he said. "That's it. Relax, now. Everything's okay. You're safe. Calm down."

Little by little, her trembling eased. A light breeze dried the sweat pouring off her. The fresh scent of crushed clover where she had thrashed about pushed away the dredged-up stench of scorched timbers and the sickening-sweet odor of burning flesh. She sat up. "Sorry. Guess I lost it."

Hank released her but kept a palm flattened against her back. "Scared the hell out of me is what you did. You sure you're all right?"

"I don't fall apart like that. Something just snapped."

"You're entitled. It's my fault, anyway. I encouraged you to talk about things."

"I'm glad you did. I feel freed from a heavy load I didn't even know I was carrying."

He looked as if he was about to say something more but checked his watch instead. "If you're up to it, we ought to be getting back."

CHAPTER NINETEEN

FARM LIFE SETTLED INTO a satisfying routine. Shelby's mornings continued to be devoted to training. During rest periods between practice bouts with Latica, she learned that Hank had been married for only a few years and that he had a daughter, now dead. But Latica never said anything about how the family had come to be on this remote farm. Nor did she mention how her husband had gotten so terribly burned or reveal anything about how Hank's wife and daughter had died.

Between lunch and dinner, Shelby helped work the farm. She learned to milk a goat, to weed vegetables, to gut and pick chickens, to drive a tractor. Leonard taught her to mend fences, repair small engines, and do preventive automobile maintenance.

At first, the hard work generated sore muscles that made getting up in the mornings a chore, but the discomfort soon yielded to physical exhilaration. Her growing bond with Hank's family warmed her. Except for missing Carmen, worrying about her despite Hank's assurances that she was well and happy, Shelby would have been content.

Telephone calls to her little sister filled part of the void created by their separation. Once each week, she donned a wig and makeup and rode with Hank to Grand Junction, where she practiced shadowing make-believe targets or melding into crowds. A call to Carmen formed the high point of each trip—leery of using the farm's satellite phone or his cell phone because the signals might be picked up, Hank insisted on making the calls only from Grand Junction's public telephones. Carmen's happiness with Sylvia and Jason Fox and their children eased Shelby's guilt over their separation.

Shelby also called Elizabeth Fontaine, her Arkansas-librarian friend. No one answered, so she left a voice-mail message explaining that she would not need Elizabeth to care for Carmen after all. "I had to run from the people I told you about, but everything's all right now. We're with friends, and we're safe."

She tried calling her friend in Arizona and learned the number had been disconnected. It seemed strange that the telephone company could not give her a forwarding number. She supposed the move that prompted the number change had taken place some time back. Directory assistance had no new number for the Reverend and Mrs. Frederick Rogers in the Flagstaff area.

Shelby and Hank spent long stretches of time together in town and on the pistol range, and they often did farm chores as a team. During their free time, they took walks. On one of the walks, she learned how he had become a professional hit man.

They had been looking for a lost nanny goat and her two kids. They found the goats an hour before sunset and, weary from tromping over the mountain, rested side-by-side on the horizontal trunk of a tree that had fallen across a creek.

"You know pretty much everything about me," Shelby said. "I don't even know if Hank is your real name."

"It's Herbert." He grinned. "You can see why I want to be called Hank. I've insisted since my ninth birthday."

"What's your family name?"

"Pekins."

"Tell me about Herbert Pekins. Where did he grow up? Does he have siblings? How did he meet his wife?"

"I have no brothers or sisters. I spent my childhood in a small town in Michigan. My dad was killed in an industrial accident when I was a teenager, and Mom and I moved to Detroit. I went to Central Michigan State University, paying my way with a part-time job and ROTC. My mother passed away shortly after I earned a naval commission and volunteered for SEAL training."

"I lost my mother when I was young," Shelby said, "so I know what it's like. It must have been especially tough, losing both parents."

"It was, yes. Anyway, the Pentagon sent me to Bosnia with a NATO detachment. A special unit, an international team with a murky chain of command, had been organized to eliminate some of the Bosnian government's violence-prone competition. They borrowed me from the navy."

Shelby slipped off her shoes and dangled her feet in the water. She jerked them out and twisted to straddle the log. "It's like ice! You might have warned me."

He chuckled. "You're definitely not in Haiti anymore." Straddling the log, he lifted one of her feet, dried it with his handkerchief, and warmed it by clamping it between his thighs.

Balancing with her hands, she leaned back and enjoyed his ministrations. "You became an assassin for your government?" she prompted as he worked.

"For the international team. I gather it was indirectly controlled by the United States, but our government's tracks were well covered. The American intelligence community had long chafed under a law forbidding assassinations." He lifted her other foot and gave it the same treatment. "They set things up so politicians could deny culpability."

"Latica was a member of your team?"

"Not just a member, my good right hand. She was a Bosnian civilian but had trained with a local militia unit and became a crack shot with a sniper rifle. A British Special Air Service commando, on loan the same as me, rounded out our team."

The pressure of Hank's thighs had warmed more than Shelby's feet. Reluctantly, she put on her socks and shoes. "It's getting chilly. Let's head back." As they walked side-by-side toward the tired-looking late-afternoon sun, she said, "Obviously, you and Latica grew close while you worked together."

"Extremely close. We might have become lovers if she hadn't been devoted to Leonard. They had married while he was on a Peace Corps assignment in the Balkans, but the fighting broke out before he could arrange for her immigration. She rebuffed my advances but introduced me to her sister. Eventually, Natasa and I married. We had a little girl. Beverly would be six now."

Shelby heard the sadness in his voice. She grasped his hand and felt return pressure from his fingers. "What led you from Bosnia to this mountain hideaway?"

"As I said, there were three of us doing wet work. Key targets started getting away, and we decided one of us was a mole. The question was, which one? Apparently, our handlers drew the same conclusion and planned a sure way to solve the problem—they ordered all three of us terminated. When their shooters burst in, we had our weapons out, arguing and waving them at each other. I guess that took the cleanup crew by surprise. We had an old-fashioned shoot-out. Only Latica and I survived. We picked up Natasa—she was pregnant then—and my in-laws and made our way to the Adriatic coast. From there we got ourselves smuggled into the United States."

"Patrick is Bosnian? How did he get an Irish name?"

"His father was Irish, an explosives expert with the Irish Republican Army. Hunted by the British, he spent the last twenty years of his life hiding in the Balkans."

Since Hank's mother-in-law was not at the farm, and since he had referred to his wife and daughter in the past tense, he clearly had not told Shelby everything. A fleeting glance at his face revealed how painful the memories were, so she decided not to press. Still holding hands, they trudged in silence through lengthening shadows toward the barn with the nanny goat and her kids trailing behind.

"Leonard was teaching school in Indiana," Hank said. "He sent us money, and we hid in Detroit. I knew the city, and we figured its size would make us anonymous. Patrick had been a doctor in Bosnia. He provided prenatal care and delivered Beverly. By then, the navy had listed me as missing and presumed killed in action, so we decided to surface with new identities. Leonard joined us in Detroit, and he and Latica rented an apartment a few blocks from ours. Patrick and my mother-in-law moved in with them. Leonard and I worked the assembly line in a nearby factory. Patrick fixed the plant's broken machinery. We led a peaceful existence for almost three years."

"But the assassins found you?"

He nodded. "Natasa had a cold, and Latica planned to take Beverly off her hands for the day. Leonard worked the night shift at the factory, so he and Latica loaded their two children and my mother-in-law into their car for the drive to our apartment. At the last minute, Latica dashed back inside to get something. While he waited, Leonard turned on the ignition. A car bomb . . . only Leonard survived."

The pain Shelby saw in Hank's eyes brought tears to hers. "You don't have to tell me."

"It's been three years. I'm nobody's model of mental health, but I ought to be able to talk about a three-year-old trauma."

"You don't have to."

"I want to. Want you to know, to understand." They had reached the barn, and he led her to the hay bale where they had sat that first day. "Two contract hit men were operating as a team. After wiring Leonard's car, they invaded my apartment. They trapped Natasa in the kitchen and waited for me to come home. I didn't show on schedule—Patrick and I had agreed to fix a neighbor's car after work—so they boiled water and held her hands in it, trying to make her tell them where to find me. One of them continued the torture while the other went outside to watch for me. There's no way to know what happened, but the gas stove exploded. Flames gutted the kitchen and the bedroom over it. Beverly was sleeping up there."

Hank's voice held steady, but twilight streaming through the barn door reflected off tears sliding down his face. Shelby stood and pulled his head to her breasts. She said nothing. She just held him.

Still sitting, he slid his arms around her. "The surviving hit man caught me as I tried to fight my way past firemen who blocked our door. He forced me into an alley between neighboring buildings and was about to knife me when Patrick beaned him with a brick. We took him to an abandoned factory and, well . . ." He released Shelby and pulled away.

She sat on the hay bale and rested a hand on his thigh. "What did you do with the man?"

"Nothing I'm proud of. He begged me to let him die. I refused, until he told me about the car bomb, described what had happened in my apartment, and explained how his operation worked. He showed me how to reach the offshore broker on his computer. I granted him his wish to die, assumed his identity, and reported the assassination contract fulfilled."

"Latica said you guys have been on the farm for three years. So you came out here right away?"

"We were officially dead, but they would still be looking for any family member that might have learned something. I told you Patrick's a medical doctor. He nursed Leonard back to health."

"You said you assumed the killer's identity. But after you trapped me and we began talking, you told me I was your first contract."

"Back then, I just wanted the guy's bank account and investment portfolio, and a way to convince the broker I was dead. The man who died with Natasa and Beverly was burned beyond recognition, so I gather they concluded it was me. I let the broker believe I was the assassin and had been injured, that I wouldn't be able to take any more assignments."

"Obviously, you changed your mind."

"We'd planned on the farm being a temporary hideout, a place to lick our wounds. But you've seen the extent of Leonard's injuries. And Latica fell apart emotionally. She seems normal, but the mere suggestion that she leave the farm brings on a relapse."

"Can't you get her counseling? Psychiatric help?"

"Talking about that triggers a sort-of . . . she goes catatonic. Anyway, the stock market turned down and I started worrying about money, so I e-mailed the broker and reported myself healed and ready for work. I declined a couple of jobs but took contracts on you and Rankin because of your profiles. I figured the country would be a better place without either of you."

Although Shelby didn't approve of the way Hank had decided to earn a living, she understood. His determination to protect Latica,

Leonard, and Patrick was a more extreme version of what she had done when she agreed to work for the CBTF, what she would do if necessary to protect Carmen. "You plan to just live here forever? To keep on killing people for money?"

He shrugged. "Inertia kept us from doing any planning. We just . . . we drifted. But then . . ."

"Then what, Hank? Tell me what you're thinking."

"Fate has a way of pushing you off center. Three months ago, everything started going to hell." He smiled and caressed her hand, still resting on his thigh. "I believe it's working out now."

"You're talking in riddles."

"Because I might have it wrong. When I know I'm right, I'll explain." He stood. "Latica will be holding dinner for us."

Shelby's weekly trips into Grand Junction, where she called Carmen from a public telephone, eased the pain of separation. And she relished the time alone with Hank. They had some privacy on the farm, but it was usually brief and never certain. The trips put them together for hours with no distractions. Always, their last stop was the storefront medical clinic Hank had visited on the day they arrived from Las Vegas. Each time, he asked her to drop him there and pick him up two hours later. And he always asked her to drive home.

The morning after their third weekly trip, while helping Latica tidy up the kitchen, Shelby could no longer tolerate the mystery. They were doing dishes, Latica washing, Shelby drying and putting away. "Why does Hank visit that clinic whenever we're in Grand Junction?" Shelby asked. "Is something wrong with him?"

Latica, squeezing the dishcloth, closed her eyes. She shook

her head.

Shelby laid her towel aside and faced the other woman. "He's sick, isn't he? Seriously ill."

"No, he's . . . I don't know. Ask him."

"Just tell me. It isn't fair for everyone to know but me."

Latica dabbed at her eyes with her apron. "He has a tumor."

Despite the kitchen's heat, a blanket of cold settled over Shelby. "What kind of tumor?"

"Primary bone cancer in his arm. It's early-stage, so he can get it removed without amputation. But he's been refusing treatment. He just took medicine for pain relief. It was like he'd lost interest in living."

Shelby thought about his pills, about the shortening intervals between them. "But he's being treated now?"

"We aren't supposed to know about it, but the doctor at the clinic told Patrick, and he talked with the consulting oncologist. Since you came to stay with us, Hank has started radiation therapy."

Their talk about death while they were in Las Vegas now made sense to Shelby. He'd been thinking about his own demise, not about killing her. "And they expect him to recover?"

"Patrick says the tumor is already shrinking. They will be able to remove it." Latica wiped her eyes again. "We're so grateful to you."

"To me? I didn't do anything."

"You have done more than you realize. So much more. Had you seen how it was before, you would understand." Latica shrugged and resumed washing dishes.

Floundering in a sea of confusion, Shelby went back to drying the dishes and putting them away. Hank had saved her life, and his family had made life worth living again. Yet they thought she had done something for them?

"Latica says you've become a darned good street fighter," Hank said during breakfast the next morning. "Says you put her on the mat as often as she does you."

"She's being easy on me. Building up my confidence."

"I did that at first," Latica said. "Not recently."

Surprised, Shelby laid her fork aside and gave the other woman her full attention. "Really?"

"The last couple of days, I've given it everything I have. You learn fast, and you're a natural athlete."

Shelby couldn't keep the grin off her face. "You were really trying?"

"My level best. And Hank says you're better with handguns than most of his SEAL colleagues were. I think we should have a celebration."

Throughout the day the family interspersed farm chores with party planning, and shortly before sunset Leonard started a fire in a backyard pit. When a bed of coals had accumulated, they roasted a young goat. Everyone took a turn cranking the spit while the other four drank home-brewed beer and whooped and danced to old audio tapes. As the night wore on, the music got louder and faster, the beer tasted better and better. Dancing with the others in a circle around the fire, Shelby started giggling and couldn't stop. With stomach muscles burning from the belly laughs, she collapsed.

Hank fell beside her, laughing just as hard. In the middle of it, he whispered in her ear, "What are we laughing about?"

"Life." She poked at his ribs. "We're laughing because life is good. I had forgotten how good it can be."

She relieved Leonard at the spit and watched as the others circled the fire in their primitive dance. Hank joined her and offered to take over. "Just help me," she said. They stood close, their hands touching on the crank as they turned the spit. "Hank, thank you."

"For what?"

"For all this. For sparing my life, of course. But even more, for introducing joy into it."

"You're the bringer of joy. I should be thanking you. We all should." He sipped his beer. "We've never done this before."

"That can't be. Patrick had brewed the beer; someone built the spit. It's been used before."

"Sure, we've barbequed and drank together. We sit around a campfire, sing and tell stories. But the joy we're sharing tonight is new. I'm not sure how, but you brought it."

"I'd like to bring Carmen."

He seemed suddenly sober. "For a visit, or to stay?"

"To stay for a while. As you said, no one knows what the future holds."

With a hand on the back of her neck, he tugged gently and kissed her forehead, then her nose. Arching his head back, he stared for a moment, and she thought he might kiss her lips. Instead, he released her and said, "We'll go get her on Tuesday."

Everyone slept late the next morning. Then the men, grouchy with hangovers, went about their belated morning chores. In the kitchen, Latica shaped patties from a crock of sausage while Shelby peeled breakfast potatoes.

"Hank told us you want your little sister to live with us," Latica said.

"For a while." Shelby barely breathed, waiting to see how the woman would receive the idea.

"She's seven, Hank said. Has she been in school?"

"In Haiti. Since we came to America her life has been . . . disrupted. Hank says the people who are caring for her are home-schooling her."

Latica wiped her hands on a dish towel and put the sausage crock back in the refrigerator. "Leonard is a teacher without pupils." She plopped the sausage patties into a heavy iron skillet on the stove's back burner. "He will be delighted to have a student again."

"You won't mind having a child underfoot?"

"Leonard and I had two boys. They . . ." Latica concentrated on the sausage patties, worrying them with a spatula. "You know about Hank's daughter? She would be six."

"He told me. He also told me about your children. About how Leonard got hurt. I hope you don't mind my knowing."

"It's three-year-old history."

"It's very private history, Latica. I felt privileged when Hank shared it with me. It made me feel more nearly a part of your family."

"More nearly? Membership is yours for the taking. So is Hank."

The casual way Latica tossed out her comment clouded its intent. "I don't know where I stand with him," Shelby said. "With you, either."

Latica flipped the sausage patties and pointed the spatula at Shelby. "You are the mystery. Hank tells us nothing about you."

"He hasn't told you why I'm here?"

"He says it must come from you."

Shelby sliced the potatoes into long slivers and set them in a bowl of water by the stove. "Do you know how he's started earning his living?"

"*Our* living." Latica's voice took on a defensive note. "He provides for all of us."

"I'm a part of that. Someone hired him to . . . they were going to pay him for me."

"You were a target?"

Shelby reminded herself that Latica had been Hank's partner, a fellow assassin in Bosnia. "He changed his mind and brought me here to protect me."

"That explains much. But you seem undecided about him."

"*I* seem undecided? He treats me like a kid sister."

Latica shifted the sausage patties to a platter and dumped the sliced potatoes into the skillet. They popped and sizzled in the hot grease until she covered them with a lid. "Hank thinks he has to take care of everyone he loves, to keep them from hurt. When he can't do that, it tears him apart inside."

"You're talking about his wife and daughter?"

"About us." Latica lifted the lid off the potatoes and poked at them with the spatula, jabbing as if she wanted to punish them. "Me, my father, Leonard. You, too."

Shelby set the breakfast table, took biscuits out of the oven, and ladled apple butter into a serving dish. Mulling over what Latica had said, she vacillated between asking the woman to elaborate and pretending she understood. The men, coming in from their morning chores, freed her from the need to decide.

Breakfast talk seesawed between the day's work schedule and banter about the previous night's party. Latica teased Leonard about overcooking the goat. Patrick received good-natured ribbing about the taste of the beer he had brewed, about liking his product perhaps too much.

Less capable of dissembling, Shelby brooded. She smiled when the others aimed jokes her way, nodded when they included her in their banter. But her mind turned endlessly on the history of her hosts, on the way tragedy stalked them and how it constricted their lives. Always, her mind cycled back to Latica's inclusion of her among those who Hank loved: *Me, my father, Leonard. You, too.*

CHAPTER TWENTY

TWO WEEKS IN FLORIDA shadowing Heber, watching him at work and at play, had been enough for Vlad to set up the hit. The cash from that job gave him the leisure to return to Chicago and finish what he had started with the nursing student he'd met there, but he couldn't get Shelby Cervosier off his mind. Finding her, using her, then disposing of her at his leisure, became an obsession. A check in with the broker revealed that no one had sent in her thumb to collect the fee and that her contract was still open.

He caught an early-morning flight to Las Vegas, the city his tracking software had identified as the source of her e-mail to Elizabeth Fontaine, the Arkansas librarian. In Las Vegas, he rented a motel room convenient to an Internet café. Using a computer at the café, he sent a message to the return address on Shelby's e-mail, pearlis@easynet.net:

Dear Pearl, I desperately need your help. This connection is not secure, so it would be dangerous to say more. Meet me at 11506 South Tupac Avenue at 8:00 p.m. It is an Internet café. Wait for me at the serving counter, and I will explain everything. Love, Shelby.

At a quarter of eight, he sat at a computer in the café, positioned so he could keep an eye on the entrance. Guessing that Pearl would be close to Cervosier's age and that, living and working in Vegas, she would be doing okay, he watched for a young, expensively dressed female. At one minute until eight, a short, twentysomething blonde with a cover-girl face slid onto a stool at the counter. Wearing his harmless-young-country-boy smile, Vlad approached and spoke in a near whisper: "Pearl?"

She faced him. A raised eyebrow questioned his right to know her name.

His heart thudded at the thought of tears streaming from those big blue eyes, of that blemish-free face twisted in agony. "I'm a friend of Shelby's. She's in trouble."

"Her e-mail said she'd be here."

"She's hiding."

"From Hank?" Pearl laughed. "He won't hurt her."

Cervosier had picked up a dude? Vlad had figured she and her kid sister would be traveling alone. "Hank's dead. It's that other guy."

Pearl frowned. "What other guy?"

"I didn't ask. Didn't want to get involved. But she's hurt, and she asked me to meet you."

"Hurt?" Pearl's voice turned shrill. "How bad? What happened?"

"It'll be better if she tells you."

"Where is she?"

"Just down the street." Vlad glanced around, deliberately looking furtive. "We need to get out of here." He headed for the door but watched Pearl's reflection in the glass.

She slid off the stool and hurried after him. Outside, she caught up. "How far?"

"Two blocks. She has a room."

The motel, a single-story, cement-block structure on its last leg, offered rooms by the day or week. As they drew nearer, Pearl's steps slowed. She looked apprehensive.

Vlad pressed the room key into her hand. "She's in one-forty-seven. Said it hurts to get out of bed. You're supposed to go on in. Good luck." He had rented an end room. He rushed around the corner from it and flattened himself against the wall.

Pearl knocked. "Shelby?" She knocked again, louder. "Shelby!"

No more sound. Vlad worried that she had decided to walk away. Then the key scraped against the lock. Straining, he heard the squeak of hinges. He rounded the corner and found her standing in the open doorway, peering inside. By ramming a shoulder into her back, he knocked the wind out of her and propelled her across the room and onto the floor. He slammed the door shut and jumped her before she could get enough breath to scream.

With a hand clamped over her mouth, he held his knife against her throat and pushed hard enough for her to feel the blade. "You make a sound, it'll be your last. You gonna be quiet?"

She nodded.

"Okay, I trust you." Twisting so she couldn't see, he laid his knife on the floor and dug a palm-sized rubber ball from his pocket. "Quiet, now." He pulled his hand from her mouth. As she ovaled her lips to scream, he crammed the ball between them, flattening its sides to force it between her teeth.

She made retching noises. Her shoulders heaved. She struggled to get out from underneath him.

He smiled, visualizing how her first gasping intake of breath had sucked the ball to the back of her mouth and triggered her gag reflex. She couldn't open wide enough to expel the ball, but he duct-taped her lips to make sure. With his weight centered on the small of her back, he twisted the knife against her neck, digging its tip through the skin. "Be still, or I'll slice you."

Her shoulders jerked with the retching, but she stopped bucking. The retching eased, so she must have worked the ball forward against her teeth.

"Sit up and pull your knees to your chest." He forced her head between her bent knees until she grunted from the strain. By duct-taping her wrists to her ankles, then looping the tape around her neck and down to her ankles again, he secured her with her head jammed between her knees. He let her fall sideways onto the floor.

Satisfied that she couldn't move, he set the bedside alarm clock for midnight and stretched out on the bed. When the alarm awakened him, he showered, did his usual all-over body shave, and ran the water to make certain no residue remained in the drain trap. He packed everything away, donned his latex gloves and wiped every surface in the room with a paper towel and spray cleaner, and eased his rental car as close to the door as obstructions permitted. Lifting and carrying Pearl as if she were a piece of luggage, he tossed her into the rear seat.

He got the address of her apartment from her driver's license, drove there, and pulled to the curb a block away. "You've made me hurt you way more than I intended," he said. "I'm not a violent man, but I make my living by finding people. I have a wife and two children to feed. Are you listening, Pearl?"

Realizing that he had her taped too tightly to nod, he turned her so he could see her face and shined his penlight in her eyes. "Wink if you understand me. Good girl. To get paid, I have to find Shelby. If I ask you where she is, you'll lie, so let's not even bother. I need a little time on your computer and some numbers off your telephone's caller ID. Then I'm outta here."

He centered the penlight on her eyes once more. "Wink again if you're gonna help me. That's my girl. Now, the sticky part is getting into your pad. Shouldn't be anyone in the lobby this late, so your only job is to get me by security." He screwed the top off a small bottle of scotch and splashed it on her. "We've been out having ourselves a ball. You're smashed, so you'll just wave and say hi to the security dude. You won't call him by name. That way, I don't have to worry about your using some oddball name to make him suspicious."

Holding his penlight so she could see his face, Vlad tried to impress her with the sincerity of his expression. "The danger is that you'll misjudge me and act up in the lobby. It isn't safe to do that, Pearl. I'll shoot the security guy and anyone else there. Then I'll shoot you. Do you think I'm lying?"

Pearl blinked and grunted.

"You're probably saying no. Saying you believe me and you'll behave. That right?"

She winked.

"Good, you're a smart girl. If you cooperate, get me the information I need, you'll be okay." He sliced through the tape that bound her neck and ankles but left her mouth sealed and her wrists taped together. "Climb up here with me." When she sat at his side, he reached for her purse and dropped it into her lap. "I'll need the key card for your parking garage."

Inside the garage, with the car's interior lights off in anticipation of camera surveillance, he cut the tape off her wrists and pulled the ball gag from her mouth. While giving her a minute to regain control of her jaw muscles, he stripped off his latex gloves. "Remember, one false move on the way in, everybody dies."

In her apartment, once more wearing his gloves, he taped her wrists together in front but left enough slack so she could twist her hands and work her fingers. "Let's see your e-mail files." He went through her current and recently deleted e-mail: nothing from Cervosier. "Where's your phone?"

Her caller ID directory showed no numbers with an out-of-town area code. "Where do you keep your bills?" She directed him to the basket where she kept unpaid bills and the drawer where she tossed them after payment. He sifted through them and pulled out telephone invoices. "I need a name for each number that's listed as out-of-area. Jot the names by the numbers."

"I have to go to the bathroom," she said. "I'm so scared."

"Finish this, and you can do whatever you want."

"I can't, I'm—oh, God." Her face took on a pained expression. A stench filled the room.

The smell, the thought of what she had done, sickened Vlad. "You filthy perv." He stepped away. "Scummy animal. Even pigs know better."

Tears rolled down her checks. "I couldn't help it. You scare me so. May I take off my panties? Rinse myself? I'll just be a minute."

"Do it!" Christ, what an animal. How could he get off terminating a bitch that smelled like shit? "Hurry, goddamnit."

Through the bathroom doorway he watched her step out of the soiled panties. She opened a drawer, and he rushed in and grabbed her wrist. "What are you doing?"

"A candle," she said, sobbing. "I'm just lighting a scented candle to get rid of the smell."

The drawer held a butane-fueled lighter and several short candles, nothing else. Vlad visualized a scene: douse the overheads, impale her with a shish-kebab skewer from her kitchen or a coat hanger from her closet, and watch by flickering candlelight while she bled out. He lit the candle, pocketed the lighter, and backed out of the bathroom to escape the stench.

She moved out of his line of vision, and the shower began running. He gave the candle a minute to burn away the odor and decided to humiliate her by watching her scrub off the shit.

As he approached the bathroom door, smoke alarms blared. At the same time, the door slammed shut.

The bitch, pulling something! He twisted the doorknob: locked. He drew back to kick it open but jumped away when gushing water from the apartment's sprinkler system drenched him. He had to get out. There would be a monitor at the front desk, probably one at the local firehouse. Cops and firemen.

Excited and angry, his clothing soaked but with the girl's telephone invoices in his pocket, he slipped out of the apartment and into the stream of residents making their way down the fire stairs. The bitch couldn't have seen his rental car's license plate. She might have noted the make, but nothing distinguished it from hundreds of other GM junk heaps. At a truck stop on the interstate, he changed out of his wet clothes and, over coffee in the restaurant, scanned the telephone invoices he'd taken from her before she tricked him. He would see her again, he promised himself as he studied the invoices. He liked the small ones best. Yeah, he'd be back.

The most recently paid invoice showed two long-distance calls. A check of the area-code map in the directory at a bank of pay phones revealed the calls were to Connecticut and Colorado. Three a.m., local; that made it six in Connecticut. He tried the number.

"Forsyth residence," said a female voice with a New England accent.

"This is Howard Levant. Sorry to call so early, but Pearl asked me to check on Carmen."

"I beg your pardon?"

"Carmen. The little girl. Pearl wanted me to call."

"There is no one by that name at this residence. Do you wish to speak with Pearl's mother?"

Vlad hung up. With nothing to do for the next few hours, and too hyped to sleep, he got back on the freeway. Guessing he would hit pay dirt in Colorado, he headed northeast until well after daylight. He stopped for breakfast in Green River, Utah, a couple of hours from the Colorado border, and dialed the Colorado number. A woman answered with a simple, "Hullo?"

"Hi," Vlad said. "This is Larry." He let silence hang on the line.

"You wanna talk to Jason? He's done left for work."

"That's okay, I'm just checking on Carmen. She all right?"

The woman's voice brightened. "Lord, yes. She's runnin' and playin' nonstop. Eats like a horse. Wish we could keep her forever."

"I'll pass the word that you're taking good care of her."

"You tell Hank we want to see him, too. Real soon."

Vlad rented a motel room, plugged into the Internet, and downloaded a reverse telephone directory for Colorado. The phone number had been issued to Jason Fox, on a rural postal route near Eldora. He loaded MapQuest and checked travel time from Green River to Eldora. Figuring he could do it in five hours, he decided to catch a nap.

An hour later, still wide awake, he showered, dressed, popped an amphetamine capsule, and hit the road. He would reach Eldora around noon.

Cruising through the Rockies near Grand Junction shortly after sunup, he thought about the little blonde in Vegas. He had her full name from the telephone invoices, so she'd be easy to trace even if she moved. If she tried hiding out, he'd get her mother's address from a reverse directory for that town in Connecticut and track the little cunt through the back door, so to speak. Drive her to a remote place so he could let her scream, take his time with her and—the blast of an air horn sounded like it was in the car with him. He wrenched the steering wheel to swerve away from the sound and, coming wide awake, realized he had drifted into a semi's path on a downhill grade.

Minutes later, his eyelids grew heavy again. He had a whole vial of amphetamines, though, enough fuel to keep him going until he finished with Cervosier. Then he'd crash for twenty-four hours before heading back to take up where he'd left off in Vegas.

CHAPTER TWENTY-ONE

ON THE DAY BEFORE Shelby's planned trip to retrieve Carmen, she skipped her morning training to help the family harvest winter fodder for their goats and sheep. With a blade attached to his tractor, Leonard had mowed a field of tall grass, and the fallen forage had baked in the sun for several days. Now, while everyone else did the milking, animal feeding, and after-breakfast kitchen cleanup, he raked the hay into rows with a tractor-drawn rake. Throughout the rest of the day, he used the tractor to pull a high-sided trailer along the rows while the family tossed in hay with pitchforks. Each time the trailer's load started spilling over its sides, everyone climbed aboard and rode to the barn, where they pitched the hay from the trailer into the loft. It occurred to Shelby that, had they been using horses instead of Leonard's versatile little tractor, they would have been reenacting a typical nineteenth-century farm family's autumn routine.

First Patrick and then Latica suggested that Shelby do something less taxing. She surprised herself by being insulted that they felt she couldn't handle the work, but within an hour her shoulders and back screamed for relief. By late afternoon, when they pitched the final trailer-load into the hayloft, her whole body felt numb.

They spent the remainder of the day on the porch, drinking iced tea and recuperating. Shelby and Hank played checkers, sitting knee to knee and balancing the checkerboard on their legs. Engrossed in the game and the pleasant sensation of his knees brushing hers whenever one of them leaned forward to make a move, Shelby realized with a jolt that the background voices were gone. "Where did everybody go?"

"Evening chores," Hank said. "Farms have a rhythm of their own. They impose it on you."

"Shouldn't we be helping?" Shelby's exhaustion had morphed into a pleasant tiredness that reminded her of the transformation daily exercise and farm work had made in her body.

"I think they planned it this way." Hank grinned. "A contrivance to leave us alone together. Romantic notions about a May-December mating, I presume."

Shelby caught herself giggling like a schoolgirl and cut it off. Her face grew hot. "That would be Leonard. He's the romantic."

"You've gotten to know the family well."

"I've grown to care a great deal for them."

"They care for you, too. Nobody will say it—sentimentality is difficult. But I hope you know that."

She leaned back in her chair. "I've always thought people who cared for one another shared their feelings. I feel left out."

"Caring is more than that. It's protecting, too."

"That's what you do, isn't it? You've parked the people you care for in this out-of-the-way place and dedicated yourself to keeping them safe."

He tossed the checker pieces into a box and folded the board. "I probably ought to lend Patrick and Leonard a hand."

"Do I make you nervous, talking about feelings?"

"Not at all. It's just that I . . ."

She waited for him to finish. When he didn't, she said, "You've pulled me into your family circle. Am I a part of it?"

"You know why you're here."

"Because we're involved, you said on the bus. But, I don't know. You act as if the present will go on forever, when we both know that's impossible."

He turned gruff. "Nothing is permanent. You're young, but you're old enough to understand that."

"I do understand. That's why I don't want things to be left on hold."

"Nothing's on hold. You're practicing, getting better every day. You'll soon be self-sufficient."

"You're taking care of me. Why do I need to become self-sufficient?"

Taut-lipped, he stood with the checkerboard and box in his hands. "Everyone else is working. We ought to help."

Lying in bed that night, Shelby continued to fret. Hank's behavior, the way he looked at her when he didn't know she was aware of it, told her he cared for her. Yet every time she tried to move their conversation to a personal level, he countered with a reference to life's uncertainty or to her youth.

Maybe it was because of his illness, the primary bone cancer Latica had told her about. But that was being treated, and Latica had said the prognosis was excellent. It could be the nature of his work, the danger involved. But surely he realized that she had adjusted to life's uncertainties.

Given the way their lives were playing out, the danger of sudden, violent termination they both faced, shouldn't they take and give whatever love and comfort they could, for whatever time they had?

Perhaps he worried that she would demand a long-term commitment: marriage, children, and the proverbial cottage with a picket fence. There should be some way to reassure him about that.

The house had grown quiet except for the occasional creak of aging timbers reacting to changes in humidity and temperature. After watching a moonbeam stab through a window and creep over the floor, Shelby stared at the ceiling and asked herself why she always waited for events to overtake her. Why couldn't she do what Hank had suggested during their road trip? In Las Vegas, he had urged her to reach out to life, to squeeze it, make it respond. "Grab life by the scruff and shake it," he'd said. But he wouldn't reach out to her any more than he already had. The next move was up to her.

She threw back the bedcovers and swung her feet onto the chilly floor. If she thought about it, she would crawl back into bed, so she refused to think. Instead, she reached under her gown to slip off her panties and tiptoed across the hall to his bedroom.

He lay on his back, stretched full-length under the covers. "Are you all right?" he asked, his voice barely above a whisper.

Standing in his doorway, she said, "I'm . . . Yes, I'm okay."

"Are you chilly? Need more cover?"

"I'm lonely. May I get in with you?"

He shifted to the side, fluffed a pillow for her, and threw back the covers. She recognized the gesture as the one she had used in Las Vegas when inviting him to share Pearl's guest bed. Feeling light-headed, she pulled the door shut and climbed in with him.

He lay on his side, watching her. "You sure everything's all right?"

"I don't know. I feel . . ." She twisted to face him. "I thought you might . . . that we . . ." Why couldn't she finish a sentence? She concentrated on regulating her breathing.

He twisted onto his back again and extended an arm. "Come here."

She scooted closer and rested her head on his arm.

Tugging gently, he pulled until their bodies touched, her head snug on his shoulder. "Better?"

"Umm." He wore pajama bottoms but no top. She let a hand trail over his chest and rest on the patch of hair at its center. Bending her knee, she slid a leg across his thighs. He was in his late forties, twenty years her senior, and had undergone three weekly radiation treatments. What if he was impotent? Would he be embarrassed? Angry? That concern vanished when her leg encountered contrary evidence.

His hand glided down her thigh to touch bare flesh where her knee-length gown had ridden up, and her heart began hammering. The hand drifted higher, pushing the gown up over her hips. "You are the most beautiful, most desirable woman I've ever seen," he said, whispering in her ear. The hand roamed over her bottom, and she shivered.

"Cold?" he whispered.

"Not even close." She craved the sensation of flesh against flesh, wanted to feel the heat of him. Grasping the bowknot on the drawstring of his pajamas, she tugged.

He worked the pajamas down far enough to push them off with his feet. On his side facing her, he kissed her. It was gentle, tentative, their lips barely brushing.

His erection, hot enough to scorch, nestled between her thighs, and her belly convulsed. *Breathe*, she reminded herself as his tongue pushed into her mouth.

He rolled her onto her back and worked her gown farther up. "Let's get rid of this."

She raised her arms so he could pull it off over her head. His chest hair tickled her nipples. He shifted again, and the hair tantalized her belly while his lips and tongue made love to her neck, her shoulders, her breasts. Her center, awash with liquid heat, felt forlorn. "Please," she murmured.

His fingertips, barely brushing flesh, danced across her belly and caressed between her thighs. He kissed her navel, his tongue dipping inside and swirling while his fingers pulled and tugged at the fringes of her sex, never quite penetrating.

She grasped his ears with both hands and tugged. "I can't . . . I need . . ."

He spread her thighs, opening her, exposing her. His lips moved again, going lower, going where no lips, no tongue, had ever been, pulling her over the edge.

Her hands, still grasping his ears, no longer tugged. Pushing now, they held him there. Melting, dissolving—oh, precious Mary. Unbearable pleasure. Howling, dying.

The room came back into focus. Hank lay between her splayed legs, his head resting on the inside of her thigh, his thumb caressing her. Her breathing had slowed, but her heart still thudded. The liquidity at her center still boiled.

He shifted, kissed her there again.

"No more, Hank. Not yet. Let me . . ."

He kissed once more, then slid up her body and eased into her, setting up a slow, predictable rhythm that her hips echoed with their thrusts. The gentle loving spawned a gradually magnifying response until it became a rush that started at the locus of contact and boiled up into her belly and spread to her limbs. It loosened her joints so that her feet and her hands fell limp and powerless on the sheet as the flame grew hotter, turning her insides molten, boneless. She hungered for hard, drilling plunges that would tap her core.

He folded her knees to her breasts. His thrusts quickened and grew forceful.

Screaming her surrender, she descended into velvety, primordial blackness.

He turned her body, lifted her, and her head rested once more on his shoulder. "I fainted," she said, whispering.

"Just in time. One of us had to call it quits."

She felt so languorous, so used, that she had to force words out. "Was I loud?"

"Wonderfully loud."

"Do you think the others heard?"

He chuckled. "Anyone within a mile."

Her cheeks burned. "I won't be able to face them."

"They're adults. They've been where we are."

"Where you are, perhaps. It's hard to believe my space has been occupied before."

What now? she wondered. The volcano had erupted; the lava had cooled. She felt wrung out, her bones liquefied. Powerless muscles still quivered. Did he feel the same way? What if he wanted her to go away so he could sleep? Just a few more minutes of warmth and safety, and she would stagger to her bed and give him back his space. She cuddled closer. Just another minute, she promised herself. Only a minute more.

Kitchen sounds, the rattling of pans, pulled her awake shortly after dawn. The smell of brewing coffee wafted into the bedroom. Hank slept on his stomach, his arms clutching his pillow. Sprawled halfway across him and pressed close, she lay with an arm encircling him. She rolled away, and he turned toward her but did not open his eyes.

Where had he tossed her gown? There, on the floor several feet away. She had left her robe and slippers in the other room, by the foldout bed. To retrieve them she would have to cross the central hallway, visible from the kitchen. She hesitated a moment longer and, shrugging mentally, swung her feet onto the floor and pulled on her gown. The entire household must have heard her last night, howling like a wounded animal. Why would anyone be surprised to see her leaving his room?

She pranced across the hallway, the floor frigid on her bare feet. In her room, she slipped on her robe and slippers and ran a brush through her hair, guilt eating at her for oversleeping. She customarily arose at dawn to help Latica start breakfast. Debauchery had turned her into a slug.

Pan-fried potatoes were an invariable breakfast dish, and peeling and slicing them had become one of her morning chores. She entered the kitchen and saw Latica doing it. "I overslept," she said. "Sorry. I can finish that."

"Almost done." Latica set a cup before Shelby and filled it with coffee. The woman's face and her voice revealed nothing of what she might have heard during the night.

Shelby ladled heaping teaspoons of sugar into the coffee. "What would you like me to do?"

"Drink your coffee; wake up. Leonard and Patrick are feeding the animals. You can have breakfast with us or wait for Hank."

If there were going to be recriminations, it would be best to clear the air right away. Better still if Hank slept through it. "We should let him sleep. I'll eat with you guys."

She had finished her coffee, bathed, flossed and brushed her teeth, and dressed by the time the men returned from their chores. Tense as an overstressed spring, she took her place at the table. The men nodded, mumbled good morning, and began devouring eggs, potatoes, and ham. Everybody acted as if nothing unusual had happened. Could they possibly have slept through her shrieking?

After breakfast, while helping Latica with the dishes, she decided to face the issue head-on. "About last night." She concentrated on her dishwashing as she spoke, and avoided the other woman's eyes. "I'm sorry if I offended anyone."

Latica paused in scraping dishes. "I told you my sister died three years ago. Told you Hank never brought anyone to the farm before you. There was only one conclusion we could draw, and none of us understood why you slept in the study."

Shelby felt feverish. She knew her face must look sunburned, and it increased her embarrassment even more. "This is awkward."

"It shouldn't be. Are you protected?"

"Hank protects me. That's why I'm—oh, you mean . . ."

Latica grinned. "No contraceptives?"

"I didn't anticipate the need."

"You should take care of that. You guys still picking up Carmen today?"

"I think so."

"Stop in Grand Junction and ask Hank's doctor to write a prescription. You'll need a morning-after pill, too."

"Morning after?"

"For last night."

"Of course." She felt like a freshman on her first day of high school. "I'll ask Hank to—" He crossed the hall into the study. "He's awake."

Latica filled a coffee cup. "He'll need this. Go."

Shelby wasn't certain how he would feel about their night, and she didn't want to be presumptuous. Maybe he regretted it or felt she had taken advantage of him. Perhaps it had just been recreation. She found him sitting at the computer and placed his coffee by the keyboard. "Good morning."

He lifted her hand to his lips. "Hi. Just about to check my mail." He sipped the coffee. "Delicious, thanks."

"You need to thank Latica. She made it while I overslept."

"She'll excuse you."

"She heard us last night."

Looking up from the computer, he gave her a crooked grin. "They probably heard you in Grand Junction."

The heat came back to her face. "I never thought I'd be a screamer."

He sipped more coffee and studied the computer screen. Shelby sat on the foldout bed, watching him work and basking in the domesticity of the moment. Memory of their night, of the unbearable pleasure that had wrenched shrieks from her and stripped away her consciousness, spawned a warm lubricity between her thighs, a heat that spread through her and made her extremities heavy and languid, her nipples stiff and tingly. Concentrating on the sensations, she barely heard Hank speaking to her.

"Message from Jason," he said.

"Does he mention Carmen?" She stood behind him with her

hands on his shoulders, her chin resting on his head, and read the message on his computer screen:

Something weird is going down. A dude telephones early this morning, tells Sylvia you asked him to check on Carmen. Sylvia didn't mention it until this chick called. She said her name is Pearl. Said some whacko beat her up, pulled a knife on her, and asked about Carmen's sister. She told him nada, but he copied her e-mails and ripped off her telephone bills. She picked up duplicate bills this morning so she'd have our number and could call. I figured you ought to know.

An icy shiver prickled Shelby's scalp. "One of Krystal's people. We have to warn Jason."

Hank composed a hasty e-mail: *The woman who called you is a straight arrow. The guy who called is probably the psycho she warned you about. He can get your address from a reverse phone directory, so you need to get out of there right away. If you have a gun, load it and keep it handy. I'll call your cell phone number within two hours.* He hit the SEND button, then stood and pulled Shelby into his arms. "We'll call them from Grand Junction. Pack a change of clothing."

CHAPTER TWENTY-TWO

THE TRIP TO GRAND Junction in the old Ford Econoline van, usually a pleasure because of the scenery, seemed interminable. When they arrived, Shelby called Las Vegas from a public phone and got Pearl's voice mail: "If you're a close friend, I'll be in touch. If you're just an acquaintance, it's been nice knowing you." The voice mail disconnected without inviting the caller to leave a message.

Hank telephoned Jason Fox and asked if his e-mail had been received. He pulled a pen and a scrap of paper from his pocket and scribbled. "We'll be there ASAP. Don't tell anyone else where you are. Hang tough, buddy."

He hung up and turned to Shelby. "Jason's boss has a ski condo in Eldora. It's empty during the summer months, and Jason checks on it from time to time. He and his family are on their way there."

"You think they're safe?"

"For now. Your friend in Arizona, the one whose phone has been disconnected. Does she know about Carmen?"

"Yes, but she doesn't know I'm running."

"Who does, besides the Arkansas librarian?"

"No one. Other than Krystal, of course."

"Did your Arizona friend know the Arkansas librarian?"

"No, but she sent me a package in care of the library when I first slipped into America."

Hank thrust the telephone receiver at her. "Call the library."

She made the call, and someone told her Elizabeth wasn't available. "When will she be there?" Shelby asked. The answer made her body grow cold. She broke the connection and turned to Hank. "I got her killed."

He caressed the side of her neck. "They say what happened?"

"Just that she isn't there anymore. Tried to get me to leave my name and number."

"Did you call or e-mail her from Pearl's apartment?"

"E-mail, while you were getting our things from the hotel. I didn't want her to worry. I asked Pearl not to tell you."

Hank grasped her hand and led her back to the van. Eldora was approximately 250 miles from Grand Junction. They headed east on I-70 at eighty miles per hour, a speed that strained the old van. Shelby sat hunched over in the seat, sick at heart for her role in whatever had happened to Elizabeth.

Hank rubbed her leg and patted. "You aren't responsible for what happened to your librarian friend." He shifted his hand to the back of her neck and massaged. "And you couldn't know the psycho would get access to her e-mail log. You did nothing wrong."

"He kills so casually. What if he gets to Carmen before we do?"

"There's no way he can find her. Even if he could, he wouldn't hurt her." Hank pulled a handkerchief from his pocket and handed it to Shelby. "He'd want her as bait."

Shelby wiped her cheeks and dabbed at her eyes. "I don't want to live if I get her killed."

"Quit inventing things to worry about."

"Inventing? I didn't invent the bastard that killed Elizabeth, that hurt Pearl. How the hell am I—" Anger had pushed aside her despair, and she realized that had been Hank's intent. Stretching, she kissed his cheek. "Have I mentioned how much I love you?"

"I haven't said the words, either. I think you know."

"I know." She kissed him again. "You're armed, I trust. Did you bring something for me?"

"In my satchel. Behind the seat."

Reaching back through the opening between the seats, she dug in his bag. Her Glock nestled there in a nylon-and-plastic holster. She pulled it free and hefted it. The weapon felt like an old friend.

"You have two full magazines," Hank said. "There's extra ammo in the bag. Your Taurus is in there, too."

"I overlooked it." She dug through the bag and came up with the little .22-caliber, eight-shot revolver. Its holster had short Velcro straps to fit around her ankle. She remembered her surprise when Hank described the penetrating power of the revolver's slender, high-velocity ammunition.

"It's loaded with hollow points," he said. "It isn't nice to think about what they'll do inside a body."

"I'm looking forward to the experiment." She strapped the little revolver to her ankle and pulled her pant leg down over it.

"This guy's a professional," Hank said. "If it comes to that, you can't afford second guesses. If you hesitate . . ."

"I won't hesitate."

He looked at her for a moment and shifted his gaze back to the road. "No, I don't believe you will. Let's talk about this psycho, as you called him. He probably has Jason's address, but there's no way for him to know where they're hiding."

"You figure he'll show up at Jason's place, expecting to find Carmen there?"

"Most likely. But we've moved fast, and he's coming all the way from Vegas. He'll be tied to airline schedules. If he drives, he'll have to stop for a nap. We'll get there ahead of him."

"Let's stake out the place the way you did Elizabeth's house. We'll wait for him, whack him when he shows up."

Hank twisted his face into an exaggerated frown. "Whack him?"

"I don't know your trade terms. What would you say?"

"How about we ice him? Bump him off? Rub him out? Zap him? Waste him?"

"You're teasing me."

"That bother you?"

She grinned. "Why don't we just shoot his ass?"

"Works for me. We'll find an inconspicuous surveillance spot. When he shows, we'll play it by ear."

They reached Jason's cabin by midafternoon. On a country road with no neighbors within hailing distance, the place looked deserted. Hank slowed but drove on by. He made a U-turn, drove back, and parked the van where they could see the cabin's front porch. "Cover me. I'll make sure we got here first."

Darting from the van to a fence post, a bush, a telephone pole, he worked his way to the porch, peered through a window, and disappeared around the house. He was gone a long time, and Shelby's tension ratcheted up until he reappeared, walking leisurely with his weapon holstered.

"Locked up tight," he said. "I scouted the area way beyond pistol range—we're alone. Take the van to the nearest store and buy blankets, water, and food for an overnight stakeout." He handed her his money clip. "I'll wait here in case he shows up."

Worrying that the killer would get there and attack Hank while she was gone, Shelby drove as fast as the curvy road permitted. She made hurried purchases and rushed back to the cabin.

Hank took the wheel and backed the van into a stand of aspen that hid it from the cabin and the road but gave them a clear view. He inspected her purchases. "You bought enough food for a camping trip."

"When I'm nervous, I eat. How long do you think we'll have to wait?"

"If he's coming, he'll get here sometime today and drive around, checking things out. Then he'll wait for dark."

"What do you mean, *if* he's coming?"

"He pumped your friends for information and got nothing but Carmen's name and a couple phone numbers. He'll have other work, a life to live. He might decide not to follow through on this."

"Maybe." She passed Hank the water bottle from which she had been sipping. "Thirsty?"

He drank from the bottle and handed it back. Then he pulled her close. "We'll just sit here and keep an eye on the cabin."

CHAPTER TWENTY-THREE

VLAD FOUND THE FOXES' cabin around noon, just as his Map-Quest route guide led him to expect. Betting that the little blonde in Vegas would contact Cervosier and she'd rush to protect her kid sister, he decided to waste the family and wait inside until Cervosier showed, but he found the place empty and locked. Figuring the occupants had gone shopping, he backed his rental car into a clump of bushes where the lane curved a quarter mile beyond the cabin. Well-hidden but able to see the cabin, he settled in to wait.

He'd been sitting there, buzzed on amphetamines and day-dreaming about how the showdown would play out, when a ratty old Ford Econoline van cruised by, turned, and eased to a stop. A man and woman: the dude driving, the bitch sitting next to him. She had the right hair color for Cervosier, but Vlad didn't get a good look. He dug out his binoculars, collapsible foldaways that took no more space than a pack of cigarettes, and focused on her. It was Cervosier, and she looked even hotter in the flesh than in her digitized photo.

The dude got out of the van, and Vlad trained the binoculars on him. The slut in Vegas hadn't mentioned that the guy was old enough to be Cervosier's daddy. Vlad tracked him with the binoculars as he headed for the cabin, holding a pistol and darting from cover to cover like a movie stuntman. When the old fart stepped into the porch, he would have been an easy target if Vlad hadn't parked so far away. Center the Smith & Wesson's laser beam on him, ease back the trigger, kablam!

When the dude gave her the all clear, the bitch would join him. They would go inside or maybe sit on the porch to wait for whoever lived there. That'd be the time to sneak up on them, put a slug through the guy's head and—*where's he going?* The guy rounded the cabin, and Vlad lost sight of him. Probably checking the back door, looking through windows.

After five minutes, the guy hadn't reappeared. He might be an ex-GI, scouting the way the army taught him. He couldn't secure a quarter-mile perimeter, though. That would take all day, and he'd know an enemy could fall back and sneak in again. He would just check possible hiding places within shooting range, a hundred yards out at most. Vlad relaxed. No possible way for the dude to spot him.

Minutes later the old guy reappeared, approaching the van from the other side of the road. He said something to the bitch, and she drove away. The dude stepped back into roadside bushes.

Vlad considered going after him. The guy wasn't that old, however, and he had a weapon. He might be waiting, planning an ambush. Better to lie low and figure this out.

The van returned maybe an hour later. The man stepped out of the bushes, took the wheel, and backed into a stand of aspen. Dumb bastard thought he could set a trap.

Vlad chuckled. They didn't realize who they were dealing with.

The hours dragged by with Vlad watching the aspen thicket where the couple sat eyeing the cabin. The people who lived there would eventually come home, and Cervosier would visit with them. She'd want them to know she and her sugar daddy were outside, armed and waiting. Maybe the sugar daddy would try to go inside with her. If so, Vlad would center the Smith & Wesson's laser sight on his head and split it like a melon. Without her bodyguard, the bitch would be easy.

The sun dropped behind a mountain peak; the temperature plummeted. Vlad's stomach growled, reminding him that he hadn't eaten in several hours. He'd emptied his water bottle, and who knew how long this standoff might last? Couldn't swallow his bennies without water, but he didn't need them anyway. The excitement was enough to keep him chugging along. When it got really dark, he'd be able to sneak up on their van. They might even fall asleep. He leaned back and closed his eyes. *Relax, give them a little time.*

A noise, some kind of bird or animal, awakened Vlad. Streaks of light on the eastern horizon—he'd slept the night away! No movement around the cabin; no lights inside. The people might be in there sleeping.

No, Cervosier would have alerted them. Everybody would be gone.

Maybe not, though. Cervosier and her sugar daddy might have fallen asleep just as he had. Or they might still be waiting in the aspen grove for the people to come home. Dim morning light had turned their hiding place from black to a gray blob, but even in yesterday's sunlight he hadn't been able to see their van through the trees. He would have to reconnoiter.

He worked the Luger's slide to jack a cartridge into the chamber and slipped out of his rental car, leaving the heavy, cumbersome Smith & Wesson revolver behind. Working his way through the underbrush along the roadway, he made cautious but steady progress toward the aspen grove. He was almost there when engine sounds wafted from their hiding place. The van pulled onto the road and accelerated away.

Cursing, he dashed for his vehicle. Ragged breath and quivering legs forced him to slow his pace to a jog; the van disappeared down the road before he slid into the rental car and cranked its engine. He spun out in the direction of their travel, pushing as hard as he dared on the unfamiliar mountain road. He'd catch up and tail them until he caught the bitch alone or got the drop on her sugar daddy. Squinting in the early-dawn grayness, he willed their taillights to appear.

There! He topped a hill and spotted round taillights characteristic of those old Fords. Wouldn't do to raise suspicion by closing on them too quickly; he tapped his brakes and trailed them for several miles, gradually shortening their lead.

They came to a village, just a wide spot on the highway, but with enough traffic so he could risk getting closer. He inched in behind the taillights, and fury ignited a dull throb in his temples. He'd been following an old Ford pickup.

Disgusted, he made a U-turn and headed back toward the cabin. So close, and he had blown it by parking too far away. He should have stalked them last night in that aspen grove. Should have blasted the sugar daddy and dragged Cervosier out of the van. Crying and begging him to let her live, she would have promised to do whatever he wanted.

One screwup didn't mean he was whipped, though. The people who lived in the cabin would eventually come home. A little of his special persuasion, and they'd tell him where to find the target.

An intersection loomed. He'd been so focused on following those taillights that he hadn't noticed the service station and café when he passed it earlier. With his growling stomach reminding him how long he'd gone without food, he slowed to turn in.

He scanned the cars parked there, and an electric current shot through him. Tromping the accelerator, he drove on by. A quarter mile down the road, he made a U-turn and crept back. There sat the old Econoline van, in full view in front of the café.

CHAPTER TWENTY-FOUR

"I'M DISAPPOINTED WE DIDN'T get him," Hank said, rubbing his thirty-six-hour whisker stubble. Sitting across a table from Shelby in the restaurant where they had stopped for breakfast, he stirred half-and-half into his coffee. "I'd like some payback for your librarian friend. On the upside, Jason's family and Carmen are safe."

Shelby tasted her coffee and ladled in another spoonful of sugar. Like Hank, she regretted missing the assassin, but not out of thirst for revenge. She needed closure, assurance that the man would not pop up after she had let her guard down. "You really think he's given up?"

"Yeah, or he'd have been here by now. Probably got another contract. Might have gotten himself arrested or killed." Hank sipped his coffee. "We talked about you and Carmen staying on at the farm. You make a decision about that?"

"I thought it was settled. We'll stay until you kick us out."

He reached across the table and squeezed her hand. "I want you more than I've ever wanted anything. But I'm in a risky business."

"I know that. I want to be with you as long as I can."

"There's something else. I'm sick."

"I know about your bone cancer, too."

"How did you . . . ?"

"I have sources. But I understand it's early stage, that they can take it out."

"Still, it's dicey. We need to think about—" The waiter brought their food, and Hank fell silent until the young man left. "We need to decide what you'll do if something goes wrong. If I'm no longer there for you."

The concern in his voice pumped a wave of pleasure through her. "You don't believe I can protect myself? I'm armed to the teeth, and you guys nearly killed me with conditioning and practice fighting."

He chuckled. "You're good, all right. I figure you could take me in a no-rules, unarmed street brawl."

"You really think so?"

"It's okay to feel smug about it. I'll tell you something else, if you'll promise not to crow."

They were eating scrambled eggs, bacon, and toast. Shelby paused from spreading jam on her toast. "Crow over what?"

"Latica compared our scores on the firing range. You're way out-shooting me with the Glock. She says you're better than I ever was."

Uncertain whether or not she should feel as good about that as she did, Shelby just grinned. They finished eating, and Hank laid cash on the table with their check.

"How far are we from Eldora?" Shelby asked as they climbed into the van. "I can hardly wait to see Carmen."

"An hour, maybe." He rolled his jacket into a tight ball and handed it to her. "Enough time for a nap. You haven't slept for twenty-four hours."

"Thanks." She reclined her seat as far as it would go and used the jacket to cushion her head against the window. But even with her body dragging, excitement over how things were working out kept her mind humming: safety, reunion with Carmen, the warmth of family at the farm, further bonding with Hank. Just under the surface there lurked sorrow and a mountain of guilt over Elizabeth's presumed death and fear about the fate of her friend in Arizona. Lacking the emotional resources to deal with those feelings at the moment, she kept them firmly suppressed. She sat up and rested a hand on Hank's thigh. "Want me to drive?"

"I'm good. Can't sleep?"

"Too keyed up. It's been four weeks since I've seen Carmen."

He grinned. "You suppose she's still mad at me?"

Shelby caressed his thigh. The feel of muscle flexing under her palm started a tingling deep inside. "No one can stay angry with you. You're too nice a guy. But she'll need lots of attention when we get her to the farm. I'll be busy for a while."

"You looking for excuses to slack off on your training?"

Her fingers slid to the inside of his thigh and worked their way upward. "I'm explaining that you and I might not have a lot of time alone."

"That mean our love life is over after only one night?"

"We'll work something out. But I'm worried about practical issues with Carmen. Medical care, education, playmates."

"Health care isn't a problem. Patrick isn't licensed in the United States, but he's as good a physician as most general practitioners. You know about his contact in Grand Junction for prescriptions."

"Latica said Leonard will do homeschooling."

"At first. After a period of adjustment, we'll enroll Carmen in public school. They have a slew of illegal-immigrant students, and the bus runs by on the road just off the farm. Patrick will tell them he's her grandfather and handle the details. That'll give her some friends, and it will give us more time together."

Shelby's fingers reached their destination, and the feel of his swelling phallus quickened her pulse. She pressed and grinned. "What will we do with this free time?"

"What we're going to stop and do somewhere along this road if you don't quit teasing me."

She pressed again and rubbed. "Who says I'm teasing?"

"I told Jason to expect us in an hour." Hank's voice had grown thick. "Should I call again, say there's been a delay?"

"I think I can relieve your tension without that." She opened her seat belt, rested her cheek on his thigh, and eased his zipper down.

He jerked. "What are you doing?"

"You concentrate on driving. What goes on down here is strictly my business."

CHAPTER TWENTY-FIVE

WITH THE SUN PEEKING over the Rockies, Vlad found it easy to follow the old van when it left the restaurant. He hung close in traffic but kept at least one car between them. On deserted stretches, he dropped back so that he lost sight of them on hills and around curves but picked them up again on the straightaways. Each time a hill or a curve separated them, he noted any crossroad or turnoff so he could double back if he didn't see the van when the road straightened or flattened.

In the service station next to the café, he had bought water and two Hershey's chocolate bars. Fortified with another amphetamine and the candy, he felt godlike. Too bad Cervosier wasn't alone. He could force her off the road on a deserted stretch and overpower her. Her profile pegged her as a killer, but that didn't worry him. Bitches were devious and could be dangerous if you trusted them, but he'd never seen one he couldn't beat into a quivering mass of obedience. Hell, some even juiced up when he hurt them. That enraged him, sluts who thought he played the game for their benefit. It never took long to get past that.

Cervosier's sugar daddy posed a problem, however. The way he'd staked out that cabin showed some smarts.

They were on a straightaway now, and Vlad let them pull ahead. As the distance widened, Cervosier twisted to face the driver. She slumped in the seat so that Vlad could no longer see her, but his imagination filled in the blank. Rage flared, making him grind his teeth. She belonged to him now. She shouldn't be going down on anyone else.

At a stop sign in the village of Eldora, he eased to a stop directly behind them. Both heads visible again. Taking out the dude would be a no-brainer: use the Smith & Wesson with its laser sight, center the red dot on the back of his head, blow his brains out. There were no other cars around, so why not do it? Waste the dude, grab the bitch, and haul ass.

Before he could decide, they pulled away from the intersection, inching along as if looking for something or somebody. They made a right turn onto a side street and pulled to a stop in front of classy condominium apartments. He parked farther down and watched in his rearview mirror as they got out and knocked on a door. When they went inside, he made a U-turn and parked three doors down from them.

CHAPTER TWENTY-SIX

HUGGING CARMEN, SHELBY WATCHED Jason and Sylvia Fox greet Hank as if he were a prodigal brother home at last. They paused long enough to acknowledge her when Hank made introductions but started fawning over him again within minutes. He stooped to embrace their children and turned again to Shelby and Carmen.

With Carmen's legs wrapped around her waist, Shelby held the child close and caressed her back and shoulders. "You remember Hank, don't you, sweetheart?"

Carmen clung tighter, pressing her face against Shelby's neck. "I don't like him. He hurt you."

Shelby stroked her little sister's hair. "Things were mixed up. He was trying to help us."

"He's mean. He took you away."

"He brought me back, though. He wants us to be together."

Carmen loosened her grip and sneaked a look at Hank. Shelby reached out and stroked the side of his face. "We hurt him, too. He just wants to help us. To love us."

Hank smiled at Carmen and asked, "Is Snaggly still with you?"

She leveled her grave, shiny black eyes on him and nodded.

"Do you suppose I could say hello to him? I've missed him a lot."

Carmen turned her gaze back on Shelby.

Shelby set the little girl on her feet. "Go get him. It's all right."

Mounting the stairs slowly, Carmen seemed to question the wisdom of the move, but she must have reached a decision upstairs. She bounded back down cradling the snaggletoothed, clown-faced rag doll in her arms. As she approached Hank, she slowed but kept moving until she was close enough to pass the doll to him.

Squatting, he turned it one way and then another to examine it. "Looks like he's doing okay." He twisted the doll to face him. "You having a good time here, Snaggly?" As if he were listening, he nodded and wrinkled his brow. "I'm sorry I acted so mean when I first met you. There was danger, and I needed to get you away from that place."

Eyes carefully focused on the doll, he nodded again. "Uh-huh. Yes, I liked you more and more as we traveled together. I really hated taking Shelby away, but it was the only way to keep you guys safe. We came back as soon as we could. Shelby loves you more than anything in the whole world, and I love her."

He shifted his gaze to Carmen. "I'm having trouble understanding what Snaggly says."

Carmen giggled. Hank held the doll out to her, and she edged closer to accept it.

"Do you think he understands why we left him with Jason and Sylvia?" Hank rested a knee on the carpet. "Why we had to stay away so long?"

"He kind of understands." Carmen hugged the doll.

"How do you think he feels about it?"

"It's okay. He likes you a little bit."

"That's good." Reaching out, Hank caressed the doll's face. "I like him a lot."

Jason pulled Shelby's attention away by saying, "That setup at the rest stop when I took Carmen, what Hank told you I'd do. I hope you aren't still mad."

Sylvia had been stooping by her daughter, talking with her. She straightened. "What'd you tell her, Jason?"

"We had to make her behave."

Sylvia turned to Shelby. "Honey, what'd they say to you?"

"They threatened Carmen."

"That precious little thing?" Sylvia's voice, already high-pitched, rose an octave. "What'd they say?"

"Now, Sylvia," Jason said, his voice placative. "We just—"

A wave of Sylvia's hand cut him off. "I asked her, not you."

"They did the right thing," Shelby said. "It didn't seem so at the time, but it was. If you know what Hank is involved in . . ."

Sylvia shook her head. "Hank's a real doll, God bless him. But I sure as shootin' don't want to know nothin' about his work. You all hungry?" Not waiting for an answer, she headed for the kitchen. Standing before the open refrigerator, she said over her shoulder, "Hank never does eat enough. Needs a woman to look after him, I'd guess." She began pulling out food and setting it on the counter. "Have you folks some bacon, eggs, biscuits, and gravy in two shakes. How's that sound?"

Shelby, not the least bit hungry, said, "It sounds scrumptious." She pulled Carmen aside and explained that they would be leaving together. She had worried about how her little sister would handle being uprooted again, but a day and a night with five people in the one-bedroom condo had apparently taken its toll. The prospect of a room of her own, layered over Shelby's description of the farm animals, made her eager to go.

Tupper, the Foxes' twelve-year-old son, followed his mother into the tiny kitchen area, open to the living room. "Got any cookies?"

"You get on outta here. Can't you see I'm busy?"

He crowded closer. "We're starving, Mom. Give us some cookies."

"You all can't be hungry; you just ate. Go on, now. Get."

"Give us cookies, and I'll take the kids outside."

"What, you're not a kid? Twelve ain't exactly grow'd up." She dug into a cabinet and pulled out a package of Oreos. "You take them little darlin's straight to the playground," she said as she worked the package open. "Don't you take your eyes off 'em."

Sylvia must have sensed Shelby's misgivings. "It's just across the street," she said. "There's a chain-link fence around it. We don't have traffic, and they've been cooped up all mornin'."

Shelby nodded, and Sylvia refocused on her son. "You hold them babies' hands crossin' the road." Counting aloud, she dropped six cookies into his palm. "Get on out. Scat." As the three children tromped out the door, she said, "They're drivin' me crazy. This little place. If we don't go home soon . . ."

Jason had been talking with Hank in the living area. He turned to his wife. "We're going today, babe. Hank says everything's all right. Can we have some fresh coffee?"

Uncertainty about her friend in Arizona ate at Shelby. The fear that Barbara's telephone had been disconnected because something terrible had happened gave her no rest. She had to find out. "Jason," she said, "do you have an Internet connection I can use?"

"I brought my laptop from the cabin." He set up the computer in a corner of the living area. "You'll have to use the dial-up modem, so it'll be slow."

Shelby logged on to Google and did a keyword search on Barbara Worthington Rogers. Her heart froze as she read headlines from a month-old issue of the *Flagstaff Daily Sun*: "Home Invasion and

Torture Deaths Stun Flagstaff." The article's first paragraph identified the victims as the Reverend Frederick Rogers and his wife of
one year, the former Barbara Worthington.

Abruptly ill, Shelby clamped a hand over her mouth and raced
upstairs to the condo's only bathroom. Squatting, she gripped the
toilet bowl with both hands and vomited. The convulsions lingered
even when there was nothing left in her stomach. She clung to the
bowl as if it were a life preserver in a storm-tossed sea.

"Shelby?" Hank knocked on the bathroom door, softly at first,
then harder. "I'm coming in."

"Go away. I'll be out in a minute."

The door opened. He knelt and wrapped his arms around her.
"It isn't your fault. There was nothing you could do." He lifted her
in his arms, lowered the toilet lid, and sat there cradling her on his
lap. "Terrible things happen. You can't carry the weight of them.
It'll pull you down, as well."

"He tortured them, Hank, trying to find me. And they had
nothing to tell him."

Hank rocked her as if she were an infant. "It's horrible, but
it isn't your fault. You have to tell yourself that over and over—*it
isn't my fault; it isn't my fault.* You've got to bounce back, sweetheart.
Can't let him win by destroying you emotionally."

"He got away with it." Anger pushed back some of her sorrow
and guilt. "He did terrible things and just melted away in the night.
He'll go on with his life, do the same to other people. There's no
way to find him. No way to stop him."

Hank stood and set her on the toilet seat's lid. He dampened
a facecloth and wiped her face. "I have to go downstairs and assure everyone you're okay. You stay here 'til you feel better. Maybe
stretch out on the bed."

"No, I'm functioning." She looked in the mirror and raked fingers through her hair. "Let's go down together."

Downstairs, she asked permission to use the shower, borrowed shampoo and a hair dryer, and went back up. When she came down a second time, Hank took a turn in the bathroom.

Shelby joined Sylvia in the tiny kitchen. "Let me help."

Sylvia patted the kitchen counter in front of a stool. "All done except gravy. You just sit here and have yourself some coffee. We can finish getting acquainted while I do the fixin'."

"Have you guys known Hank a long time?"

"I met him when I dropped out of high school. Jason, he's known his Uncle Hank since . . . why don't you tell her, Jason?"

He had joined Shelby at the kitchen counter. She turned her gaze on him. "Uncle?"

"Not my real uncle. He and my father were high school chums. Hank went on to college, and Dad joined the army. When I was born, he was somewhere in the Middle East. Hank stood in for him, did the Lamaze thing with Mom, assisted at my birth, the whole bit. Dad was an only child, and Mom just had a sister. They drafted Hank as my uncle."

Shelby felt a stab of envy. She had known Hank such a short time, and Jason had known him forever. "Even for nephew and uncle, you seem close."

"When I was in high school, Dad served another tour in the Middle East. He got killed. Mom needed help, and I guess I needed guidance. Hank was there with both."

"You needed guidance?" Sylvia laughed. "An ass kickin' was what you needed." She had sprinkled flour into hot bacon drippings. As she talked, she poured milk into the skillet while stirring furiously. "Jason was fightin', stealin'. He near 'bout raped me.

Got me pregnant when we was fifteen."

Uncomfortable with the conversation, Shelby stared into her coffee cup. *Come downstairs, Hank.*

"I was pretty wild," Jason admitted. "Hank straightened me out about Sylvia and the baby. He was best man at our wedding. He started checking my grades, giving me hell when they lagged. He practically shanghaied me into college. Helped with finances all the way through. He's godfather to both our kids."

"You folks getting along all right?" Hank said from the stairway. Downstairs, he kissed Shelby and sniffed her freshly shampooed hair. "You smell good."

A dab of shaving cream had stuck to his ear. She speared it with a finger and wiped it on a napkin. "I'm learning about your previous life."

He clapped a hand on Jason's shoulder. "Don't believe anything this juvenile delinquent tells you."

"Ex-juvie," Sylvia said. She poured the gravy into a bowl and set everything on the table. "After Hank got on his case, you wouldn't believe what a straight arrow Jason turned into. Got his college degree in three years. Done so good they asked him to stay and get his master's free of charge. He works at the Boulder Institute for Natural Habitat Studies, figurin' out where wild critters live."

Shelby listened and picked at her brunch, trying to be a good guest. After the meal, Hank and Jason huddled over another cup of coffee. Then Hank declared it was time to leave. "If we start now, we can reach the farm before dark."

Sylvia asked Jason to herd the children back inside to say good-bye. "They've got to learn manners." While waiting, she shared her secret of mixing bacon and sausage drippings to put extra flavor in gravy. After several minutes she said, "Where's Jason and them kids?"

Shelby grew uneasy waiting for Jason to bring the children in-side. She knew her anxiety was just an echo emotion from learning what that man had done to Barbara and her husband, and she tried to ignore it. Yet minutes ticked by, and the anxiety surged.

Hank finished his coffee and slid off his stool. "We need to hit the road."

Sylvia pulled a sweater off a peg by the door. "I'll walk with you. Jason's probably out there playin' with the kids. Sometimes he acts like he ain't fully growed up."

As Hank reached for the doorknob, it turned. The door opened, and Jason stepped inside gripping his son's arm. Polly trailed be-hind, staring at the floor.

Shelby's heart slammed against her ribs. "Where's Carmen?"

Looking down at his son, Jason said, "Tell them what you told me."

CHAPTER TWENTY-SEVEN

AFTER PARKING SEVERAL DOORS down from the condominium, Vlad fidgeted for half an hour, keeping his eye on the front door. Abruptly, his prospects improved and his mood lightened: kids coming out. A boy, preteen, with two baby bitches. He guessed the girls to be somewhere between five and ten years old, about right for Cervosier's kid sister.

Holding hands, the children trooped across the street to a fenced playground. The girls climbed onto the outer ledge of a circular platform and grasped a metal bar. The boy scrambled over the platform and into the spokes that held everything suspended from a central pole. He pushed; the platform turned. The girls squealed their delight.

Vlad jotted his stolen cell phone's number and a brief note on a scrap of paper. From his overnight bag he chose a wig with curly black hair. He popped another benny and poured his remaining bottled water onto the ground to create mud, which he smeared on the rental car's license plate to obscure the number. He eased the vehicle next to the playground gate and called the boy over. "I'm Constable Fielding. This playground's closed. You kids have to leave."

"Why is it closed?" the boy asked.

Vlad shrugged. "They told me to make sure nobody uses it."

"We're just playing for a few minutes, so the grown-ups can talk."

"You have to leave now. Otherwise, you're all under arrest."

Keeping a tight lid on his temper, Vlad waited with his car door open while the boy talked to the girls. All three walked slowly toward the gate. The boy looked sullen, the girls apprehensive. They had to form a single file to walk between the car and the playground's chain-link fence. When the gate swung shut behind them, Vlad blocked their way. He handed the note to the boy. "Give this to your sister."

The boy passed the note to the blond-haired girl, and Vlad grinned at the dark-skinned one, some kind of mixed breed. To the boy he said, "You know the man and woman that went into your house a few minutes ago? You and your sister give the woman that note."

He let the boy and the little blonde ease by, but he grabbed the mongrel and threw her into his car. It was a two-door, so tossing her into the rear seat left her trapped. As he drove away, his heart beat extra fast. They wouldn't dare call the cops, but he would stay on back roads and keep moving to play it safe. Payday, a long time coming, was just around the corner.

CHAPTER TWENTY-EIGHT

"Go on," Jason insisted, nudging Tupper. "Tell them what happened."

"A man took her," the boy said. He had been crying and was barely understandable through gasps and hiccups. "Said to give you that note."

Jason clutched a slip of yellow paper. He handed it to Hank.

Hank scanned the note. "How long ago?"

"A little while." Tupper started crying again. His sister joined in. "We were too scared to come in," the boy sobbed. "I knew I was supposed to take care of her."

Shelby snatched the note from Hank. As she read, she couldn't get enough air. Printed in block letters that looked like a child's scrawl, the message started with a telephone number. Below the number, Carmen's abductor had scrawled, "CaLL me iF you WaNt the BaBY BitcH to Keep BReathiNG."

Hank tried to get a description of the man, then of the car, but gave up. Tupper could only say the man had shaggy black hair and the car was a dark color and looked new. When they tried to question Polly, she just cried harder.

"Ohmagod," Sylvia cried. "We gotta call the cops."

"No," Hank said. "If the police stop him, he'll murder Carmen in a heartbeat." He dialed the number and handed the phone to

Shelby but leaned close to hear.

"Cervosier?" a male voice asked.

"Yes," Shelby said, keeping rigid control of her voice. "Who are you?"

"What's important is who I have with me. Can you hear her?"

Carmen's sniffles in the background made Shelby want to scream into the telephone, to demand that the pervert leave her sister alone. Clamping down on the impulse, she kept her voice level. "What did you do to her?"

"Belt-whipped her ass. She's a sharp little bitch, learns fast. Right now, she's licking my balls. Guess what she's gonna do when I hang up?"

"I . . . you . . ." Shelby's mind shut down. She was barely aware of Hank lifting the phone from her hand. He talked, but his words didn't register. She felt cool dampness on her face and realized Sylvia had sat beside her, was wiping her forehead with a wet cloth.

Sylvia pulled the facecloth away. "Feelin' better?"

Shelby rubbed at her damp forehead with the back of her hand. "What does that man want?"

Hank, squatting before her, gripped her hand. "He wants you."

Of course he wanted her. And he had won by zeroing in on her weak spot. "Okay."

Frowning, Hank chewed his lip. "I can't let you—"

"He beat Carmen," she said, cutting him off. "Said he's making her—" Shelby's voice broke. She took the washcloth from Sylvia and wiped her own face.

Hank massaged her hand, patted it. "He lied. Trying to get to you."

"Call him back. Tell him—" The ringing of the phone cut through her words.

"He said he'd call back," Hank said. "You've got to be tough." He handed her the phone. "Keep it together for Carmen's sake."

She clutched the phone. "This is Cervosier."

"I figure you're too smart to call the cops," the man said. "But I'll keep this short to be safe. You know what I want?"

"I know."

"If I don't get you, I'll train the kid to be a kinky fuck and sell her."

"She's just a baby."

"That's what makes it profitable."

Hank's hand on her shoulder, his fingers squeezing, steadied her. "Let her go," she said, "and tell me where to meet you."

The man laughed. "You're insulting my intelligence."

"An exchange, then. A neutral spot with no one around. Carmen and I both start walking."

"Like in those old spy movies? I'll get back to you."

"Wait! Let me speak to . . ." Realizing that she was talking to empty space, she let the phone dangle.

Hank took it from her. "You can't ransom her with your life. It won't work."

"I don't know what else to do."

"He has no reason to harm her. But killing you will earn him twenty-four grand."

"What he's threatened to do to her is worse than death."

"If he's a person who would do that to a little girl, what makes you think he'll give her up when he gets you?"

"I'll depend on you to make sure he does."

Hank paced the condo, running his hands through his hair. "Jason, you could make the exchange. I'll hide in your car. When he shows, I'll pop the bastard."

Jason pursed his lips. "If you miss, he'll kill somebody."

"If I can't get off a clean shot, we'll follow him. He'll keep Shelby alive while he looks for a disposal site. Long enough for me to take him out."

"He might *plan* on keeping her alive. That'll change if he spots a tail."

"We'll have to make sure he doesn't. Can't chance losing him, though."

"We could rig a GPS tracking device."

"What's that?" Shelby asked.

"Global Positioning System," Jason explained. "Microchip gets a signal from three satellites, triangulates, and tells where you are. The gizmos are small. We could plant one on you."

"We might be able to buy a setup in Denver," Hank said. "We'd have to stall this guy until tomorrow."

They wanted to leave Carmen with that madman overnight? Shelby's heart, already galloping, shifted into overdrive. "We can't wait that long."

"No need," Jason said. "At the research station we track wolves to study their range. We've got these GPS collars we put on 'em. A satellite beams their coordinates to our station. Just stall the guy for a couple of hours while I bring a collar home and cut the electronics off. You carry that sucker, we'll get a fix on you every five minutes."

As it turned out, they didn't have to stall the kidnapper. He insisted on waiting until nighttime to make the exchange. "I know your driver will be armed," he told Shelby. "I'm not dumb enough to give him a target. I'll call you back after dark, give you a location."

The GPS collar looked like a heavy dog collar with a small transponder attached. Jason used hedge clippers to cut away the leather. "The battery lasts about a week," he said as he worked.

"What's the range?" Hank asked.

"That isn't a problem. A communications satellite picks up the signal and transmits the coordinates to our server. It'll work anywhere except underground or in a cave or a building with a dense roof, like thick concrete. The problem will be getting the information to you. I'll have my buddy monitor the computer and pass the coordinates on."

"How's he going to do that? This guy will head into the mountains. You get a few miles off the freeway, there's no cell phone service."

"My SUV's got a two-way radio. We might hit some dead spots, but you'll be able to pick up his signal most of the time."

"I don't like it." Hank pursed his lips. "Not much choice, I guess."

"There's another wrinkle: the GPS location coordinates are in latitude and longitude." Jason held up a government survey map. "We can find them on this, but translating them into positions on a road map could get dicey."

The kidnapper called an hour after midnight and told Hank to drive to a freeway off-ramp deep in the mountains. "Carry a cell phone. Call me when you're in position, and I'll lead you to the exchange site."

"You called it right," Jason said. "He's picked an ultimate location where cell phones don't work. Guess he didn't think about radios."

"He'll probably stay in shadows during the exchange," Hank said. "No way to get a shot at him. Be nice to have you as a backup anyway."

Jason nodded. "However you want to play it."

"Why don't you follow me in another vehicle? Hang back so the guy doesn't spot you. We'll stay in radio contact."

With Sylvia's help, Shelby taped the tiny GPS transponder to the inside of her thigh. The only tape in the condo was an old roll of medical adhesive, and they had trouble anchoring the device to her skin. It made a slight bulge under her loose-fitting jeans, but not enough to be obvious. In the dark and with the tension the kidnapper would be under, everybody agreed he was not likely to notice. On the ankle of her opposite leg, she strapped the holstered, .22-caliber snub-nosed revolver Hank had designated as her back-up weapon. They decided the Glock would be too obvious, and it might prompt the kidnapper to search for other weapons. "He doesn't know you've been trained," Hank said. "Let's not give him any clues."

They traveled in a two-car convoy, Shelby and Hank in a radio-equipped Chevy Blazer borrowed from the research institute, Jason in his old Volkswagen Camper. Two miles from the designated off-ramp, Hank called Jason on the radio. "Pull over and douse your lights."

"Wilco. Standing by."

Hank dialed the kidnapper's cell phone. "We're almost to the off-ramp."

"Exit there and head south," the kidnapper said. "Stay on the line."

Hank made the turn, and the man said, "Blink your lights." A dark-colored sedan pulled onto the road behind them, accelerated, and whipped around the Blazer. "Follow me. When you see my blinkers, stop and turn off your lights."

While Shelby held her palm over the telephone, Hank called Jason on the radio. "We're heading south on State Road One-oh-three. Let's give the GPS a trial run."

Another voice came over the radio. "Ralph here, at the station. I've got the signal." He read off latitude and longitude in degrees and minutes.

Silence for several moments. "That would be right," Jason said. "I figure it close to Highway One-oh-three and maybe four miles off the freeway."

They followed the sedan for several minutes, and *No service available* appeared on the cell phone's display. At a spot where the winding road straightened and leveled for a short distance—Hank guessed they were five miles from the freeway—the lead car's blinkers began flashing. Hank stopped on the edge of the road but kept the engine running. The kidnapper backed, turned, and eased his sedan forward until it faced them maybe fifty yards away. He put his headlights on high beam.

Hank patted Shelby's knee. "Here we go." Leaving the Blazer running and its headlights on, he slid out and stood by the door.

Shelby followed but stepped in front of the Blazer's lights so Vlad could see her. A three-quarter moon in a cloudless sky painted the mountains with a hard, silvery luminescence, but the headlights' glare made everything seem dark outside their arc.

"I'm Vlad the Impaler," someone shouted from the void behind the other vehicle's headlights. The voice was high-pitched but recognizably male. "You made a big mistake fucking with me."

"I'm Ivan the Terrible," Hank shouted back.

No response for a moment. "All right, smart guy. You just

upped the slut's pain quotient. Turn off your lights."

"So you can see to take a potshot at me? Not likely."

"You try following me after we make the switch, I'll gut her, let her die real slow."

"Let's get on with it."

"Start walking, bitch. Arms stretched out shoulder high."

"I walk when Carmen walks," Shelby said.

With Vlad's headlights behind her, Carmen appeared as a silhouette. Shelby stepped back to give Hank a hug and started to turn away.

He held onto her. "I don't like this," he whispered.

"It's all we can do, Hank. You'll pull it off." She twisted free and walked toward Vlad's headlights. As she and Carmen neared each other, she said, "Walk on by me, sweetheart. Hank's waiting for you. When you're behind me, run to him."

Carmen didn't answer. When they were mere feet apart, she flung herself at Shelby.

Squatting, Shelby hugged her.

Engines revved. Vlad's headlights moved.

"Run, sweetie," Shelby urged. "Run to Hank."

Carmen, her body shaking, clung tighter.

Aware that the Blazer had also started moving, Shelby snatched Carmen off the ground. Hank was trying to cut Vlad off, but he was too late. The psychopath would reach them first.

As Vlad's headlights closed on her, she feinted to the left. The headlights veered in that direction, and she leaped to the right but tripped and fell. Holding her trembling sister close, she shut her eyes.

Engine sounds became deafening. Headlights seemed blinding even through her clenched eyelids. She had the sensation of lying on a busy freeway.

Eyes open again, headlights no longer blinding her. Vlad had missed them. Hank passed them also, veering to the other side.

Stunned by the brush with death, Shelby scrambled to her feet. She held Carmen in her arms and stood frozen.

Glowing taillights. Tires skidding on gravel as the vehicles ground to a halt. Both vehicles moving again, one turning, the other backing. Which way to run?

Hank's Blazer hurtled in reverse, engine screaming, tires spinning and then grabbing traction. It broadsided Vlad's sedan. The crash sounded as if the world had cracked open.

Both vehicles together now, their rear wheels off the road. Headlights washing away the night. Hugging Carmen to her breasts, Shelby dashed for a ditch on the other side of the road.

Gunshots. Bullets kicked up gravel in her path.

She skidded to a halt and crouched on the road, her chin tucked against her chest, her arms squeezing Carmen. Moisture on her hand, slick where it gripped her sister's thigh. She glanced down, and her heart froze. Carmen had been shot.

CHAPTER TWENTY-NINE

"STAY WHERE YOU ARE," Vlad shouted. "You try to run, the next round goes in her back."

Squatting, Shelby tried to shrink in the headlights' glare. The vehicles sat on the edge of the road, coupled where they had collided, their rear wheels in the ditch, their headlamps angling across the road, bathing it in light.

Hank crouched in the protection of the Blazer's front fender, peeking over it to see Vlad's wrecked sedan. If he tried to help them, he would also be highlighted by the headlamps, an easy target. "Hank," Shelby said, "stay there."

The blood running down Carmen's leg did not extend above thigh level; that would be where the bullet had entered. How much damage had it done? Hank's lecture during her introduction to firearms flashed though Shelby's head: shock keeps a wound from hurting for thirty minutes or longer. "Carmen," she whispered. "Can you hear me, sweetheart?"

No answer, but the thin little arms tightened around her neck. She returned the pressure. "That's right, baby, hang on to me. You're going to be okay."

"If you get up off that road," Vlad screamed, "you and the kid are buzzard meat."

Shelby hugged Carmen tighter and whispered in her ear, "Don't be scared. Hank will help us."

"Back off into the trees," Hank called to Vlad. "It's your chance to keep breathing."

"Cervosier," Vlad said, "leave the kid on the road and walk over here." The shrillness had disappeared from his voice. He sounded confident. "Tell her to stay put. If she moves, I'll shoot both of you."

In the headlights' glare, Shelby checked Carmen's wound. Blood trickled from a hole in the child's thigh and gushed from an exit wound on the other side. Looking in the direction of Vlad's voice, she said, "I'll do what you say."

"Stay where you are," Hank shouted. "If he shoots you, I'll take him out. He can walk away and live. It's a trade-off."

"She's bleeding, Hank." Shelby spoke to Carmen in as soothing a voice as she could manage: "Wait here, sweetheart. Hank will take you to a doctor." Carmen whimpered but obeyed, and Shelby kissed her for what she knew was the last time. "Don't try to stand. Just sit still until Hank picks you up."

"You try to run," Vlad shouted as Shelby pushed to her feet, "I'll snuff the kid. When you're over here, your sugar daddy can get her."

"Take care of her, Hank," Shelby said as she walked past where he crouched. "I love you." She rounded the vehicle where Vlad waited. The curly black hair Tupper had described had been a wig; the man was bald. Even so, he looked young. She guessed late twenties.

"Turn around," he ordered. "Face away from me."

A tearing sound, and he wrapped tape around her wrists, binding them behind her. He slapped tape over her mouth and, with an arm around her throat, backed her into the darkness where trees blocked the moonlight. More strips of tape. He wrapped one around her neck to make a collar. Another became a leash. He used it to drag her into the undergrowth.

No sounds of pursuit. Hank would be tending to Carmen.

Crossing the mountainside in a headlong dash without her hands for balance, dragged along by the makeshift leash, Shelby fell repeatedly. Each time, Vlad used her hair as a handle to jerk her to her feet. The tape over her mouth forced her to depend on what air she could get through her nose, and her lungs burned. Her racing heart felt as if it might burst. She was going to pass out, and the lunatic would kill her right there on the mountainside.

She drifted in and out of consciousness, but managed to keep walking. They paused at the foot of a grass-covered slope. Vehicle sounds, the roar of trucks—a highway.

Vlad dragged her up to the road and flung her down on the shoulder inches from the side stripe. "You try to move, I'll put a round through your knee." He crouched behind a guardrail that hid him from the road.

Approaching headlights shifted to the inside lane as they closed on Shelby. A tractor-trailer rig whooshed by and moved back to the outside lane. In the abrupt darkness following the wash of light and air, Shelby twisted, trying to reach her ankle holster. No good, her fingertips barely touched the weapon.

Another set of headlights approached. The car zinged by within an arm's length and braked with a drawn-out screech of rubber on pavement. The driver backed along the shoulder and stopped a few feet away. He leaped out. "Hey," he shouted, and walked toward her.

She wanted to scream a warning, wanted to tell him to get back in his car, lock the doors, and go, go, go. All she could do was grunt through the tape over her mouth.

"You sick?" the man asked. He leaned over her. "My God. Somebody tied you up. You okay?"

He reached for the tape on her mouth, and Vlad shot him through the head. Five quick steps took the killer to the car. He jerked open the passenger door and dragged out a writhing, screaming woman. "Be still," he said, and shot her in the face.

Another set of headlights appeared. Holding the pistol behind his back, Vlad smiled and waved. The car whizzed past, and he shot the woman again.

He rolled both bodies down the freeway embankment. "Transportation," he said cheerfully, and jerked Shelby to her feet. He hustled her to the car, shoved her in through the driver's side, and slid in beside her.

She wriggled all the way across the bench seat. Turning her back to the passenger door, she tried to open it with her taped hands.

Vlad slammed the butt of his pistol against the side of her head. When she regained her senses, he had taped her ankles together and fastened them to her wrists behind her. She lay facedown on the floor between the engine's firewall and the seat with her head on the hump that divided the driver and passenger sides. The car bounced and accelerated. They were back on the freeway.

"Buick Roadmaster," Vlad said. "Big land yacht. Handles like a truck but rides like a waterbed."

Lying on her stomach with her head twisted to the side, Shelby could see nothing but his foot on the accelerator. Her mind centered on Carmen, bleeding in the glow of headlights from wrecked cars. Then her thoughts skipped to the man and woman the psychopath had just shot. Were they dead, or perhaps lying there wounded and alone in the weeds below the freeway, suffering as their lives drained away? Would Hank get Carmen to a hospital before she bled to death? This man killed so casually. If the GPS worked, he would probably shoot her the instant he realized Hank was tracking him.

Vlad got her attention by dangling her little .22-caliber revolver between his thumb and forefinger an inch from her nose. "What were you planning to do with this? You even know how to use it?" He pulled it away and patted her cheek. A muted click, and music drifted down on her. He found a classical station and sighed. "May as well relax. We've got some ground to cover."

She lost track of time. Her head felt numb where he had hit her, as if someone had injected a Novocain shot into her temple. Blood trickled from her hairline across her cheek. The numbness dissipated, and her head throbbed. They turned off the freeway, and every bump and pothole threatened to wrench her back and scramble her brain.

The car made a sharp turn. Crunching sounds from the wheels: a gravel road. The engine labored and then idled as they went up and down steep grades. Shelby counted, trying to establish a time interval between turns, but the road twisted so much she couldn't distinguish between an intersection and a switchback.

Vlad braked hard, then eased the car forward. A clattering sound filtered through the floor, reminding Shelby of the loose-planked bridge her chauffeur had crossed daily when driving her to and from parochial school during her childhood in Haiti. The clatter stopped. Within seconds they turned onto a rutted, potholed road and eased down an incline that required constant braking. The road twisted like a writhing snake. It leveled and straightened, and the Buick's engine labored; they were climbing again, slowly.

They stopped. Vlad turned off the engine and the headlights and clicked on a flashlight that was no larger than a bulky pen. He flashed the beam in her eyes and ran it over her bindings. "Make yourself comfortable while I check our accommodations." He slid out of the car and walked away, whistling.

Hank had promised to track them with the GPS, but the Blazer had looked too badly damaged to operate. With only one usable vehicle, he and Jason would have to choose between following Vlad or taking Carmen to a hospital. The way Carmen was bleeding, surely they had chosen the hospital. "Please, God," Shelby prayed, "let her be all right."

If they had driven to a hospital, it would be several hours before they picked up Vlad's trail. *I'll be dead by then.* But they were in radio contact with the man at the research station, and the GPS would tell him the shooting's exact location. Hank might have asked him to send an ambulance and left Jason with Carmen. He could be slipping up on Vlad that very moment.

Then again, maybe not. Jason had warned that translating the GPS coordinates into locations on a road map would be tricky. Hank might have gotten lost.

Having found her ankle holster, Vlad would eventually search her for other weapons. If he found the GPS transponder, he would know their movements were being monitored. He would disable it and drive away or set a trap for Hank. She had to get rid of it, hide it in the car in case they started moving again. Straining until her muscles screamed, she tried to reach the device. No luck.

She and Sylvia had fastened it to the inside of her thigh with adhesive tape, but they'd had trouble making it stick. Rubbing her thighs together, she tried to loosen it. Again and again she rubbed. Her thigh became raw, but the transponder seemed to be shifting. She paused, concentrated on forcing air through swollen nostrils, and started again.

The passenger door opened, startling her. The courtesy light blinded her. Vlad jerked the tape off her mouth. "What's making you antsy, cunt?"

She gulped great mouthfuls of fresh mountain air, and her lungs wanted to sing. But her heart misfired with the realization that the transponder still clung to her leg.

"You dancing to an inner tune?" Vlad asked. "Can't be still like a lady?"

"I need to pee. You have to untie me."

"Piss in your pants, pussy." Laughing, he grabbed her ankles and pulled her out of the car.

Her chest and stomach slammed against the ground, knocking the breath out of her. Not pavement or gravel, more like hard-packed dirt. A looming shadow—a building. No lights anywhere. Her head wound throbbed anew.

He cut the tape that bound her ankles. With her hands still taped behind her, he hauled her to her feet. "Let's go."

Her legs refused to work. She started to collapse.

He steadied her. "You gonna walk? Or do I drag you?"

"I'll walk." Circulation returning to her legs sent needle-sharp pains through them, but they supported her. She concentrated on moving them.

Trailing behind her, Vlad directed her over a wooden foot-bridge. He shoved her along a narrow pathway toward what moonlight confirmed was a building. He illuminated the trail with his penlight, but the three-quarter moon, hanging like a giant lamp in the western sky, rendered it superfluous.

The GPS transponder, no longer securely taped to her thigh but not entirely free, wobbled and bobbed. Swinging her hips, she rubbed her thighs together with each step, trying to loosen it further. It dropped a couple of inches inside the leg of her jeans, as if hanging by a single piece of tape. Two more thigh-scraping steps, and the tape gave way. The device worked its way down her leg, falling a few inches with each step. At some point it would drop onto the path, directly under Vlad's feet.

It slid past her knee. Holding her breath, she faked a stumble as it hit the side of her foot. She collapsed on the path, sitting back so Vlad would have to stop or step over her. Scraping the path with her hands, still taped behind her, she felt for the little device. Nothing there.

"Get up, you clumsy piece of tail." Vlad twisted his fists in her hair and lifted.

She made herself a deadweight and dragged her fingers across the path. Her scalp felt as if it was separating from her head. She screamed in frustration and pain.

He laughed again. "Make all the noise you want. Nobody's gonna hear." Pulling harder, he lifted her just as her fingers touched the transponder.

Unable to grasp it, she slapped at it as she came to her feet. Stumbling and shuffling, she tried to kick where she had slapped with her fingers. No contact. Was it on the path, or had she knocked it off the walkway?

A shove from Vlad, and she stumbled on. The building that had been a dim outline became a looming, moon-washed ruin of raw wood and corrugated tin. "What is this place?" she asked.

"Old mine. It played out a long time ago, but nothing rots in this dry air." He laughed. "You'll have company. About a year ago, I brought a date up here. Dumped her in the shaft after I finished. She lasted a long time, though. I'd love to have gotten her on tape."

A shudder racked Shelby as she imagined a woman much like

herself, frightened and alone with this fiend, screaming away the final hours of her life. Now, it was her turn. *Don't give up. Hank is out there somewhere.*

Vlad forced open the shed's squeaky-hinged door and ushered her inside. Moonlight stabbing through an empty window frame made the inside seem darker. Vlad played his penlight's beam over the interior, an empty, high-ceilinged and dirt-floored square maybe fifteen-by-fifteen feet.

He faced Shelby, and his penlight's beam reflected off a knife in his other hand. Her heart flip-flopped. *He's going to butcher me.*

"Be still," he said, and began slicing her clothing. In less than a minute she stood naked except for her socks and shoes and the empty ankle holster. He flashed his penlight into a corner. "Sit over there."

Awkwardly with her hands still taped behind her, she eased her aching body to the ground, stretched out her legs, and leaned back against the wall. The rough-hewn planks scraped her back, and pebbles on the dirt floor dug into her, but exhaustion dulled her senses. She just wanted to rest.

Holding a three-foot length of wooden plank, Vlad knelt before her. He propped his penlight on the floor and whittled the board's ends into arcs. Duct tape completed circles to create stocks that imprisoned her ankles and held her legs apart. He hooked her duct-tape collar to something on the wall behind her, immobilizing her. Humming as he worked, he pulled off her shoes and socks.

"You made it really hard on your friends, Shelby, running from me the way you did." He flashed the penlight on her face, blinding her. "That one in Arkansas, the librarian, was a tough old bird. Almost took me out. Not so tough at the end, though. I cut off her air and held her eyes open so I could see the moment her soul took wing."

He focused the light on Shelby's vagina. "Your cunt reminds me of that preacher's wife in Arizona. Same hair color, lips puffy like hers." He hefted a breast with the back of the knife blade. "She had bigger tits. Humongous nipples. You should have heard her when I worked on 'em with my pliers. Ever hear a boar hog squeal when they're cutting his nuts out? That's how she sounded."

Shelby bit her lip to stay quiet. He wanted her to fall apart. She wasn't going to give him that satisfaction.

Keeping the light focused on her face, he worked the knife's handle into her vagina. "I straightened a coat hanger, cut off its tip at an angle to make it sharp." He twisted the knife handle to force apart dry tissue. "I rammed it—goddamnit!"

He had dropped his penlight. It rolled into a hole dug by an animal or eroded by storm water. Cursing again, he withdrew the knife and used it to reach into the hole, which ran under the building's wall. The penlight was beyond his reach.

He shoved the knife into its scabbard and got to his feet. "Be right back." Moving slower without the light, he left the shed.

Shelby pulled with all her strength, testing the tape that held her wrists and her neck. No give, no chance. Where was Hank? Had the plan to follow her with the GPS failed? The whole thing had seemed so complicated: the satellite transmission, the conversion from geographic coordinates to road map locations, the radio relay. Too many variables. Too many ways for things to go wrong.

Tiny pebbles on the dirt floor had merely irritated her when she first sat. Now they felt like jagged boulders. Her shoulders ached. Her thighs cramped from the way the homemade brace held her legs apart. The temperature dropped, and she shivered. To keep blood circulating, she shifted her hips and twisted her legs in tandem to the left and right. *Come on Hank. Ride in like one of your*

American cowboy movie stars. God, her mind was going.

The door had drifted closed in Vlad's wake; creaking hinges announced his return. Moonlight flooding through the window frame revealed that he carried an armload of wood, a mixture of scrap lumber and broken-off branches or roots. He dumped it on the dirt floor and arranged several pieces in a neat pile. Using dried grass and a twisted piece of newspaper for kindling, he lit the pile. "A bit primitive," he said as he stacked on more wood to build the flame higher. "It lends atmosphere along with light, though."

He pulled a two-foot splinter of plank from his wood pile. No more than an inch or so across, it narrowed to a point at one end. "I'm not sure modern technology is a net gain," he said as he worked on the narrow end with his knife, sharpening it in the firelight. "You get some benefits, but there are offsets. Take radio antennas. They're my favorite impaling tools, but that Buick we borrowed doesn't have one. I think they build them into the window or the roof or something. No coat hangers up here, of course." He held the sharpened stake out to her as if offering it for inspection. "This will have to do. How many inches you figure you can take?"

On his knees beside her, he dragged the sharpened end of the stake across her lower belly, and a mewing sound, like a distressed kitten's, bubbled from her throat. She tried to cut it off and found that she couldn't. Eyes closed, she prayed silently for a quick death.

"That's for later. Sort of a *coupy de gracy.* Did I say that right?"

She opened her eyes. He had laid the stake aside and was holding the blade of his knife in the fire, turning it slowly in the flames.

Their gazes met, and he flashed a friendly smile. "I know you're scared. Know I've hurt you. But have you cried or begged? Not a tear, not a word." He withdrew the knife and, holding its fire-blackened blade close to her face, eased it toward her right eye.

It singed her eyelashes. She reared her head back until it bumped the wall. Twisting, she tried to turn her face away.

By fisting her hair, he held her still. "You gonna beg?"

"Please," she whimpered. "Have mercy."

"Now, that's better." He touched the hot blade to her face an inch below the eye, pressed for a moment, and moved it away. It left a searing streak of pain in its wake.

He held it in the fire again. "No scream, though. I really, really want to hear you scream." He pressed the heated blade to a nipple, held it there.

She did what he wanted. Once it started, she lost control. The scream became a drawn-out, animalistic howl.

"That was so beautiful." He laid the knife aside and stood, stretching. "Let's give the tit a chance to hurt. They tell me it gets worse for several minutes. Air hitting it and so forth. We'll see some tears yet."

He was right about the pain getting worse. It flared moments after he pulled the knife blade away. Then it grew more intense. The nipple pulsed.

Squatting, he fed more sticks into the fire. "We've got work to do, you and me. Before we're finished, you'll be a different, better piece of ass. Then we'll share the ultimate intimacy—the draining away of your essence. It will be the most intense experience of your life."

He resumed turning the knife blade in the flame but paused with his head cocked sideways as if listening. Shelby heard only a buzzing in her head and the drumming of her heart, but something had his attention.

He walked to the shed's only window, or rather the opening that had once been a window, and cocked his head again. "I believe we have company."

She heard it then, an automobile engine laboring up the steep grade. The sound distracted her from her agony and restored hope.

Vlad stepped outside. A car door slammed, and he came back carrying a semiautomatic pistol, similar to those with which she had practiced on Hank's firing range, and a larger weapon that looked like a cross between a revolver and a rifle. It had a sight that she at first thought was telescopic but recognized as a laser when he activated it and a red dot raced across the wall of the shack.

"Sounds like your sugar daddy found us," Vlad said. "He'll check the car first. The laser will make it an easy shot."

CHAPTER THIRTY

SHELBY STRAINED TO IDENTIFY the engine sound as it grew louder. Then it died.

Vlad barred the door by dropping a piece of timber into ancient cast-iron braces. The shed's single window opening was on a side wall at a ninety-degree angle to the door. Holding a weapon in each hand, he crouched there in the moonlight and peeked out, licking his lips.

Shelby waited, tension building in her gut, giving the driver time to work his way closer on foot. Then she shouted, "Hank, he's in the shed."

Vlad dashed over and aimed a kick at her stomach.

Shock flooded through her. Vomit filled her mouth. Spilling out, it coated her chin and dribbled on her stomach. She spat to clear it from her mouth.

He taped her lips shut and glared at her. "Know what that earned you, bitch? An extra half hour of roasting before your lights go out." She thought he might kick her again, but he turned away and shouted through the window, "Hey, I've got your cunt in here. Way she's bleeding, I figure she's got five minutes left."

No response. Maybe Hank wasn't even out there. It could be anyone.

"Let's do this the John Wayne way," Vlad shouted. "Strap on

our six-shooters and meet halfway. If you win, there's still time to save your bitch."

"I have a better idea," Hank called out. "Why don't you leave her there and drive away? Why get yourself killed for a measly twenty-four grand?"

"You must be the guy they sent to Arkansas," Vlad shouted back. "Couldn't take her out, huh?"

"I'll buy her from you," Hank said. "Half the contract fee, and you won't have to deal with a corpse."

"It won't be that much trouble, fellow. What's she to you?"

Shelby's spirits had spiraled; now they plummeted. Hank had made a mistake. He'd let the maniac know she was important to him.

"Like I said," Vlad yelled, "disposal's no problem. But I'm a reasonable man. You lay your weapon where I can see it and drive away. That buys the bitch an easy death. A bullet through the brain. Here's what the hard way sounds like."

He ripped the tape from her mouth and pulled a stick from the fire. He held the glowing end to her burned nipple.

The breast felt as if it were aflame. She couldn't stop screaming even when he pulled the fire away. By degrees, she reined in the shrieking, letting her mouth hang open to accommodate air that ravaged her tortured throat as it rasped in and out.

Vlad dropped the burning stick into the fire and slapped the tape back over her lips. Now she couldn't get enough air.

"Let's recap," Hank called in a calm voice. "You can collect half the fee and drive away. No muss, no fuss. That cuts my payday in half, but I have some fun with the target. Or you can have the fun, after which I kill you, take the target dead or alive, and make an extra twelve grand. Either way is all right with me."

"You're lying," Vlad shouted, his voice turning shrill. "You've got the hots for this bitch. That scream you heard—I rammed a stake up her cunt. She's bleeding like a stuck pig."

Shelby labored to force air through her swollen nose. She had to do something. If the bastard wrenched another scream from her, Hank might rush the shed. He would be gunned down.

She could twist her lower body, move her legs even though the plank holding her ankles apart forced her to move them in tandem. The fire had burned down to a bed of glowing embers. Straining, she rammed her bare feet into them and kicked the embers against the century-old, kindling-dry, wooden wall. Vlad, his attention focused on Hank, did not turn around.

Again, Shelby tensed and twisted. Her feet, scorched by the first effort, blistered as they swept through the fire a second time, propelling glowing coals and flaming wood scraps against the opposite wall.

Smoke curled from the first wall. Flames glowed. Cursing, Vlad dashed over and kicked the burning planks, breaking them away.

The other wall ignited. Flames climbed toward the ceiling. When Vlad noticed it, the fire was too far along to douse by kicking loose the flaming planks. Cursing, he aimed one of his pistols at Shelby, holding it inches from her face.

She closed her eyes, waiting for a bullet. Nothing happened, and she looked at him.

He grinned. Smoke drifting in an ashen haze blurred his features. "I need a thumb for my payday. I'll take that first." He wiped his eyes, laid his pistols aside, and fisted his hunting knife. "Then I'll cut you open. Let your sugar daddy find you with your guts on the floor." Coughing and wheezing, his face partially obscured by smoke, he leaned over her.

A thump against the door made him drop the knife and grab his pistols. He fired several rounds into the door and dived through the window. The ensuing hail of gunfire sounded like a war zone.

Except for the hiss and sputter of flames working their way up tinder-dry walls to lap at the ancient ceiling, the night turned abruptly quiet. Smoke billowing over Shelby's head began to settle. She would asphyxiate before she burned. She was grateful for that.

More thumping, and the door fell off its hinges. A figure, smoke-shrouded and indistinct, dashed across the room. Holding a handkerchief to his nose, Hank stripped the tape off her mouth and used his switchblade to saw through the tape holding her neck to the wall.

Unable to balance, she fell sideways. "Hank," she gasped between coughs. "Hank."

With his hands under her arms, he dragged her across the room, out the door, across open space where air—pure, clean, cool—beckoned, and into a shallow ditch that paralleled the dirt road. On his stomach at her side, he sliced through the tape binding her wrists and cut the spreader plank off her ankles. "You holding up?" he asked, massaging her shoulders.

She tried to raise an arm but couldn't. "I'll live. Where is he?"

"Out there. I might have hit him. I don't know."

"Are you all right? Any wounds?"

"Not a scratch." Hank's eyes swept up and down her body. "That low-life bastard. What'd he do to you?"

"Nothing I'd like repeated. No permanent damage." Concentrating to make her arms work, she raised them shoulder high and, slowly, painfully, moved them back and forth. "Tell me about Carmen."

"Tough little lady. That bullet missed the bone and went all the way through her leg. Looks like the guy's using full metal jackets—

no massive tissue damage."

"She was bleeding."

"A pressure bandage did the trick."

"You took her to a hospital?"

He shook his head. "Bullet wounds get reported to the cops."

"Infection, Hank. She might—"

He stopped her with a finger on her lips. "Patrick and his medical bag will be at the Foxes' condo before noon. Sylvia's picking him up at the Denver bus station. But we've got a more pressing problem. That madman's packing firepower."

"Two weapons," Shelby said. "One looks like a nine-millimeter semiautomatic. The other is a long-barreled revolver with a laser sight."

Hank flashed his pistol. "I've got this and my backup."

"Ammo?"

"One more clip for the Beretta. Just what's in the backup's cylinders."

"Won't the burning building attract attention? Rangers watching for forest fires?"

"I doubt it," Hank twisted onto his stomach for a quick peek over the lip of the ditch. "It doesn't seem to be spreading, and the building isn't that large. Rangers will figure it's a bonfire built by tanked-up campers. They'll watch until it dies down, then go back to their TV. Let's figure how we're gonna do this."

"Any idea where he is?"

"Only cover out there is a stand of aspen. I'd lay odds he's hiding in it." Hank raised his head to peer over the ditch bank again, and a shot rang out simultaneously with a loud ping. He grunted and curled in the ditch with both hands clamped to his eyes.

"Are you hit?" Shelby asked. "Hank? Hank!"

"Shit, shit, shit." He took a hand away to pull a handkerchief from his pocket. The hand dripped blood. In the waning moonlight it looked black.

Shelby concentrated to keep her breathing steady. "How bad?"

"I can't see."

Shelby, her arms working sluggishly now, put her hands on the sides of his head and turned it so moonlight fell on his face. The upper half was a bloody pulp. "It doesn't look bad," she lied, struggling to keep her voice calm.

"I don't believe I'm hit." He dabbed at his eyes with the handkerchief. "It's rocks or gravel. Like shrapnel."

She took the handkerchief from him, wet it with her tongue, and wiped blood from his eyes.

The cloth touched an eyelid, and he winced. "Damn!"

"Sorry." Shelby checked the other eye and gasped; the lid was almost torn away. The socket dripped blood. She wrapped her arms around him and ran fingers through his hair as she rocked him.

He pushed her away. "He's in a stand of aspen to the right of the cabin. No way to know if he'll fight or run." He touched an eye but hissed and jerked the hand back. "Can't see a damn thing."

"I don't think he'll run." Hank's bleeding had slowed to a mere oozing, but the possibility of permanent eye damage chilled Shelby. "It's more than the bounty. He seems . . . obsessed."

"All that combat practice you complained about—today's your final exam. You see my Beretta?"

He had dropped it when the rock chips splattered his face. She picked it up and dusted it off. "I have it."

"Make sure the slide's working. The dirt . . ."

She pushed the lever that let the magazine drop into her hand, jacked the slide to eject the bullet from the chamber, and checked the barrel for dirt. "It's all right." She cleaned the ejected bullet on his shirt and loaded it back into the magazine. "Only four rounds. You said you have another clip?"

He fished the spare magazine from his pocket. "That's it. Make every shot count."

She slapped in the fresh magazine. "I'm barefooted. Bare all over, actually. I won't move well across this rocky terrain."

"Take my shoes and socks."

Her feet were blistered where she had dragged them through the fire. She bit her tongue to keep from gasping as she pulled Hank's socks over the burned tissue. His lace-up Rockport hiking shoes were so big that even with the eyelets pulled all the way together they wouldn't stay on her feet. "Let me have your shirt."

"You'd take the shirt off my back? I should have expected it." He unbuttoned the shirt and slipped it off.

"I need your knife." She cut the shirt's seams and ripped it apart to make wrappings for her feet. When she finished, her feet were half-again their normal girth and the shoes fit reasonably well.

"I have my backup piece," Hank said while she worked. He pulled the little .22-caliber revolver from its ankle holster. "I'll shoot at any nearby noise, so you make sure I know it's you when you come back."

"I'll call out. You lie still." She kissed his nose and then his lips.

He wrapped an arm around her. His palm caressed her bare skin. "Better take my undershirt."

She slipped on the V-neck T-shirt. The world's shortest mini, but it made her feel less vulnerable. Where the fabric rubbed her burned nipple, however, it felt like fresh fire. "Let me have your knife again." She cut a plug out of the T-shirt so the breast would not touch cloth, put the folded knife in his hand, and kissed him once more. "Thanks for everything."

"Be careful," he said. "And be smart."

She started to peek over the lip of the ditch but thought about Hank's experience and changed her mind. Instead, with the Beretta in one hand and the half-empty spare magazine in the other, she crawled along the ditch until she reached the footbridge she and Vlad had crossed to get to the mine shack. She wriggled under the bridge and looked out on the other side, where scrub bushes offered concealment.

No sign of Vlad. Flames still danced where the shed had stood, but it had collapsed and the fire had consumed most of it. She surveyed their prospective battlefield, gray and hazy now in morning twilight. They were on a plateau half again as large as a football field; a ridgetop that miners had leveled, she guessed. No vegetation other than the aspen grove.

The road they had driven up was a single-lane, dirt trail that hugged one side of the plateau. The drainage ditch in which she was hiding paralleled the road but petered out where it began its descent off the plateau.

She was about twenty yards from the Buick Vlad had hijacked after capturing her. If she made it to the aspen grove and stalked him, he might somehow get to the vehicle and drive away. She could disable it by shooting out the tires on her side, but the muzzle flash would reveal her location. He could pin her down.

Looking for Hank's vehicle, she scanned the narrow road down the steep incline that had forced his engine to labor. There it was, maybe halfway down—the ancient Volkswagen camper Jason had been driving. Hank must have borrowed it after wrecking the Blazer. If she could reach it and turn it sideways on the road, she could block the Buick. Leave it there and work her way around the plateau to the aspen grove.

She shuddered at the prospect of crawling back to Hank to get the ignition key. Her knees were already raw. No other strategy occurred to her, so she reversed direction and started the long, time-consuming journey.

"Hank," she called as she approached his location. "It's Shelby."

"No engine noises," he said, "so he didn't get away. No gunshots, either. You scare him to death?"

"Don't be a wise ass." Was he as frightened as she was? Trying to front for her benefit the way she was for him? "I need to block the road so he can't get away. Give me your car keys."

"They're in the ignition. I left them in case we needed a quick getaway."

She had crawled back for nothing? She tried to stay upbeat for Hank, but a groan escaped her anyway.

"Come closer," he said. "Let me touch you."

She rolled until they were nose to nose. "How're you holding up?"

"Nursing the mother of all headaches." He ran his hands up and down her arms. "Crawling in that gravel is a bitch, huh?"

"Not a picnic."

He unbuckled his belt and unzipped his jeans. "Take my pants."

"And leave you here in your skivvies?"

"I'll lay odds your knees are bleeding. You want to stay mobile, you need some protection." He pulled the belt out of its loops and handed it to her along with his knife. "You'll have to punch a hole to make it fit."

She struggled to twist the knife's tip through the leather. By then, he had his jeans off. They swallowed her, but with the belt cinched up and the legs rolled into gigantic cuffs, they were wearable. She dropped the knife and the Beretta's partially empty spare magazine into a pocket. "If he sees me in this outfit, maybe I will scare him to death."

"I'll bet he isn't used to targets fighting back. Keep your cool; remember what you've learned. You can take this guy."

Another kiss on Hank's nose, and she crawled away. The denim protecting her legs made a world of difference. Once more using the bush next to the footbridge as cover, she surveyed the terrain on both sides of the ditch and studied the aspen grove. Dawn had fully broken; in thirty minutes to an hour, the sun would appear. No sign of Vlad, but he shouted to Hank as Shelby made her way along the drainage ditch until it flattened on the slope and gave no protection.

His voice came from the aspen grove. "You still there, fellow?"

"I'm here," Hank answered.

"Is the bitch worth dying for? Make her walk over here, and you can leave."

Hank laughed. "You had your chance to live. I'm taking you out now."

Vlad would be concentrating on Hank's position, Shelby figured. Maybe she could roll out of the ditch onto the road and get behind the Buick. With the car as cover, she could dash to the other side of the road, where the terrain dropped away from the plateau. From there, she could safely make her way downhill to the VW.

"You're old," Vlad shouted. "Eyes aren't what they used to be. Reflexes shot. Don't hear real good, I'll bet. You really think you can take me?"

"If you believe I'm worn out, why don't you try . . ."

Scrambling over the ditch bank and dashing to the Buick, Shelby missed the rest of what Hank said. She paused, squatting in the protection of the car, and caught her breath.

"Tell you what," Vlad shouted. "I've got water over here. Got some trail mix. Let's just sit tight. Let me know when you decide to trade the bitch for a get-out-of-jail-free card."

As Shelby worked her way downhill, bending low to keep the road surface between her and Vlad, the voices became too faint to make out. She darted across the road to the VW camper. No way to tell if Vlad saw her. If he did, he wouldn't waste a bullet trying to hit her at this distance. He might make a break for the Buick, however, thinking she was trying to get away. She cranked the VW and waited, hoping he would try. She would goose the camper and catch him midway between the aspen grove and his car.

He didn't come out, so she eased the VW forward until she had covered half the distance to the Buick and wrenched the steering wheel hard left to turn it sideways on the trail. At the slow speed and with no power steering, the wheel resisted. As she leaned to put muscle into it, a shot rang out and the windshield spiderwebbed. She flopped down on the seat and stomped the brake pedal.

That big revolver with the laser sight. She'd forgotten he had a long-range weapon. If she hadn't leaned to force the steering, she would be dead. The road might not be completely blocked, but she didn't dare rise up to try again. She clicked off the ignition and slid out on the side opposite the aspen grove.

She studied the terrain in fresh morning light. The trail hugged one edge of the plateau. The mine shack, now just smoldering cinders and curled roofing tin, had set on the other. On her side of the trail, the terrain fell away sharply and dropped into a ravine dotted with trees. Immediately behind her, the trail descended into the ravine. In front of her, the plateau was about a hundred and fifty yards long. At its end, a bluff towered thirty or forty feet.

Having gotten a fix on her environment, as Hank had preached in countless demonstrations and lectures at the farm, she focused on the VW. It sat at an angle across the trail, not blocking it as well as she would have liked, but she doubted the big Buick could get by. And with the drainage ditch on one side and the drop-off on the other, Vlad wouldn't be able to drive off the road to get around the obstruction. But she had to take him out before he screwed up his courage and tried to sneak up on Hank.

"You're a real smart fellow," Vlad called out. "Distracting me while you sent the bitch for your car. Dumb slut drove right up to my doorstep, though." A shot rang out, and the VW's right rear tire blew. Another shot, and the right front tire went. "Your raggedy ride isn't going anywhere now. You come out of that ditch, I'll do your head the same way. Care to try me?"

Shelby took two deep breaths and dashed to the side of the road opposite the aspen grove. She dived for the protection of the embankment.

Her move must have surprised Vlad, because he didn't take a shot. "There goes the bitch," he called out. "Making a break for it. Want to call it a draw, help me look for her?"

"Why would I want to do that?" Hank shouted.

"If she gets away, there's no payday for anybody. We can split the cash."

"I like that. You're a peacemaker now."

Shelby lost track of their mutual taunts as she slogged across the steeply sloped terrain below the trail to reach the foot of the bluff. A minor landslide had scattered rocks, some waist-high, where the bluff towered over the plateau. Using them as cover, she crossed to the other side. With only momentary exposure between rocks and bushes, she jogged to where the mining shack's burned-out remnants hugged the rim. Behind the shack's ashes, the terrain dropped off into a ravine partially filled with mine tailings. She worked her way along the slope several feet below the rim, careful not to trip in her oversized shoes. A miscalculation would send her tumbling to the bottom of the ravine.

She could not see over the lip of the plateau, but she stopped where she calculated the aspen grove should be off to her right. No vegetation to use as handholds, no way to pull herself back up to the top. She turned on her side to protect her burned nipple, flattened her body on the hard-packed slope—it was slippery with loose rocks and gravel—and began pushing her way up by digging with her fingers and toes.

Almost there—she could reach over the edge now. She pressed her palms on top of the ledge and pulled, taking some of her weight on her arms, careful not to drag her scorched nipple on the rocks. *Keep talking, Hank. Center his attention on you.* She poked her head over the top and saw that she was no more than five feet from the aspen grove. The eastern sky had turned bright orange, and the aspen trembled in a slight breeze. No way to guess where among the slender saplings Vlad might be lurking.

With her upper body flattened on level ground, she tried to lever her trunk over the ledge by pushing with a foot against a small boulder. It dislodged and tumbled into the ravine, maybe fifty feet below, taking an ever-growing number of smaller rocks with it. To Shelby, the clatter sounded like thunder.

If Vlad investigated, only speed could save her. She scrambled to her feet and dashed for the tree line, pulling Hank's big semiautomatic from her pocket as she ran. Crouching, she waited with all her senses on hyperalert.

Dim light inside the grove. Noise off to her right. She spun and pointed the weapon. A fawn stared into her eyes for a moment and bounded away, crashing through the aspen.

Laughter behind her. "You outsmarted a deer. Don't turn around before that weapon hits the dirt."

CHAPTER THIRTY-ONE

SHELBY FROZE. SHOULD SHE drop the weapon, or try to get a shot off before she died?

Making a stand now would be suicide, and she might yet get a fighting chance. She clicked the pistol's decocking lever and let it drop.

"That's a good girl. Lace your fingers together behind your head. Get on your knees."

She knelt, and in the process let her fingers hang looser.

"Your sugar daddy must be hurt pretty bad to let you run around like this. Can you think of any reason why I shouldn't do you now?"

"Just one."

"Really? What's that?"

"You said you wanted to see tears. That hasn't happened."

He chuckled. "You're on your knees, a gun pointed at your head, and you can still be a smart-ass. I like that. And I like the way your barbequed tit hangs out of your shirt. Sore, huh?"

"It's pretty bad."

"Probably a good place to start working on those tears. Hold your position." Still behind her, he came closer, and she guessed he was picking up her weapon. He pressed a gun barrel against the side of her head and grasped the back of her neck in a pincer grip.

"It's okay to scream. I expect you to."

Pressure on her neck. Pain shooting through her like electric current. Abruptly, she was bathed in sweat. Her bladder voided. A hissing sound from her throat morphed into a loud groan.

The crunching pressure became a gentle caress. "Let's have that scream. See if we can't lure your sugar daddy out of his ditch." A hand slithered around to cradle her exposed breast. Grasping the burned nipple, it squeezed and twisted.

She screamed. Her shoulders shook. Her head snapped back— and his pistol barrel no longer pressed against her skull. Before he could adjust, she reached back and grabbed his ankles. As she jerked them forward, she heaved her head and shoulders backward into his legs and groin.

His weapon's discharge next to her ear sounded like a cannon blast, and her world became eerily quiet. He landed on his back. She spun and fell on top of him.

Accepting that he was stronger, she did not wrestle for the pistol. Instead, she slammed the heel of a hand up under his chin. His head flew back, and she chopped at his Adam's apple. Her other hand dug at his crotch, trying to reach his testicles.

He twisted, turning his back to her. He still held his weapon but used the gun hand to support himself on hands and knees as he tried to scramble to his feet.

From behind him, she reached under his left arm to grab his right wrist, his gun hand. Her other hand grasped his right ankle. She lifted the ankle while tugging on his wrist.

Without the support of the arm and leg, he collapsed. His shoulder slammed against hard-packed earth. His weapon was under him now, useless unless he could roll over.

Determined not to permit that, Shelby dug her toes into the dirt and put all her strength into lifting his ankle. Her ears began working again, and she heard his deep breathing, heard her own grunts of exertion.

He braced his free hand on the ground and tried what was in effect a one-armed push-up.

She grabbed the arm with both hands and twisted it behind him, doing her best to break it.

"Goddamn," he shouted. "Shit, oh, shit." With his face pressed to the ground, he could not resist the pressure as she pushed his arm further up behind him. "Here," he shouted, and extended his gun hand, relaxing his fingers on the pistol's butt. "Take the fucking gun. Ease up."

Holding his arm with one hand, she made sure the semiautomatic was cocked and pressed it to the back of his head. "I hope you try to turn around."

"I'm not trying anything," he said. "I think you broke my goddamn arm."

"I hope so." Why not put a round through his head right now? That's what Hank would recommend. He had warned her not to be tentative.

Before she could decide, Hank called to her. He sounded too close to be in the ditch where she had left him. "I'm all right," she shouted. "I've got him. Stay where you are." If he still couldn't see, he might walk right off the edge of the plateau. "Stay th—"

Vlad screamed and twisted, jerking his head away from the pistol.

His sudden spasm threw her off balance. She fell to the side, and her shoulder slammed into a tree trunk. The shoulder went numb, but she held on to the weapon. She rolled so Vlad couldn't reach it.

He didn't try. Instead, he crashed his way through the aspen grove and out of sight before her numbed shoulder let her level the pistol.

She fired twice in his direction, hoping for a lucky shot. The crashing continued, and she struggled to her feet. She started to follow him but stopped when Hank shouted her name again. She couldn't let him stumble around on the unfamiliar terrain, couldn't risk having him walk off the edge of the plateau. "Hank," she shouted. "Stay there. I'm coming."

Gripping his little .22-caliber backup revolver, he stood roughly midway between the drainage ditch and the aspen grove, close enough to the mining shack's still-smoldering ruins to feel the heat. He pointed the revolver in her direction as she approached.

"It's Shelby," she shouted. "Don't shoot."

"Those shots," he said. "You hit him?"

"Don't think so." She hugged him. "I told you to stay in the ditch."

"You screamed."

"Like a girl, huh?" She hugged tighter and released him but kept a hand on his shoulder. "And you were going to rescue me?"

"Stupid move, I know. What's the situation?"

"I'm pretty sure I dislocated his shoulder. Maybe broke his arm. Not his shooting arm, and he still has weapons."

"Take me back to the ditch. I'll stay put this time."

The pistol she had taken from Vlad proved to be the one she'd been using when he got the drop on her: Hank's Beretta. She stuck it in a pocket and led Hank back toward the ditch. Halfway there, they heard an automobile engine roar. Hank dropped to the ground and shouted, "Go, go."

She sprinted toward the vehicles. The sun, peeking over the horizon, flashed against metal and glass as the Buick backed down the slope toward where the VW camper blocked the single-lane road. The Buick's engine screamed as the heavy car accelerated. Its rear end slammed into the camper with an explosive *Ker-bam*. For a moment the two vehicles moved together as if joined. Then the Buick broke free. Rocking violently, it careened on down the slope.

By the time Shelby dashed to the old camper, Vlad had reached the bottom of the slope, stopped, and turned. The big sedan made a sound as if a wheel was grinding against metal. Vlad pulled away slowly, babying it.

The VW had taken the impact just aft of its rear wheel. Its bumper stuck out like a metallic pretzel, and sheet metal that had covered the rear-mounted engine lay on the ground. No way to tell whether or not the engine had been destroyed.

It made no difference, Shelby realized as the Buick limped under the bridge that spanned the ravine. With two of the VW's tires shot away, she couldn't follow. Eyes closed, she turned her face skyward in frustration.

As Vlad made the turn that would take him up to the road on top of the ridge, where he would cross the wood-planked span, Shelby's mind replayed the horrifying nighttime ride to this place, hog-tied and lying on her stomach with her face pressed against the Buick's carpet near his feet. They had been on a gravel road and slowed to cross a loose-planked bridge—the bridge over the ravine, she was certain. A snakelike road from the bridge to the bottom of the ravine required the Buick to inch along. They had driven under the bridge and accelerated up the slope to the mine.

Vlad was nursing the limping Buick up the gravel road from the ravine to the top of the ridge. Then he would cross the bridge and turn onto the main road. It had taken them maybe three minutes to get from the bridge to the bottom of the ravine. She had lost at least a minute already, so she had about two minutes before he crested the ridge, drove across the bridge, and escaped.

The camper was old, and it had taken a massive hit next to its engine compartment. How much damage? She climbed in and pumped the accelerator. Mumbling, "Start, little engine," she twisted the ignition key.

The ancient, air-cooled power plant turned over sluggishly, as if the battery was almost dead. It coughed into life, clattering and pinging.

No room to turn the rig around, and with both right tires flat, it would handle like an amusement park ride. She shifted into reverse and, gripping the steering wheel with sweaty palms, mashed the accelerator.

The camper listed precariously to the right, and it wanted to swerve in that direction. The flat tires thumped and bumped along the rough dirt trail, but the vehicle picked up speed as it backed down the slope. The faster it went, the more it insisted on swerving to the right. Too fast, and Shelby would lose control. Too slow, and she might as well forget it.

How much time had passed since the big Buick disappeared under the bridge? Two, maybe three minutes? Tension would distort her perception, but Vlad must be almost to the top of the ridge. Then he would drive across the bridge and turn onto the main road.

Gritting her teeth, she floored the VW's gas pedal as the dirt trail flattened and she neared where it went under the bridge. The bridge was supported by slender wooden pilings. They were her target.

Impossible to control the lurching camper. All she could do was aim it. She missed the piling on her side of the bridge but managed to ram the one on the far side.

The world seemed to stop. She had the sensation of being flattened against the seat, of having all her internal organs liquefied. She blacked out.

When she regained consciousness, the struggle to get air into her lungs tightened a band around her chest. A gray haze floated in the morning air: dust particles suspended inside the camper. The world seemed absolutely still and silent, except for the sound of her labored breathing and an automobile engine in the distance. The dust settled enough for her to see that the bridge piling she'd hit had cracked and bent but held.

She had to get out of the camper. What if it caught fire? What if the bridge collapsed on top of it?

Her door wouldn't budge, but the passenger door was already open, sprung and gaping several inches. She put her feet against it and pushed. With a drawn-out metallic protest, it opened a few more inches and froze. She squeezed through, surprised at how hard it was to make her body move. Everything hurt. She took a step and stumbled. On one knee, with a hand braced against the ground, she concentrated to keep from blacking out again. Then she labored erect and held onto the car door while another wave of dizziness washed over her.

The engine sounds were above her now. The Buick idled with its wheels barely on the bridge. The cracked bridge piling bowed outward and creaked. The beam over it sagged.

Vlad eased the Buick forward. He made it halfway across before the bridge groaned like someone in pain, and the cracked piling snapped. The sagging beam dropped several more inches.

The Buick stopped. It began backing as the beam sagged still more.

The bridge tilted crazily. The car slid against the railing, which gave way. The big sedan dropped into the ravine.

It landed upside down and turned onto its side slowly, as if it were a dying animal trying to get to its feet. Loose planks rained down on it, setting up a clattering din. Silence returned to the ravine as dust settled around the car's hulk.

Fascinated, Shelby watched from her position near the wrecked VW. Realizing her mouth was hanging open, she snapped it shut. As a precaution in case Vlad could still function, she eased down onto her stomach among scattered rocks and sparse weeds. Pain shot through her, a reminder to baby herself.

With Hank's semiautomatic cocked and ready, she waited for Vlad to climb out of the wreck. He didn't, so she inched closer, trying to see inside. The morning sun, slanting its rays into the ravine, created stark contrasts of light and shadow. The sun in her eyes transformed the shadows into black holes.

The Buick had been stationary when it fell, the drop was no more than twenty feet, and Vlad was protected by airbags and the vehicle's frame and metal shell. Even so, he might have been too badly injured to climb out. Trapped inside, maybe.

Or he could be playing possum.

Gripping the Beretta, Shelby used her elbows and toes to inch forward on her stomach. If she crawled back under the bridge, the sun wouldn't blind her and she could see better.

She had covered about ten feet when a gunshot caused her to press her body hard against the ground. She crawled a few more feet and, shaded now by the bridge, saw the wreck clearly. From this angle, however, weeds blocked her view at ground level.

"How you doing out there, cunt?" Vlad shouted. "Your barbequed tit feel good?"

One question answered: he was functioning. He might be trapped in the wreck or just afraid to climb out. The smart assumption was that he could move if he wanted to.

"Remember that stick I promised to ram up your pussy?" he said. "Maybe I'll do that yet."

He wanted the sound of her voice. Wanted to get a fix on her. *Keep wanting, hotshot.* When she moved, he might see the weeds around her waving, but she had to find protection. Several rocks, ranging from basketball size to small boulders, were strewn five or so feet to her right. Her problem was to get over there without being hit. She tucked the Beretta into her pocket, took a deep breath, and rolled.

She was almost there when shots rang out and a bullet kicked up gravel inches behind her. A second bullet ricocheted off the protective rocks as she stopped rolling.

Unless he changed positions, she was safe here. With both of them at ground level he couldn't hit her, because of the rocks. To get off a shot, however, she would have to expose herself. That would work if he didn't know her location or if he were an amateur. But he did know, and the way he had taken out Hank showed how good he was. Hank had peeked over the lip of that drainage ditch for only a second and ducked back down. It had been enough for Vlad to pinpoint him in moonlight.

She studied the terrain and the wrecked vehicles, looking for a way to get a clear shot without giving him one. Flat on her belly but protecting her injured breast with a palm, feeling less pain now, she snaked her way through the scattered rocks and sparse weeds. The Buick lay on its side. Facing it at an angle that permitted her to see its undercarriage, she pulled the Beretta from her pocket. She braced her elbows on the gravel and, grasping the weapon with both hands, put two rounds in the exposed fuel tank.

Hard to tell in the shadows, but it looked like gasoline was leaking out, staining the metal as it trickled down. Yes, she could see it spreading. It reached as far down the tank as she could see. Unless the ground was porous, it would pool below. Volatile fumes, heavier than air, would hover over the pool. She counted to ten, slowly, and fired a round at rocks below the overturned vehicle, angling the shot to create a ricochet and, she hoped, a spark.

No flame. She tried twice more, aiming for metal near the fuel tank. Despite the angle, the rounds went through instead of ricocheting. Five rounds gone. The magazine held ten, and she had fired two when Vlad got away from her in the aspen grove. Three left, plus four in the spare magazine.

"We're both in a jam, here," Vlad shouted. "It's time to think about helping each other."

Wriggling through the rocks, careful not to expose herself, Shelby looked for another approach. From her new position she could see where the fuel trickled, splattering a flat rock. She rolled onto her side to get the Beretta at as low an angle as possible and fired a glancing shot at the rock, placing the round in the puddle of fuel.

No spark, no fire. The fuel, as volatile as it was, might nevertheless have suppressed the spark.

She fired again, aiming at dry rock just inches in front of the oozing fuel. She tried once more, and ejected the semiautomatic's empty magazine. As she slammed in the spare with its four rounds, blue flame drifted across the flat rock and climbed the trickling gasoline to the holes in the fuel tank.

The tank erupted with a dull *whomp*. The shock wave jarred her.

"Oh, shit," Vlad mumbled, barely loud enough for her to hear. He raised his voice: "Cervosier, we've got a fire here."

Shelby crawled several feet to her right and twisted to get a view of the vehicle's broken windshield. She braced the pistol, ready to shoot if he climbed through.

"I'm coming out," he shouted. He stuck an arm out where the windshield's glass used to be and waved the long-barreled revolver with its laser sight. "Look at this. See? I'm tossing it." He pitched the weapon in her direction. It landed roughly midway between them.

"The other one," she said. "The automatic."

He held up the weapon and tossed it. "I'm unarmed. You won't shoot an unarmed man, will you?"

She waited with the Beretta centered on his windshield.

He stuck both hands out. "See? Nothing to fight with. I'm coming out."

"Not all the way," she said. "Head and shoulders, then stop. I have to know you're unarmed."

"Whatever you say." He wriggled through the broken windshield, favoring the arm she had twisted.

"Stop," she commanded when his shoulders were outside the vehicle. Keeping the pistol trained on him, she stood and hobbled close. Black smoke poured out the Buick's windows. Inside, orange flames danced. "Tell me again what you did to my friend in Arizona."

"It's burning," he said, desperation kicking his voice up to soprano.

"Describe once more how it felt in Arkansas, watching Elizabeth's eyes as she died."

"You've got to let me out."

"Why do I have to do that?"

His fingers dug into the soil, and he started pulling his body out of the wreck.

Aiming carefully, Shelby put a round through his shoulder, shattering the joint.

He muttered a low-pitched "Umph," but kept wriggling, pulling with one arm.

She put a round in his other shoulder. With the Beretta lowered, she backed away from flames that were now spurting out the windows.

"Kill me," he begged. "In God's name, shoot me."

"I could do that, but what if there's no hell?" She let the pistol hang loosely at her side. "This might be your only chance to burn."

"Mercy," he screamed. "Have mercy."

She turned away, heading for the wrecked VW. His shrieking followed her, and she hesitated.

He screamed again.

Despising the weakness that compelled her, she turned back.

He looked up at her and begged, "Shoot me. Don't let me burn."

She aimed at his head. Her finger tightened on the trigger, but she could not squeeze.

"Please," he pleaded. "In the name of God, do it. Be merciful."

It was the right thing to do. Letting the psychopath live would be an act of aggression against society, but deliberately making him suffer would lower her to his level. Taking careful aim, she squeezed off a round.

A hole erupted in his forehead, and his head thudded on the ground. The only sound on the mountainside was the fire's crackle and an occasional pop.

With her mind numb but her body screaming, Shelby squeezed back through the VW camper's partially opened passenger door. She flicked the power switch on its two-way radio. When an LED above the switch glowed, she keyed the microphone. "Jason? Are you there?"

"I'm here." He sounded unreal through the tinny speaker. "You're broadcasting. Don't use names."

"Is my sister all right?

"She won't be running any footraces for a while, but she'll be fine. Probably have a battle scar to brag about. She's with your in-house doc, doped up and feeling great."

Despite her pain, her exhaustion, and her worry about Hank, Shelby felt a loosening of tension throughout her body. "Do you have my location?"

"Roger that. I'm at the lab. Ha . . . the big guy told me to stay here 'til he calls."

"He won't be calling. Will you come get us?"

"I can be there in an hour, maybe an hour and a half. He with you?"

"He's here. We need dressings for wounds, pain medicine, salve for burns. And bring me something to wear. Socks, too. With thick soles. Hurry."

"First aid kit, aspirin, burn salve, clothing, athletic socks. Wilco."

"Not aspirin. A strong painkiller. As strong as you can get."

CHAPTER THIRTY-TWO

SHELBY WORRIED THAT, ON top of the recent cabin fire, smoke from the burning Buick would attract forest rangers. Nothing she could do about it, and she couldn't leave telltale fingerprints in the VW camper—no clues that would tell the CBTF she had been here. Using a cloth dipped in sand for its abrasive qualities, she scoured every surface that she or Hank might have touched, rubbing hard to obliterate or at least smear their prints. Then she hobbled to where Hank waited. "It's me," she called out when he started to raise his weapon at the sound of her feet on the gravel.

He lowered the weapon. "You okay? Did he wound you?"

"No, I'm fine."

"You're not hurt?"

"I hurt all over, sweetheart, but I'm not wounded. He's dead."

"Knew you could do it." He started walking toward her, feeling carefully with each foot before putting weight on it.

They hugged for a long time, and the racing of his heart told her he'd been more worried than he wanted her to know. As she led him to the foot of the ruined bridge, she told him what had happened and described their situation. "Jason won't be able to cross the bridge. We'll have to climb up there. It's a steep slope. Can you make it?"

"I rested while you did all the work. I'm good to go."

Working through her exhaustion, Shelby struggled up the slope, pausing to direct Hank after finding each foothold. His feet bled on the rocks, but he refused to accept his shoes back. They climbed to just below road level and stopped, hoping they wouldn't be spotted in the weeds if rangers showed up ahead of Jason.

After what seemed an eternity, Jason arrived and stood on the road by his SUV, scratching his head and studying the tilted bridge. He spotted Shelby and Hank limping toward him and swooped down on them. "Holy Bejesus," he said, "you guys want me to call med evac?"

Hank shook his head. "Just get us the hell away from here."

"I second the motion," Shelby said, giddy with relief at Jason's arrival.

Jason pointed to the wrecked vehicles in the ravine below the bridge. "What about my VW?"

"There's a dead guy in the burned-out vehicle," Shelby said.

"A de . . . get the hell away, right." Jason grasped Hank's free hand and started to pull him to the borrowed SUV.

"Easy does it," Hank said. "My feet."

Jason glanced down. "Oh, shit, sorry. Listen, I can carry you."

"Just lead me. I'm blind, not crippled."

They climbed into the SUV, and Jason backed and turned. "We're out of here," he muttered as he dropped the shift lever into drive. When they reached the paved road and had covered several miles, he slowed. "I need to do some medicating?"

"Hank's face," Shelby said. "I can't tell how bad."

Jason parked on the roadside and, at Shelby's insistence, tended to Hank first. Using gauze soaked in hydrogen peroxide, he swabbed Hank's forehead and around his eyes. When the cleaning revealed the extent of eye damage, Jason's jaw clenched. He spread on an antibiotic salve and bandaged Hank's forehead and feet. Then he turned to Shelby. "Looks like the dude tried to roast you." He dug out a vial of pills and a water bottle. "Aspirin with codeine. It made my wisdom tooth extraction a breeze."

Shelby washed two of the pills down with the water. She offered the vial to Hank, but he asked for plain aspirin.

Jason opened a tube and punctured its seal. "Anesthetizing salve for burns." He squeezed the tube and used a finger to spread the salve across the knife print branded into Shelby's cheek. The salve-covered finger hovered where her burned nipple poked through the T-shirt. "I'm not sure how to go about this."

She took the salve from him and slathered it over the nipple, sighing as the medication cooled the burn.

He pulled clothing from a bag: sweat socks and a used but freshly laundered warm-up suit. "Brought you something to wear."

"Thanks." She slipped off the clothing she had borrowed from Hank.

"Oh, my God," Jason said as he took in her bloody knees.

She tried to laugh. It came out as a rasping gasp. "Raw liver, huh? Feels that way."

He squeezed a ribbon of salve onto each knee and paused with an extended forefinger. "This'll hurt."

"It already hurts, Jason."

After he had spread the salve and put some on the heels of her hands, where the skin was also torn away, she asked him to bandage her burned breast so it would not rub against her clothing. She slipped into the warm-up outfit and helped Hank back into his clothes. "Let's go home."

When they got within range of a cell tower, Jason phoned Sylvia. A neighbor had taken Polly and Tupper, and he asked Sylvia to leave them there so they would not see Hank or Shelby before they were cleaned up. Then he called the sheriff's office and described two vehicles stolen from the research station: his VW camper and a Chevy Blazer that belonged to the institute. No, he didn't have the license numbers handy. He promised to drop by the nearest substation and fill out a report.

At the condo, they parked the SUV as close as possible to the back door, so inquisitive neighbors would not see the bandaged warriors limping inside. Sylvia seemed on the verge of shock at their appearance. "It's mostly dirt," Shelby said. The anesthetizing salve and the codeine had ratcheted her pain down to a tolerable level.

Patrick was there with his medical bag. He had cleaned and sutured Carmen's bullet wound, he told them. He'd given her antibiotics and a sedative. She was sleeping. He sat Hank in a chair under a bright light and examined his eyes. "A specialist for this we need."

"What about your physician buddy in Grand Junction?" Hank asked. "Can he get an ophthalmologist to check me with no questions asked?"

"That he can do, for sure. Fix you good they will."

"Who else is here?"

"In the room with us?" Shelby asked, caressing his neck. "Jason and Sylvia."

"Jason, can you tolerate all of us in this little condo overnight?"

"No problem."

"How's Carmen going to handle the way we look?"

Jason laughed. "Way the kid's doped up, nothing's gonna bother her."

"All right. Put us where Polly and Tupper won't see us when you bring them home. We'll head out before they wake up."

The next morning, when they were seated in Patrick's old Ford Econoline van for the trip to the farm, Hank reminded Jason to wipe down his van and the condo to obliterate his visitors' finger-prints. "Just a precaution, in case the cops get suspicious when they find the bullet-riddled vehicles you reported stolen. Use a cleaning solution and do a thorough job. Then leave lots of your prints on the surfaces so it won't be obvious they were wiped."

"You think the cops will doubt my story?" Jason asked.

Hank shrugged. "Best to cover all bases."

Once they were on the road, Hank fell silent. He spoke no more than half a dozen words throughout the six-hour drive to the farm. Carmen slept the whole time. Shelby filled Patrick in on events and listened to his assurances that Hank's injuries were minor, that Carmen would heal both physically and emotionally, and that all would be well.

CHAPTER THIRTY-THREE

UNDER PATRICK'S EXPERT CARE at the farm, everyone's injuries began healing. Leonard's melted face and disfigured limbs frightened Carmen at first, but by the end of their first full day, the two had become bosom buddies. An ophthalmologist in Grand Junction examined Hank's eyes and declared that surgery could restore partial vision. Hank brooded for a while but seemed to adjust.

On several occasions, he asked Shelby to keyboard for him and to read the screen so he could take care of business on his computer. During their first session, he dictated an e-mail to the broker announcing that he was hot on Shelby's trail and wanted to defer any new contracts until he caught her. "That ought to keep them from sending anyone else to look for you," he said. He gave her the password and screen name to access his offshore bank accounts and checked to make sure the broker had transferred payment for the contract in Las Vegas. In subsequent sessions he gave her the passwords and personal identification numbers to access his investment accounts and asked her to check the statements. He explained his investment strategy and the meanings of various notations as they worked their way through the screens. "Why don't you jot all this down?" he said after showing her how to transfer funds to pay off a credit card. "That way, I won't have to dictate to you each time."

They had been home two weeks when Patrick asked Shelby to

take an early-morning walk with him before he drove Hank into town for a follow-up consultation with the ophthalmologist. "With the operation," Patrick said as they walked the path behind the barn, "farming Hank can do. But contracts? Finished he is with those."

Hank hadn't told her that. "But the doctors can restore enough sight for him to . . . to read, and to work around the farm? Maybe to drive?"

"Driving, probably not. Reading, yes, with the big print. But a problem we are having with Hank about this."

"There's another problem?"

They paused by the goat pens while Patrick cleared ash from his pipe by banging it upside down against a fence post and packed it with fresh tobacco. Using a kitchen match, he lit it and concentrated for several moments on getting it started. Then he pulled it from his mouth and spoke to her through a haze of aromatic smoke that hung in the still morning air. "No, says Hank. No operation."

When Shelby asked about his trip to the doctor, Hank had assured her everything was proceeding nicely, that he was healing. He hadn't mentioned the need for an operation, much less a decision not to have it. "Surely he wants to see. Even imperfectly."

"Seeing he would like. But this country's blue protection he does not have."

"Blue protection?"

"The cross that is blue and has the shield."

She guessed he was referring to Blue Cross and Blue Shield. "Do you mean insurance to cover medical costs?"

"The costs, yes. Grievous they are."

"But, to save his sight . . ."

"And the tumor." Patrick touched his arm where Shelby knew Hank's bone cancer was located. "This also is grievous in cost."

"How much, Patrick? Do you know the total cost?"

"For the eyes and the arm, we are calculating four hundred thousand dollars."

It would have to be cash, Shelby realized as she and Patrick retraced their path to the house, because Hank could not submit a credit report or ask for a government subsidy. She had seen his bank balance and his portfolio when she helped him with the computer; the operations would leave the family broke.

They reached the house and stood together for a moment on the front porch. Shelby patted the old man's arm and said, "Thank you, Patrick. We'd better go in."

The rest of the family had started eating breakfast. Carmen was smothering a stack of pancakes with maple syrup. Shelby kissed her cheek and said, "Good morning, sweetheart. How does your leg feel?"

"Sore." Carmen rubbed her thigh, which bulged with a fresh wraparound bandage. "Look what Leonard made for me." She set the syrup pitcher aside, stood on her good leg, and hefted child-sized, homemade crutches. "He said they're hobble sticks, but he's just teasing. They're really called crutches. Watch me." She used the crutches to swing herself single-legged across the room and back.

"Now that I can walk, Leonard's taking me to the barn. He's going to show me the goats. Did you know their babies are called kids?" She laid the crutches aside and sat back down. "When my leg is better, Leonard's going to hitch the billy goat—that's the daddy—to a cart. I'm going to drive it. Next spring, we're building a dam and a . . . a . . ." She turned a look of distress on Leonard.

"Dam and spillway," he said in a stage whisper.

"A dam and a spillway on the creek, so we can swim. We might get a puppy."

Shelby hugged her. "That's great, sweetheart. I'm sure you'll have loads of fun." She hugged Leonard and kissed his cheek. Then she loaded eggs, ham, biscuits, and apple butter on a plate for Hank and prepared one for herself.

After breakfast, Patrick and Hank headed for Grand Junction. Shelby assisted Latica with kitchen cleanup and, afterward, helped Leonard with a fence-mending job that required four hands. They finished at midafternoon, and Shelby found Latica and Carmen on the front porch eating cucumber-and-tomato sandwiches. She accepted a sandwich and said, "I'd like to go for a walk. Do you mind?"

"We'll be fine," Latica said. "Take all the time you need."

Moving slowly, still babying her burned feet, Shelby strolled to the stream where she and Hank had talked the day they searched for the missing nanny goat and kids. Sitting on the fallen tree again, straddling it at first, then shifting to a sidesaddle perch and staring into the frothing water, she thought about the twists her life had taken since Haiti's internal security thugs massacred her students.

If Hank hadn't saved her, she would have been dead long ago. And his family had healed her emotionally. She owed them her life as well as her sanity.

Now they needed her. Hank would give up his eyesight and let his tumor run its course rather than bankrupt the family. She couldn't let him do that, and the solution was a continuation of his business, assurance of a steady income.

With her decision made, she returned to the house and found Carmen and Latica, still on the porch, playing checkers. She kissed Carmen and hugged Latica. "I'll be in Hank's study."

She booted his computer and, using the codes and screen names he had suggested she jot down, sent an e-mail to the broker referencing the contract on her life. "Contract fulfilled," she typed. "Wire balance of fee to my account."

After another hour's walk, she checked for e-mail and found the broker's response: "Appreciate your perseverance. I'm negotiating another assignment for you. Funds for the completed contract will be wired as soon as I receive the evidence."

Shelby leaned back in the swivel chair and stared at the computer screen. When she sent the evidence, she would be officially dead. She could walk away, abandon these people and look after herself and Carmen. She would still be an illegal alien, but Krystal's hired killers would no longer be looking for her.

That wasn't really an option, though. She had only one path available. Hank's comments when he had talked to her about his work ran through her head: "I get to pick my assignments . . . Targets whose deaths make the world a better place."

"Evidence is on its way," she typed. Figuring she would need a month to recuperate, she added, "I sustained a minor injury. Defer new contracts for thirty days." She logged off and searched the computer's files until she found the contact profile the offshore broker had sent on her. It included a shipping address for the evidence.

In the kitchen, she found Latica preparing dinner while Carmen sat at the table working a jigsaw puzzle and stroking her kitten, asleep in her lap. Shelby washed her hands at the sink and turned to Latica. "Let me help. Just tell me what to do."

"Tell you what to do?" Latica paused from trimming the edges off a piecrust. "Oh, you mean about dinner. Only you can decide about other things."

Shelby laughed, and her exhilaration surprised her. "That's what I've been doing—deciding. The only uncertainty left in my life is how to help with the cooking."

Patrick and Hank returned from Grand Junction shortly before dinner. Hank said he felt drowsy and wasn't hungry.

"Have a nap," Shelby said. "I'll fix you a plate later." When he went into the bathroom, she asked Patrick to give him something to put him under. "I'd like him to sleep until morning."

Patrick nodded. "Good for him will be the extra sleep. But tomorrow he could sleep and today be with you. In your hands is his future."

The family had worked through the same issue she had, Shelby realized. They had recognized the same alternatives.

"I want him to sleep straight through," she said. She caught herself fisting her left hand, flexing and wriggling its thumb as she talked. She forced the fingers open and willed herself to relax but realized she was balling the fingers and working the thumb again moments later. "That way, there's no possibility of interference. I need you to perform a surgical procedure."